BURNING
FAITH

CHIP BRISTOL

All profits from this book will go to The Blair Project,
a charitable fund seeking to make a difference in the world,
one check at a time.

This book is a work of fiction. All characters come from my
imagination and are based upon "people" within me. Any
similarities to others is coincidental.

Cover art by Nathanial Rogers
Chapter art by Hank Bristol

BURNING FAITH

CHIP BRISTOL

*Features Study Questions
for Book Clubs and Individual Reflection*

This work is dedicated to
The Reverend Edward Stone Gleason

A man who taught me continuously,
inspired me regularly,
and loved me unconditionally.

At its heart most theology,
like most fiction,
is essentially autobiography.

—FREDERICK BUECHNER
The Alphabet of Grace

"Fire, fire, and then the scratch of pen on paper.
There are always some who
have to set it down in black and white."

—Frederick Buechner
A Room Called Remember

Table of Contents

PART I: Destruction

Part II: Preparation

Part III: New Life

DESTRUCTION

— 1 —
CHAPTER

Christmas Eve

Emmett Hodges needed a sermon. The Christmas Eve service was hours away, and he had nothing to say. Looking down at the empty yellow legal pad, he scratched the words "For behold." The words weren't even his. They came from angels long ago. He crumpled the page and tossed it on the floor with the other false starts. Christmas sermons used to come easy to Emmett. No more.

The sky brightened as Emmett rose from the table and poured another cup of coffee. The outline of the trees across the town common were visible, as was the spire of St. John's Episcopal Church where he had served as rector for the last 41 years. He'd never expected to stay so long. He thought he was destined for greatness, that St. John's would be the first step along the way to an impressive ministry, but now it was clear St. John's would be his first and last ministry, his legacy. The thought caused him to shake his head in disgust or disappointment—he wasn't sure which.

Emmett looked at the painting hanging on the wall above where his wife used to sit. It was a painting she'd done of their cabin in the mountains, purchased soon after arriving at St. John's. They always planned to retire there, but since Abby's death, he had been wondering if he'd stick with the plan. She was supposed to paint on the porch while he read. The dream was harder to hold when only in his hands.

He reached for his spoon and stirred his coffee. The doctor had forbidden cream and sugar years ago, but Emmett was a creature of habit. He lifted his spoon from his coffee and traced the watermark on the table in front of Abby's seat. They had spent every morning together at this table, and Emmett was determined to keep her memory alive.

The first snowflakes of a promised storm slowly descended. It's not Christmas without snow, Abby used to say. He watched it fall on the town's Christmas tree and crèche. Emmett welcomed the snow. He hoped it would bring the Christmas spirit.

The grandfather clock in the hall, his prized possession bought for their tenth wedding anniversary, announced it was time for Emmett to begin his day. Even though the church offices were closed, he was going to walk over and check on things. Volunteers had decorated the church with their usual flair. Each windowsill had a flower arrangement and candle, and garlands adorned the balcony railing. The tree beside the lectern was decorated and ready to welcome a full church. Now, it was up to him to lead an inspirational service. He knew it was really up to God, but God seemed busy with other things.

By the time he put on his coat and boots, snow covered the sidewalk and blades of grass were taking their last gasps of air. A gust of wind caused Emmett to shield his eyes and lower his head. "Simmer down, *Ruach*," he said as he closed the front door. *Ruach* was a favorite word from his seminary days. It was the word the Hebrew people used to describe the wind in which they felt God's presence. Emmett just liked the way the word sounded. He tightened his scarf and began the short journey across the common to the church.

The brick facade and white steeple made St. John's look more like a Congregational church than an Episcopal one, but Emmett had grown to love it. It was the oldest church in New Hampshire, and Emmett often joked that George Washington would have worshipped there had he made it that far north. The sanctuary standing before him was the third one built on the site. Founded in 1774, the church had documents that claimed the builders could hear cannon fire from Bunker Hill. St. John's, like its rector and members, stood proudly in the center of Webster.

Beside the church was Cutter Hall, a colonial home renovated into a parish center. It housed the church offices as well as the parish hall and Sunday school classrooms. Its purchase and renovation marked the largest capital campaign and building project during Emmett's tenure, and Emmett was proud of the accomplishment. Secretly, he hoped the parish hall might bear his name, but the Cutter family, who made the lead gift, wanted the building named for Josiah Cutter, one of the town's founders and earliest members of St. John's. Emmett understood but rarely looked up at the name above the entrance.

Emmett stomped the snow off his boots and removed his jacket and gloves as he looked over at Alma Peters's desk. His assistant was the most organized person Emmett had ever known. Together, they were the balance of nature, they joked, and Emmett knew he'd be lost without her. Emmett's office was down the hall. Once the den of the home, the office featured a fireplace with bookcases on either side, a large mahogany desk used by each of the five rectors of St. John's, and two leather wingback chairs suggesting a pastoral style Emmett no longer possessed. Since Abby's death, Emmett preferred solitude. His office had become a refuge from parishioners who always seemed to have something to complain about. He'd become a shepherd who wanted to eat his flock rather than lead it.

The shelves were filled with his father's library that he had inherited. His father had been the Bishop of Virginia, and his bishop's crozier, which Emmett called his father's "walking stick" when he was young, leaned against the wall in the corner. Emmett had hoped to follow in his father's footsteps, but it never happened. He ran for bishop once, but losing the election was something Emmett tried not to think about. Emmett hoped his father's books and mementos would inspire him, but they were more like reminders of what he hadn't done, of who he hadn't become.

His desk was covered with piles of paperwork and books, which might suggest a busy man, but Emmett knew better. The message light on his phone blinked, and he reluctantly listened to Mrs. Nesbit apologize for having missed the outreach committee meeting earlier that week, Carl Edmunds, a neighbor, call about a tree limb dangling precariously over his garage, and Jim Adams, the church's insurance agent, reminding Emmett that the church insurance bill was overdue. Emmett deleted the message without paying attention. Finances were always tight at the end of the year, and Emmett had decided to wait until after the Christmas offering, the largest of the year, to pay the larger bills. They could wait a few extra days, he told himself.

A file with the night's worship bulletin and a list of announcements sat on the chair. The file was lighter than usual because it contained no sermon. Emmett decided to give it one more try. He sat in one of the chairs by the fireplace and twisted the signet ring on his right pinky finger, something he always did when he was nervous or agitated. He tried to think about something new to say about Christmas. The idea of God with us, the incarnation, had become difficult for Emmett to believe. A nice idea, he thought, but God had never felt so absent.

Emmett remembered how much he loved Christmas when he was a child. It wasn't so much the presents as it was the idea of God coming and "sitting beside us," as he liked to say. One time, after his father spoke of modern-day incarnations, Emmett walked down the street and greeted everyone enthusiastically, thinking that they might well be Jesus. When people laughed at the enthusiastic boy, Emmett stopped.

It was clear Emmett would have to resort to what he vowed he'd never do: use an old sermon. "A recycled sermon is a recycled ministry," his father often chanted. Still, Emmett had no choice. He went over to the file cabinet and picked a sermon he had delivered as a seminary student. People had liked it, and, with some changes, Emmett thought it would work.

Just as he finished making the edits, he heard an old truck. The sputtering engine and creaking door let Emmett know Mac Ellis had arrived. Looking out the window at the rusted truck with the "No Whining" bumper sticker, Emmett watched as his one-man building and grounds committee lifted a toolbox out of the back, brushed off the snow, and sauntered toward the sanctuary. Emmett decided to make a detour on his way back to the rectory.

"Hello," Emmett called out.

"Be right there," Mac grumbled from somewhere in the back.

A retired Navy man, Mac looked as if he might have played on the defensive line at Annapolis years ago. Dressed in bright-red suspenders and disheveled khakis, Mac was a fixture at St. John's. Several years ago, Emmett was desperate for help and asked Mac if he would help with the church buildings. Mac agreed, under certain conditions: he did not need or want any help, and he wouldn't sit on any committees. "Just let me do what's needed," he declared before leaving Emmett's office. Emmett had no choice but to agree to Mac's conditions—and never regretted the decision.

While Emmett waited for Mac to finish whatever he was doing, Emmett looked around the church. St. John's had been his spiritual home for more than half his life. The first time he smelled the old wood and saw the sunlight shine through the stained-glass windows, he wanted the job. Rubbing his hand along the pew where he had held vigil for Abby during what turned out to be her last cancer surgery, Emmett remembered his one-word prayer. "Please!" It wasn't answered, but Emmett claimed he wasn't mad at God.

"Look who the angels dragged in," Mac said as he wiped his hands on the soiled red rag usually stuffed in his back pocket.

"Came by to make sure you weren't burning down the place."

"Trying to prevent it, actually," Mac said gesturing toward the furnace, which he called Bessie. "She's good to go, not that you'll need heat tonight. The place is a sauna when it's full."

"Does that mean you'll be joining us?"

"Hell, no," Mac replied. "Tonight's for amateurs, like New Year's Eve. People come out of the woodwork for Christmas. I'll be back when there's room again…like next week."

"Who knows? Maybe they'll stay, and we'll have to bring out folding chairs every week," said Emmett.

"Yes, and pigs will fly around the steeple," Mac said under his breath.

"Even so, thanks for your help getting things ready."

"No problem," Mac replied. "You okay? You don't look so good."

"Thanks. Good to see you, too."

"Just sayin'. Don't worry about tonight. Go home and get some rest. It's not like anyone's going to remember the service, anyway."

"Always the encourager," Emmett said with a smile.

"Tonight will be fine," Mac said as the two turned and walked toward the door. "What's that thing you always say? Work as if it depends on you and pray as if it depends on God."

"I hate it when you quote me," Emmett said, nudging Mac with his elbow. Rectors are not supposed to have favorites, but with Mac, Emmett was glad to make an exception.

After lunch, Emmett lit a fire and poured a glass of sherry. He wanted to enjoy the last bit of quiet before the chaos to come. It wasn't long before sleep took hold.

The sound of shovels scraping the sidewalk outside the rectory awakened Emmett. He was surprised it was dark. When he realized the service was in less than an hour, he panicked and scrambled upstairs to dress as quickly as possible. His fingers struggled to attach the plastic clerical collar to his starched black shirt. From the bedroom window, he could see people arriving. The unsettled priest could hear the brass ensemble warming up as he raced across the common and tried to blend in with the parishioners entering the church.

Simon Jackson, the head usher, spotted Emmett and looked relieved. "Glad you could make it," he said. "I was beginning to get nervous."

"Overslept," Emmett whispered. "Everything okay?"

"Yup. Just needed you. Gladys seems flustered about something, but that's nothing new."

Gladys Fitzpatrick was the head of the altar guild and ran things with the precision of an army general. She stood with her arms folded at the door of the vesting room, where Emmett and the other service participants put on their robes.

"I'm here, I'm here," Emmett said as if trying to avoid a mother's reprimand.

"I'm not looking for you, though it's nice you decided to show up," Gladys said looking behind Emmett for someone else. "It's the youngest Prescott boy that I need."

"Trey," Emmett said.

"He's the other acolyte."

"He'll be here," Emmett assured. "He's always late."

Gladys sighed and shifted her weight as she waited for the last member of her liturgical team. Gladys and the rest of the altar guild liked things decent and in order, as they often said. It felt like they had used extra starch on Emmett's vestments as he dressed for the service. Placing his father's gold pectoral cross around his neck, he looked at his reflection and took a deep breath. Emmett felt like a fraud dressed up as a priest.

"Anything wrong?" Gladys asked. "You don't look like yourself."

"I'm fine," Emmett replied. "Just a bit nervous."

"It's not like you haven't done this before."

Emmett joined the choir and acolytes as they walked to the back of the church. The church had filled since he arrived, and Simon and other ushers were unfolding metal chairs along the aisles. David Livingston, the organist, played the prelude, giving Emmett a chance to survey the congregation. All the regulars were there. Tom and Alice Jenkins sat in "their pew," as they referred to it. Sara Pierce was in her usual seat beside the window she gave in memory of her parents who were both killed in an automobile accident when she was only 20. Several children were home from college, and Emmett struggled to remember their names.

A commotion at the front door caused Emmett to turn. Robert J. Prescott Jr. arrived, followed by his wife, Millie, and their three sons. Gladys grabbed the youngest and led him to the vesting area. Those looking for seats stepped aside as Robert marched like Moses through the Red Sea. The son of one of St. John's founding families, Robert thought of himself as congregational royalty, and Emmett respectfully nodded as Robert and his family walked to the pew that might as well have been reserved for them.

Gladys brought Trey Prescott back just as Simon pulled the rope so the church's Revere Bell could announce the beginning of the service. Emmett walked behind the pews to deliver his traditional opening sentences: "For behold, I bring you good tidings of great joy, which shall be to all people. For unto you is born this day in the City of David a Savior, which is Christ the Lord."

With that, the organ swelled, the congregation rose, and Emmett took his place at the back of the procession as everyone sang, "O Come, All Ye Faithful."

The Christmas Eve service had always been Emmett's favorite. He liked the constancy: the bidding prayer and the nine lessons and carols were always the same. Leaders of the parish participated, reading the different lessons, with the rector always reading the last one, the prologue of John's Gospel, before delivering his sermon.

The congregation was particularly attentive when Emmett lifted the Bible and began. "In the beginning was the Word, and the Word was with God, and the Word was God. He was in the beginning with God. All things came into being through him, and without him not one thing came into being. What has come into being in him was life, and the life was the light of all people."

This reading, unlike the others, was more like poetry than story, and Emmett did his best to deliver it with lyrical precision. The words may have been harder to understand than readings about shepherds and wise men, but people revered it. The parish was named for the author, after all. In fact, the sign out front featured a quotation from this reading: "The light shines in the darkness, and the darkness has not overcome it." Emmett always slowed his delivery at that moment to watch as people made the connection between the reading and the sign. With a dramatic flair, Emmett raised his voice to deliver the final line, one he considered the most beautiful in scripture: "And the Word became flesh and dwelt among us, and we have seen his glory, the glory as of a father's only son, full of grace and truth." After a dramatic pause he added, "The word of the Lord," to which the congregation replied, "Thanks be to God."

Emmett climbed the historic pulpit steps and offered a prayer before his sermon. "Lord, make us masters of ourselves, so that we may become the servants of others. Take our lips and speak through them. Take our minds and think through them. Take our hearts and set them on fire. Amen." He took a sip of water and opened the file as people took their seats.

"We gather tonight in this beloved and sacred space to hear again the message of the angels, and in heart and mind to go even unto Bethlehem and see this thing which is come to pass, and the Babe lying in a manger. These words, familiar to us all, remind us of the eternal wonder, the joy, and, most of all, the hope of this season. It is the season when we proclaim the good news that shall be for all people, for unto us..."

Emmett paused, transfixed as an awkward silence filled the church. He looked down at his sermon as if he had lost his place, then up at the congregation with a bewildered look. People shot worried glances at one another. Emmett closed the file slowly.

"I can't do it," he said, placing his hands on the closed file. "It's Christmas. I know I'm supposed to deliver one of those feel-good sermons, the kind about peace on earth and good will to all, but I can't."

The silence in the church seemed palpable. Some shifted in their pews as Emmett stared off in the distance.

"Sometimes it's hard to still believe. We are here in this church tonight to recall God's coming into the world and dwelling among us, but when I look around, I see little evidence that what happened long ago has made much of a difference in the world today. To be honest, I find it hard to find God's presence anywhere."

"Here at St. John's, we're called to be the Body of Christ. We're supposed to proclaim Christ's birth, in word and deed, but I don't see much that would suggest we're doing that either. Do we really love God? Do we really love our neighbors as ourselves?"

"What was the point of sending that baby anyway? What did God hope to achieve by coming and being among us? For the life of me, I can't figure it out. I've spent close to 65 years trying to understand, and tonight, I'm sad to say, I've come up empty. And to be empty on such a night as this is sad indeed."

Someone near the front grumbled something to his wife, and Mrs. Nesbit grabbed her cane and stormed out. "I can't blame you, Agnes," Emmett said as she dismissed him with a wave of her hand. "Part of me wants to join you. Maybe it's time to admit we've come here tonight more from habit than belief. Maybe we're here to please our parents or to live up to the Christmas cards we send. Some, I'm sure, are here because deep down they believe the good news, which shall be for all people. If you are one of those, I'm envious."

"We sing 'O Come, O Come Emmanuel,' each year, but is that just wishful thinking, some unanswered prayer? What does it mean to the couple on the brink of divorce? What does it mean to the widow spending her first Christmas alone? What does it mean to those who have lost their hope that God cares, that God loves us no matter what, that God is with us through thick and thin?"

"Yes, come Emmanuel. Come. Please." Emmett said softly, as if offering a prayer. "I dare you." There were gasps from the congregation followed by an uncomfortable silence. Emmett turned and descended from the pulpit.

"He's lost it," someone whispered.

"I didn't know Scrooge was preaching this year," someone added.

The choir quickly stood and began to sing the hymn, "O Little Town of Bethlehem." As beautiful as the melody was, those gathered found it hard to concentrate.

> Yet in thy dark streets shineth,
> the everlasting Light.
> The hopes and fears of all the years
> are met in thee tonight.

The congregation offered a final prayer before the lights dimmed and candles lit for the singing of "Silent Night." Even in the darkness, Emmett could sense the scowls. Twisting the ring on his finger, he looked down at his hymnal and let the words of the hymn take him away from the gathering storm.

> Silent night, holy night
> All is calm, all is bright
> Round yon virgin mother and child
> Holy infant, so tender and mild
> Sleep in heavenly peace,
> Sleep in heavenly peace.

Emmett didn't look up as he followed the acolytes and choir down the aisle singing "Joy to the World." Joy was the last thing on peoples' minds after such a sermon, and he knew it.

Emmett stood at the door to greet parishioners, as always. Some were gracious; others asked if he was feeling all right. A few walked by without shaking his hand, as if they were in a rush to get home. The ushers began cleaning up as the last parishioner departed, and Emmett noticed Mac standing off to the side with a broad smile across his face.

"Look who decided to show up," Emmett said.

"Glad I did, too. Don't see that every day."

"Too much?"

"For some, maybe. Not me. Made me think."

"Is that a bad thing?"

"Nope, just new."

"I'm not sure what got into me," Emmett confessed.

"Emmett Hodges, rogue priest!" Mac said as if reading the headline from the *Webster News*. "Who'd have thought it? I never dreamed you'd go off script like that." Mac patted his friend on the back before following the others out into the winter night. "Merry Christmas, spontaneous one. You can always come live with me when they fire your ass."

Emmett tried to laugh. "You all go home," he said to the ushers and acolytes. "Go be with your families. I'll close up."

Trey Prescott and the other acolytes were happy to obey and raced down the aisle. "How'd we do?" Emmett asked as Simon handed him the offering plates.

"Not as much as last year, but it should fill the coffers."

"It better," Emmett replied. "I'll put it in the safe. You go home."

Once Emmett was alone, he took the offering plates and slid into the back pew. Wedging them between his knees, he began counting the money like a bootlegger. When it was clear there was more than enough to cover the bills, Emmett placed the offering plates beside him and sat back to look at the church. "It is finished," he whispered. He wasn't sure whether he was referring to the service or his time at St. John's. Perhaps both.

Cleaning could wait until the morning, he decided, so he draped his robes, stole, and father's cross and chain over the offering plates and walked toward the doors. He turned off the lights and locked up without looking back. If he had, he might have seen the candle burning beneath the antique tapestry.

— 2 —

CHAPTER

Christmas

Sirens woke Emmett from a deep sleep. Thinking they were his alarm clock, he reached over to turn it off and saw lights flashing around the edges of his bedroom curtains. He leaped out of bed and pulled the curtains open. The church was on fire.

"Oh, my God!" Emmett shouted as he gripped the curtains so tightly they fell to the ground. Someone was pounding on the door. Emmett turned and ran downstairs, still in his pajamas.

"What the hell?" Mac said when Emmett opened the door. "I thought you were dead."

"What happened?" Emmett asked as he scrambled to put on his boots and coat and join Mac to head back to the church. He could feel the fire on his face, and the smoke caused him to wince.

CHAPTER 2

"I don't believe this," he said. Flashing lights bounced off the trees and houses near the church. Police and firefighters ran every which way. Flames attacked the eaves and began to climb the roof. Smoke billowed from the bell tower into the starless night.

"Stand back," a police officer said as he unrolled yellow caution tape in front of the church.

"I'm the rector," Emmett protested.

"Sorry. You have to join the others over there," the officer said, pointing to a crowd huddled under a streetlamp across the street. Mac took Emmett's arm and led him toward the others.

"Emmett," Sara Pierce cried as she broke from the group and ran toward her rector.

"It'll be all right," Emmett said. He wasn't a hugger, but he held Sara gingerly. "It'll be all right." Joining the others, he added, "Does anyone know what happened?"

"The fire company got a call sometime after midnight." Mac replied. "Unfortunately, it was pretty much out of control by the time they arrived."

"Who called?" Emmett asked.

Mac pointed to a man in blue jeans and a red-and-black checkered jacket standing by one of the firetrucks. He looked like he'd just come from a construction site and couldn't have been more than 30 years old.

"Who is he?"

"No idea," said Mac. "Just wished he'd called sooner."

Emmett turned and faced the burning church. The crackling and popping of the fire made Emmett sick to his stomach. The flames crawled their way up the roof toward the steeple, hungry for the cross at the top.

"How could this happen?" Emmett asked to no one in particular.

A firefighter with an axe rushed toward the front doors. "Wait!" Emmett exclaimed as he rummaged through his coat pocket. "I've got the keys!"

The firefighter didn't hear Emmett, and it wouldn't have mattered if he had. Mac looked at Emmett dangling his keys and couldn't help but laugh. "Like that's gonna help," he said, which made others, including Emmett, see the absurdity of it all. Laughter provided a strange release, like a joke at a funeral.

When the man with the axe broke the doors open, flames bounded from the church like escaped prisoners. Smoke poured out like tar. The firefighter moved aside while others rushed in carrying hoses. Soon they heard a hissing that sounded like thousands of snakes. "It's the water hitting the flames," Mac said, leaning toward Emmett.

"Sounds sinister," someone said.

The putrid smell caused everyone to bury their faces in their jackets, and the man with the axe ran to the side of the church.

"Not the windows," Sara cried.

"They have to," said Mac. "They need access to the fire."

"But can't they…" Sara began, but the sound of shattering glass stopped her. Collapsing against Mac, she cried, "It's gone."

A loud cracking sound caused everyone to look up at the steeple listing to one side. Shouts from below caused the firefighters to scatter, and the steeple fell onto Cutter Hall before crumbling onto the snow-covered ground. Sparks and flames danced in the sky when the church bell crashed onto the entrance, rolled out the front doors, down the granite steps, and rested on its side against a pile of soot-covered slush.

Immediately, two ladders rose above the church, and firefighters pointed hoses toward the hole where the steeple had been. A section of the roof collapsed next. Even from across the street, it was clear the firefighters were losing.

"Will they be able to save any of it?" Emmett asked desperately.

"It doesn't look good," Mac replied, placing his hand on Emmett's back.

"What caused it?" Emmett asked.

"No clue. Could have been anything."

Another section of the roof fell into the sanctuary, followed by a portion of the southern wall.

"To think we were in there worshipping only hours ago," Emmett said shaking his head. "I suppose we should be grateful no one was hurt."

"Praise God," someone said, and Emmett reached over and grabbed Mac's arm. He could tell his friend wanted to respond to the idea that any of this could be worth praise.

"That's whipped cream on horse shit," Mac whispered. "This kinda thing shouldn't happen, especially to churches."

Over the next two hours, the rest of the roof and most of the walls collapsed. Without fuel, the fire began to die down, but the building was destroyed. People eventually wandered back to their cars. Soon, only Mac, Sara, and Emmett stood in front of the remains of the church. Two hoses sprayed water on the smoldering pile, while other firefighters packed up. It was then they realized how dark it was without the flames. It was colder, too. The three moved closer to one another.

"It's like we're standing at the foot of the cross," Sara said into the darkness.

The fire chief came over and explained that someone would stay and make sure no hot spots flared up. He expressed his sympathy over not being able to do more.

"There's nothing more you could have done," Emmett assured him. The chief forced a smile before returning to the church. Sara hugged Emmett and Mac before leaving.

"I guess we should go home too," Emmett said looking at Mac. The two were about to leave when the man in the red-and-black checkered jacket walked over.

"I thought I should introduce myself," he said as he reached out his hand. "Jake Davidson. I'm the one who..."

"Called 911," Emmett said shaking the stranger's hand. "Yes, Mac here told me. Emmett Hodges. I'm the rector."

Jake looked surprised and gazed at the pajama bottoms below Emmett's winter jacket.

"Oh, Lord," Emmett said as he looked down. "Look at me, standing here in pajamas. I'm so embarrassed. Forgive me."

"Don't worry about it."

"We're in your debt, Jake," said Emmett.

"Not at all. Drove past and saw light flickering through the windows. I could tell it wasn't good. Wish I'd driven by sooner."

"Me too," said Emmett, looking back at the church.

"Anyway, wanted to say how sorry I am for your loss."

"Thank you," Mac and Emmett said in unison.

"It looked like a beautiful church," Jake said as he walked away.

"It was," Emmett said with renewed sadness.

It was impossible to wash away the smell of the smoke. After a long shower, Emmett tried to sleep but couldn't. He went downstairs and wandered aimlessly around the rectory, unsure of what to do. It's Christmas morning, he realized as he poured his coffee and took his seat at the kitchen table. Looking out the window, the emptiness caught him by surprise.

"The church is gone," he repeated as if to get the news to sink in. After his second cup of coffee, he felt like he had to do something, so he decided to go back over and see the damage in the daylight.

The snow in his front yard glistened in the morning light and created a haunting contrast to the soot-stained ground across the common. The air tasted like smoke, and Emmett paused before crossing the street. The church sign still stood proudly in front of mounds of ash. Emmett shook his head in dismay as he walked toward the three granite steps that used to serve as the church's entrance. Out of habit, he reached down and moved a tree branch from the path.

Beyond the steps was a scene from a battlefield—with no doubt who lost. Ash and debris filled what used to be the sanctuary; off to the side, Cutter Hall looked like someone had sliced through it with a knife. Emmett could see into the meeting room on the second floor. Its chairs and tables were still neatly arranged, and a picture of St. John's still hung crookedly on the wall.

Emmett could see the houses on the next street now that the church was gone. Dark ground surrounded the church, and the remaining snow in the distance was gray as death. Lying on its side, the Revere Bell looked like a corpse. Emmett reached for one of the twisted iron railings and gasped for air. He felt like clay being squeezed. "Why," he asked out loud. "Why? Why? Why?"

The ash inside the sanctuary looked like symmetrical waves; he figured they had been the pews. Beams and other fragments of the church jutted out, and the portions of the walls that remained gave hints of where the church had once been. The altar, pulpit, and organ were gone.

A gust of wind blew ash in Emmett's face, forcing him to look away. The scene was overwhelming. He reached up and wiped the ash from his eyes, leaving smudges across his face.

"Where are you? How could you let this happen?" Emmett cried, looking up into the sky.

Mac's truck pulled up, and Emmett tried to clean his face. Two cars arrived soon after. Like Emmett, people wanted to see the devastation in the morning light.

"Oh my God," Mac grumbled in disbelief.

"It's worse in the daylight," Emmett said. He tried to think of something to say to make everyone feel better, but he had no words. Instead, he climbed down the steps and stood beside the growing crowd in silence. Sara Pierce arrived and walked down the path with her hand to her mouth.

"So, it really did happen," she said. "I hoped it had been a bad dream."

Virginia Harris and her husband, Todd, were the last to arrive. Virginia didn't bother to close her car door. She ran toward Emmett and held him like a lost child. "I don't believe this," she said in tears. "How on earth did this happen?"

"No one knows," Emmett replied.

"We were at Todd's parents' place in Vermont," Virginia explained, "but we came back as soon as we heard the news. I can't believe it. I'm so sorry we weren't here."

"There's nothing you could have done. There was nothing any of us could do," Emmett said. "It's just a tragedy, an awful, horrible, tragedy."

"I'd use more descriptive words if it wasn't Christmas morning," Mac mumbled.

"I have no doubt," Emmett said, looking at his friend.

The group looked around in silence. They tried to absorb the scene and imagine the church as it had been. Virginia spoke about the day she and Todd were married; someone else recalled their children's baptisms. A litany of memories followed as the small congregation moved closer to one another for warmth.

"What are we supposed to do now?" Sara asked, trying to sound strong.

"We rebuild," Emmett said.

"Yes, we pick ourselves up and carry on," Virginia added.

"No," said Sara, "I mean, what should we do right now? I don't want to go home." People looked at one another for an answer.

"We should have a service," Virginia said.

"What?" Emmett asked. "Here? Outside?"

"It's Christmas morning," Virginia reminded everyone. "We should have a service."

"We can't," said Emmett sounding confused. "We don't have…"

Virginia interrupted. "We don't have a building, but we do have a church."

"I don't have my robes or stole, not to mention my prayer book or Bible," Emmett protested.

Virginia walked over to Emmett and pulled the scarf from under his jacket and draped its two ends on either side before patting Emmett tenderly on his chest. "There's your stole. You can wing the rest."

"That's right," Mac said with a grin. "You're good at winging it."

Virginia, who had missed Emmett's spontaneous sermon at the Christmas Eve service, was confused. Sara whispered that she'd explain later.

"Mac," Virginia said, clapping her hands to get everyone's attention, "you and Simon go find two pieces of wood and lay them down in front of the steps in the shape of a cross. The others, come help me push some snow in a pile to make an altar."

"You're serious," Emmett said, realizing for the first time that he was going to have to lead a service in a few minutes.

"Yes, I'm serious," said Virginia, "so get ready."

Despite his heavy coat, Emmett felt naked. He watched as his parishioners created a makeshift worshipping space and tried to come up with something to say. When they were done, people took their places and Emmett stood before them. He spread his arms and said, "The Lord be with you."

"And also with you," the others replied.

"Let us pray. Almighty God, we gather this morning with heavy hearts. The church we love has been taken from us, and we don't know why. On Christmas, we usually celebrate your coming among us, but this Christmas you feel nowhere to be found. Come, Lord Jesus, come. Be with us this Christmas morning. In our darkness, we pray you bring your light. In our sadness and fear, we pray you bring the peace which passes all understanding, the peace your angels promised was for all people, including us. Through Christ our Lord."

"Amen," the congregation replied.

"At this point we'd usually sing a hymn, but since..."

"How about, 'O Come, All Ye Faithful?'" Sara suggested. Virginia thought it was a perfect choice and started singing with Sara. Others quickly joined. No one was sure about the words to the second verse, so Emmett said one verse was enough.

"Without a Bible, I'm not sure I'll get this right, but I've always loved the poetry of the Christmas story." Emmett began reciting the story from memory.

CHAPTER 2

"And there were shepherds in the fields keeping watch over their flock by night. An angel of the Lord suddenly appeared, and the glory of the Lord shone around about them, and they were sore afraid. The angel said, 'Fear not; for behold, I bring you good news of great joy which will be for all the people; for unto you is born this day a Savior, who is Christ the Lord. And this will be a sign unto you: you will find a babe wrapped in swaddling clothes lying in a manger.'"

Emmett stepped closer and looked down at his boots in the snow as he thought of something to say. "The words are familiar, but this Christmas, it's as if I've never heard them before. The idea of celebrating Christmas when we've lost our church seems absurd. A babe lying in a manger seems like a cruel joke when you look behind me. But maybe this is a chance for us to enter the Christmas story in a new way. Maybe we can stand beside Mary and Joseph and know what it feels like to feel alone and completely unprepared for what has happened. Maybe we can wonder with the shepherds, 'Why us?'"

"God moves in mysterious ways, people often say, but this isn't mysterious. It's cruel. Like you, I'm confused, hurt, and sad. If I'm honest, I'm also angry. I don't understand what's happened. I'm mad that our church has been taken away. I long for answers or, at least, a faith that can see beyond the ashes, but I don't have that kind of faith. At least I don't this morning. All I see is a church in ruins and a group of wounded souls standing beside one another. Where is God in all of this? He's certainly not in what lies behind me. No, this Christmas, the manger is far away. There's no babe wrapped in swaddling clothes. We have each other, though. That'll have to be enough."

Virginia leaned her head on her husband's shoulder, and others moved in closer as Emmett spoke. Sara and Virginia led the group in a verse of "Angels We Have Heard on High" before Emmett offered a closing prayer. The small congregation greeted one another but didn't know what to do next. The awkward silence was broken by an unfamiliar voice.

"Good morning," Jake Davidson said as he walked over.

"Everyone," Emmett called out, "This is Jake Davidson. Jake was the one who noticed the fire and called 911. We are in his debt."

Virginia and the others expressed their gratitude, but Jake repeated his regret over not having seen the fire sooner. "I'm here to invite you to come have breakfast," he announced. "There's a small army at a place called Maria's, and they've sent me up here to fetch anyone I can find."

"Maria's?" Mac responded. "It's not open on Christmas."

"It is this Christmas," Jake said with delight. "Maria heard about the fire, called around, and got some of her staff to come in. It's full of firefighters and police right now—and you, if you're interested."

"I'm in," Mac said enthusiastically.

"Me, too," said Virginia.

Jake led the procession down to Maria's, but Emmett wasn't sure he'd go. Virginia and Sara turned and slipped their arms in his.

"We're not going without you," Virginia said as she squeezed Emmett's arm.

Maria's was packed and smelled like a mixture of bacon, coffee, and smoke. Ash-stained yellow coats lined the wall, and first responders and their families filled the tables. It was not where anyone imagined celebrating Christmas, but Emmett was glad to have the chance to thank everyone for their hard work.

Maria greeted the new arrivals and directed them like a traffic cop to a table she had set up off to the side.

"You are some piece of work," Emmett said to the woman he'd come to love over the years.

"It's the least we could do."

"But on Christmas..."

"Not one person I called refused," she said proudly.

"I don't know what to say."

"You don't need to say anything. Get over there and I'll bring you some coffee."

"Make sure you bring me the check for all of this, too," Emmett said, but the look on Maria's face told him the request was out of the question. Emmett stopped to say thank you to those at each table. Their love and concern for his church was comforting.

When he finally reached their table, he took his seat between Virginia and Jake as the coffee and food arrived. Emmett stood, picked up his water glass, and tapped it with a spoon. The diner went silent.

"I want to say, on behalf of all the people of St. John's, how much we appreciate each and every person here. Last night was a tragedy beyond words, but you worked tirelessly to save our church. Even though you weren't able to save St. John's, we'll forever be in your debt. I'm sorry we've taken you from your homes on this special morning, but I want you to know how much we appreciate all you tried to do for us and be the first to wish you a merry Christmas."

"Merry Christmas," everyone replied.

"I also want to thank Maria and her staff for this spontaneous Christmas feast. Even though this is not how any of us would want to celebrate Christ's birth, I feel blessed to be sitting among you for this unconventional, yet wonderful, eucharistic feast."

"Hear, hear," everyone said lifting their mugs. Emmett took his seat, and Jake passed him the bread. "Want some toast?"

— 3 —

CHAPTER

This Is It

Emmett lost his appetite in an instant. The conversation moved from what a memorable Christmas morning it had been to what the parish needed to do now. "At least the church was insured," Sara said, and Emmett almost dropped his fork. He pushed his seat back from the table and took a sip of coffee as if he was dying of thirst.

"What's wrong?" Virginia asked.

"Nothing," he stuttered. "Just remembered something I need to do." He stood and excused himself and wished everyone a Merry Christmas.

"Need help?" Jake offered, looking up at Emmett.

"No, but thanks. I hope you'll take me up on my offer to spend the night at the rectory before heading out of town. You need sleep. We all do."

Once outside, Emmett mistakenly headed toward the church. It was where the church checkbook was—or had been. He turned toward the rectory and tried to remember the message Jim Adams had left. He was sure there was still time to pay the insurance premium. Surely, there's a grace period, he told himself. He thought about going over to Jim's house but not on Christmas. He thought about post-dating a check and putting it in the mail. Instead, he decided to be at Jim's office first thing Monday morning.

Despite his exhaustion, Emmett didn't sleep well that night. His mind raced. He thought about the church burning, the sound of the water spraying out of the hoses, and how the roof and walls collapsed. Questions about the insurance caused him to climb out of bed. His pajamas were soaked with sweat, and his heart thumped. He went downstairs, and, instead of turning on the light to read, he sat in the dark. "Help me," he whispered.

A thud upstairs reminded Emmett he had a house guest. Jake had accepted his invitation to spend the night, and the two had talked for hours over lasagna and wine. Still, Emmett was surprised to hear a guest. No one had stayed in the rectory since Abby's funeral.

"Morning," Emmett said as he stood to greet his guest and usher him into the kitchen. "There's coffee over there and milk in the refrigerator and sugar if you use it. Mugs are in the cabinet above. I'll make some eggs."

"You're a regular bed and breakfast," Jake said with a smile.

"'Be not forgetful to entertain strangers' it says in Hebrews, 'for thereby some have entertained angels unawares,'" Emmett said as he pulled a frying pan from the rack above the stove.

"Hardly," Jake said with a smile, "but thanks." Jake went over and looked at the large collection of coffee mugs. Most had sayings or pictures.

"My sister started the collection years ago," Emmett explained, "It's become a kind of joke. Pick whichever one you like."

Jake picked a black mug with "World's Greatest Son" printed on it.

"See what I mean," Emmett said looking away. "She's the sarcastic one in the family."

"I love your house," Jake said looking around the kitchen.

"Not mine. Belongs to the church," Emmett said as he began scrambling eggs. Nodding at Abby's painting of the cabin, he added, "That's the only place I own."

"Where is it?"

"Squam Lake. About an hour and a half from here.

"Looks amazing. How long have you had it?"

"Bought it from a parishioner soon after we first arrived. It's quite rustic, but it sits on 25 acres overlooking the lake and surrounding mountains. I love the place."

Jake drew closer to the painting. "Must be worth a lot." He turned and took what used to be Abby's seat. Emmett almost said something but didn't.

"That's what the realtor who keeps calling tells me, but, for me, it's more about the memories than the money. I'm going to retire there."

"When will that be?"

"Not sure. Thought I'd make it to my seventieth birthday. Now I'm not so sure. St. John's needs someone new, someone younger, particularly now that it faces this monumental challenge, but I'm not sure anyone would want the job with the church burned down."

"I guess you'll just have to stay and be younger," Jake joked.

Emmett smiled as he carried breakfast to the table and took his seat beside Jake. "Easier said than done."

"So, what's the next step for you and the church?" Jake asked.

"I don't know," Emmett said as he nervously reached for the plant at the center of the kitchen table and began pulling off dead leaves. "The vestry's having an emergency meeting tomorrow afternoon, and I'm meeting with the fire marshal later this afternoon to go over what he needs to file his report."

"What's a vestry?" Jake asked.

Emmett looked at Jake with surprise. "I forgot that you're not Episcopalian. The vestry's the governing body of the parish. They're the ones with all the authority. Technically, I work for them."

"I thought you worked for God," Jake said with a grin. "Sounds more like a business than a church."

"That's how it feels, sometimes," Emmett said with a sigh while he continued to pluck leaves from the plant. "Anyway, we're meeting at Virginia's house, the woman next to me at Maria's. She's the senior warden, which is what we call the head of the vestry."

"Senior warden? Sounds like she runs a prison."

"It does, now that you mention it. We'll decide next steps at the meeting," Emmett said. "Tell me more about what you do."

"I told you most of it last night. I grew up in Maine. My dad was a cabinet maker, and I learned the basics of carpentry from helping him. One summer, we restored a cabin down the road from our place. I loved it and have been restoring buildings ever since."

"So, you're an architect?" Emmett asked.

"I have a degree in architecture, but I specialize in restoration. I was on my way back from a project in Savannah, Georgia, an old synagogue, when I stopped in Webster for gas. The synagogue was a disaster, but we eventually restored it. Now, it's being used as a library for an art school there. Took three and a half years."

"Now you're headed home?"

"Yes. Mom died a few years ago, and Dad's getting on in years. Still works part-time, though. He won't stop and refuses to think about moving to one of those retirement places."

"What about you? Do you have a job lined up?"

"Not at the moment. A group in Cincinnati is interested in restoring an old theater, but they're a few years from having the money."

"Wish you could stick around here and help us," Emmett said, half-joking.

"I do restoration," Jake said, looking across the common, "You're going to need to start from scratch. Speaking of scratches," Jake said as he rubbed his hands on the surface of the kitchen table, "I love this table."

Emmett smiled. "Me, too. It was the first antique Abby and I bought after we were married. The grandfather clock in the hall was the second. I've begun every morning at this table since we arrived."

"I love old wood. Look at these marks."

"I do, every morning," Emmett said.

"Each has a story to tell, I'll bet," Jake said, touching the water ring in front of him with his finger.

"That's from Abby's coffee mug," Emmett explained.

Jake looked up at Emmett before taking his dishes to the sink. "I like that. It's like she's just left the room." Emmett stared out the window while his guest did the dishes. "I hope things work out for you all," Jake said, breaking the silence. "And don't worry about the insurance. I'm sure that'll work out too."

Emmett didn't remember mentioning the insurance to Jake. He must have said something about it the night before. The two agreed to stay in touch, and Emmett saw Jake to the door before rushing down to Jim Adams's office.

"I thought I'd be seeing you today." Jim said as he fished for the key to the door. "I can't begin to tell you how sorry I was to hear about the fire." Jim ushered Emmett upstairs to his office above Miller Hardware Store. "How're you holding up, Emmett? Can I get you some coffee?"

"No thanks," Emmett said as he took a seat, twisting the ring on his finger. "I apologize for arriving unannounced, but given all that's happened, I thought it was important to see you right away."

"Not at all. How can I help?"

"Well, as you know, our insurance premium is due. I've come to make us current."

"Due," Jim said. "It's past due. I called…"

"I know," said Emmett, "but with Christmas and all, I got delayed. I'm here to make the payment."

Jim looked down at his desk and moved a paper clip off to the side. "I appreciate that, Emmett, but I'm afraid it's more complicated than you showing up this morning."

"What do you mean?" asked Emmett.

"I mean, the payment was due over a month ago."

"But there's a grace period, isn't there? Certainly, a one-month delay is not a deal breaker, particularly for a client that's been with you for so long."

"You're right, there is a grace period, but I'm afraid you blew past it. I called and left a message telling you we needed a payment by last Friday. Didn't you get the message?"

"I did. I just thought if I was here first thing this morning, I could slip under the wire. Christmas is always such a busy time of year."

"I'm afraid the church's policy was canceled at midnight on Friday."

"Canceled? Surely you can make an exception this once. St. John's has been a customer since you opened this office. That should count for something."

"The church has been a wonderful customer, and I can't begin to tell you how sorry I am to tell you this. But once a policy is canceled, it can't be reinstated. We'd have to start over, and I'm afraid that won't help with your current situation. The fact is the church was uninsured when it burned."

"You must be joking," Emmett gripped the arms of the chair. "After all this time, you're washing your hands of us?"

"I'm not washing my hands. I tried to keep this from happening, but when it comes to things like canceling policies, it's out of my hands once the deadline passes."

"Isn't that convenient," Emmett growled. "Just when the church needs you, you throw your hands up and hide behind some technicality."

"I understand you're upset, but this is more than a technicality. To be frank, I wasn't the one who put off paying the premium. In fact, I called several times. I'm sorry, Emmett, there's nothing we can do."

Emmett knew, as a minister, he shouldn't say anything more. He stood, thanked Jim for his time, and was soon wandering Main Street trying to make sense of what just happened.

A knock on the window at Maria's startled him. Mac waved for him to come join him. Emmett reluctantly entered the diner and politely nodded to people he recognized.

"You look like someone's just run over your prayer book," Mac said, trying to amuse his friend.

"Sorry," Emmett said. "Just came from Jim Adams's office."

"I bet that was an expensive visit," Mac said. "This is going to cost them a pretty penny."

Emmett looked away. "It's not going to cost them a cent."

"What are you talking about?" Mac asked.

"I delayed paying the insurance, and the policy terminated before the fire."

"What?" Mac said in a tone that caused many sitting at the counter to turn around.

"Shhh," Emmett said, as he leaned closer. "The policy was up for renewal. I told Alma to hold off paying the bill until after the Christmas service and the end-of-year gifts came in. Seems I waited too long."

"There's a grace period, isn't there?"

"There is, or I should say, there was. Apparently, I missed that, too."

"There's got to be a way around it," Mac said. "Can't they make an exception, given the holidays, or the fact that we've been customers for so long?"

"I tried that," Emmett said as he took a sip of coffee, "but Jim assured me there's nothing he can do. The reality is the church was uninsured when it burned, and I'm the only one to blame."

"Holy shit," Mac said, reaching for his coffee. "Does the vestry know?"

"Not yet. There's a meeting tomorrow afternoon at Virginia's."

"This is bad," Mac said.

"You don't need to tell me. I wanted to meet with Jim first to see if we could work something out before the vestry gathered."

"They're gonna be pissed."

"I know," Emmett said.

"People were court-martialed in the Navy for less."

"You're not helping," Emmett said before declining Mac's offer to buy him breakfast. He took a last sip of coffee and excused himself. He claimed there was someplace he needed to be, but what he needed was time alone. He needed to figure out a solution. The walk back to the rectory seemed particularly long. Climbing the steps to the front door, Emmett realized Mac was right. He needed to come clean sooner rather than later. He didn't need Mac to point out that he might lose his job over this. That was more than likely.

Emmett wanted to cancel the meeting with the fire marshal but knew the investigation into the fire was time-sensitive. He was grateful to see Mac's truck parked by the church beside the fire marshal's and the police chief's. "I thought you could use some support," he said, standing at the curb. "You've already had a bad day."

Emmett offered a half-hearted smile as the two turned and walked up the path toward the stairs where the city officials were waiting. "Thank you for agreeing to see us so soon after the fire," the fire marshal said as he shook their hands. "We're all so sorry about the fire and wish we'd been able to save at least some part of the church." Emmett and Mac nodded. "We thought it would be good to go over next steps so we can finish our report, and you can file your insurance claim."

Mac looked over at Emmett, but Emmett refused to make eye contact. Instead, he looked down and shuffled his boots in the dirty snow.

"Our job is to figure out what happened. We don't suspect foul play, but we can't rule anything out at this point. Most likely, it was some sort of mechanical issue, or human error. Just don't know at this point."

"I can assure you, it was not a mechanical issue," Mac stated emphatically.

"Perhaps not, but we can't rule anything out."

The three walked toward the debris. Emmett noticed them looking at the charred wood arranged like a cross and the pile of snow that looked more like a melted snowman than an altar.

"We had a spontaneous Christmas service yesterday morning."

"I see. Best to stay away from this area until we finish our report," the fire marshal said.

"What will you need from us?" Emmett asked.

"Time and room to do our jobs. That, and any records you might have on the furnace and wiring—and a list of any work you've done recently. We'll take it from there and do our work as swiftly as we can."

Emmett promised to get him whatever he could but knew whatever records the church had were buried under the ash. Mac left soon after the others, and Emmett returned to the granite stairs, the only things left of the church.

"This is it," he said as he looked out over the ruins of the church. It was clear his time at St. John's had come to an end. The church was gone, there was no insurance, and it was all his fault. After a deep breath, Emmett stood and climbed down the stairs. He paused to look back once more, before returning to the rectory to compose his letter of resignation.

— 4 —

CHAPTER

An Undeserved Gift

Emmett sat in his car outside Virginia's house, his phone
against his ear as if taking an important call, while he
watched vestry members arrive. Despite his hands shaking,
he'd been surprised by the relief he felt in writing his letter of
resignation. Now, the moment had come to offer it, and his hands
were shaking again.

Stanley Fitzpatrick was the first to arrive, as usual. Stanley
never missed a meeting and always arrived early. Sara Pierce
was next. She waved to Emmett as she made her way toward the
house. Emmett put the phone down and reached for the door
handle as Robert Prescott's Range Rover arrived. Always one to
make an entrance, Emmett decided to let Robert enter first.

"All right," Virginia said as she greeted Emmett at the door, "now we can get started." She invited everyone to her dining room table where she and Emmett sat at the far end beside each other. The others took their seats, Robert claiming the seat at the opposite end of the table. He looked ready for battle.

Robert had expected to be asked to serve as senior warden when the position became available, but Emmett asked Virginia. St. John's had never had a woman lead the vestry, and Emmett felt it was time. So did Abby. Virginia was a bright, capable woman who had been married at St. John's, and she and Todd had been faithful members ever since. She was hesitant to accept the position, but Emmett assured her he would guide her through the responsibilities. "It's only a formality," he had told her. "I'll handle the day-to-day operations." Virginia had proven a good choice, but Robert still resented being passed over.

"I appreciate you all coming on such short notice," she began. "We've got so much to discuss, but before we get to the crisis at hand, I'd like to ask Emmett to begin the meeting in prayer, then we'll take a few minutes to share our thoughts and feelings about all that's happened."

Emmett smiled as he watched Virginia lead. He marveled at her many gifts and talents. She'd need them in the days ahead, he thought. After his opening prayer, people shared their reactions to the fire and memories of St. John's. There was anger and fear, sadness and confusion. People spoke of special moments they'd never forget, but with each memory came renewed sadness.

"If you'll excuse me," Robert said, "I don't wish to sound insensitive, but we have a lot to discuss. I know we're all grieving, but it is up to the people around this table to put our emotions to the side while we figure out what the parish needs to do. I, for one, want to know how on earth this happened."

"We all do," Virginia responded, "but our emotions are important, too."

"Yes, but they won't tell us what happened, nor will they get us to where we need to go."

Emmett reached over and lightly touched Virginia's arm.

"I met with the police chief and fire marshal yesterday," Emmett said. "They told me they'd have a report soon."

"Do they know what caused the fire?" Sara asked.

"No. It's too soon, but they did say there was little reason to suspect foul play. It was more likely a mechanical failure or human error."

"The sooner we find out, the better," Robert bellowed. "Once we know, we'll be able to figure out our next steps."

"Steps? What kind of steps?" Simon asked.

"He means whether to sue someone or not," said Terrance Adler, the head of the finance committee. He was one of the few who was not intimidated by Robert Prescott.

"If someone was culpable or a product was defective, then, yes, we should seek reparations," Robert said.

"Can't we just be sad," Sara asked quietly, "before we talk about suing people?"

"Right now, we need to figure out what we're going to do in the short term," Virginia said, trying to keep the tension from escalating. "We'll wait for the report and see what it shows. Until then, we need to focus on finding a temporary home."

A lengthy conversation ensued about the kind of property they needed. Someone suggested the high school gymnasium, another the vacant supermarket outside of town. "It'll take time to find the right space," Emmett said. "We'll need to figure out what to do in the meantime."

Virginia asked Simon and Terrance to explore possible spaces and come back to the vestry with the best options. "And

Emmett, would you be willing to work with others to figure out what we can do until then?" Emmett nodded reluctantly, as he felt the envelope in his pocket grow heavier.

"I'll help determine next steps once we hear back from the fire marshal," Robert said, as if licking his chops.

"Terrance, we need you and your committee to figure out where we stand, financially. How much money do we have, and how long will it last?" Despite its impressive history, St. John's had spent most of its endowment and struggled to meet its expenses.

"Someone needs to be working with the insurance company, too," Robert offered, and everyone at the table agreed. "It will take time, but having a point person for that process is crucial."

"Before we go any further, there's something you need to know," Emmett said as he slowly stood. "I'm afraid it's rather bad news." He paused and looked around the table.

"As vestry members, and as Terrance and the rest of the finance committee can attest, you know our finances are always tight at the end of the year. Parishioners wait until the last minute to pay their annual pledges, and we always end up riding on monetary fumes to the end of the year until our coffers are filled with the Christmas Eve offering and end-of-year pledge payments.

"This year was particularly challenging, and I need you to know I took it upon myself to hold off paying certain bills until we had more money in our account. It was not my position to do so, and I accept full responsibility for the decision."

"So, we have some late fees," said Simon. "That's not a big deal."

"What bills are you talking about?" Robert asked.

"What are you telling us?" Virginia added.

"One of the bills I waited to pay was the insurance premium."

"What?" a few people asked at the same time.

"Oh my God," Robert sighed loud enough for everyone at the table to hear.

"I waited to pay the insurance premium, and it seems I waited too long. Our policy was canceled."

"When?" asked Virginia.

"Last Friday, at midnight."

After a brief pause, she continued. "But the fire was on Sunday, Christmas morning."

"That's right," Emmett said.

"I am sure there's a way around this," said Robert. "I deal with insurance companies all the time. There's a deadline, yes, but there's also a grace period before the policy is terminated."

"That's true," Emmett replied. "I went and met with Jim Adams first thing yesterday morning, but he said there was nothing we could do. Seems I waited too long. The grace period expired."

"So, what you're saying is the church wasn't insured when it burned. Is that right?" Robert asked.

"I'm afraid so," Emmett replied, looking down at the papers on the table.

"You've got to be kidding me," Stanley growled.

"I wish I was."

"I don't believe this," Robert said with a crimson face. "First, we lose our church. Now you're telling us it was uninsured."

"That's correct. And, as I said, the fault is completely mine. Neither Terrance nor the finance committee knew anything about my decision to withhold the premium payment. It was beyond my authority to do so."

"This is not good," Robert said to no one in particular.

"No, it's not, Robert," Emmett replied. "It's tragic. Because of my actions, or inactions, as the case may be, I put the parish in peril, which is why I'm offering you this." Emmett pulled the envelope from his jacket pocket and slid it toward Virginia. "It's my resignation, effective immediately."

"No," said many at the table.

"Yes," Emmett replied. "There's no other choice. You, as the vestry, need to separate yourselves from me and what I've done in case there are legal implications." Virginia took the envelope but did not open it. "Before I leave, though, I need to express my deepest regret over what I've done. I doubt you'll be able to forgive me. I don't know if I'll be able to forgive myself. I wish there was some way I could make things right, but there isn't. This is not how I ever imagined leaving St. John's. I always hoped to leave a different legacy, but now, well…"

Emotions overwhelmed Emmett, and he knew he needed to leave. He gathered his things, and he looked up at the vestry and added, "It has been my profound honor to serve as your rector. I ask God's blessing upon you and the work you have before you. I'm so sorry for what I've done."

The vestry sat in silence as Emmett walked away from the table toward the front door. Once in his car again, Emmett put his hands and his head on the steering wheel and closed his eyes. "Thank you for getting me through that," he sighed.

The next hours were a blur for Emmett. He thought Virginia would call, informing him of the vestry's decision about his resignation, but the phone was silent. He sat in his study and waited. Reaching over, he lifted the prayer book and Bible from the table beside his chair, remnants of when he began each day reading the Daily Office. The bookshelves around the study were filled with books and mementos from his ministry at St. John's.

He could see the picture of his first Sunday at St. John's. Abby looked radiant, and he looked ready to take on the world. Beside the picture was a communion set the congregation gave him at his installation. The last time he had used it was when he took Abby communion in the hospital. A shovel from the Cutter Hall groundbreaking ceremony stood in the corner.

Emmett went into the kitchen to fix some dinner and decided he might as well start organizing things for when he began packing in the morning. He grabbed an empty box from the garage and brought it into the house. As he made his way back to his study, he heard a knock at the front door. Tempted to ignore it, he reminded himself that he was still the rector until the vestry accepted his resignation.

Standing on the rectory doorstep was Virginia with the rest of the vestry behind her. You could have called, Emmett thought, but he greeted them as warmly as he could.

"We've been meeting ever since you left," Virginia began, "and I must admit it hasn't been fun. You put us in a terrible position, Emmett. The easy thing would have been to accept your resignation and move on. Not paying the insurance was wrong, and it has devastated the parish, financially. To be frank, we're not sure we'll be able to crawl out from this deep, dark hole."

"I understand," said Emmett. "As I said, I'm..."

"But the fact is," she continued, "we want you in the hole with us. Whether we make it or not, we want you beside us. You should know, the decision wasn't unanimous, but it's official. As senior warden, I'm here to inform you that we do not accept your resignation. Emmett Hodges, you are still the rector of St. John's Episcopal Church."

Emmett stood in shock as the late-night visitors shook in the cold.

CHAPTER 4

"I don't know what to say," he began.

"How about, 'Come in. You must be freezing'?" Terrance suggested.

"Of course, of course. How rude of me," Emmett replied, waving his arms enthusiastically. As they entered, he thanked each vestry member for the undeserved gift of their faith in him.

The evening soon took on the look and feel of a late-night cocktail party instead of a reconciliation. Virginia, Sara, and Simon went to find refreshments, while Emmett led the others into the living room where he knelt and lit the fire. When he stood, he bumped into Robert who was standing behind him, eager for a word.

"I need to tell you: I was the one who voted to accept your resignation."

"I see," said Emmett, looking away. "I appreciate you telling me that, Robert."

"But I also need to tell you that I accept the vestry's decision and will not say another word about it."

"That's very kind," Emmett said, not sure he believed him.

When everyone returned to the living room, Virginia used her wedding ring to clink her wine glass and proposed a toast. "Before we lift our glasses and roll up our sleeves, I want to say how truly blessed I feel to be in this with all of you. I know this is nothing any of us signed on for, and we don't have a clue about what lies ahead, but we'll find a way, together. We've been told, 'God working in us is able to accomplish far more than all we can ask or imagine.' I guess we're going to find out if that's true. So, here's to God working in each of us!"

"Amen," said a united chorus as they lifted their glasses. Emmett did his best to go to each person and express his gratitude, but everyone seemed more interested in talking about what to do next. Without Virginia having to assign duties, people were volunteering to help with an assortment of tasks.

"What's that?" Virginia asked, looking at the cardboard box in the hall.

"Oh that," Emmett responded, unsure what to say.

Smiling, Virginia placed her hand on Emmett's shoulder. "You can put that away, now."

Virginia and Sara stayed behind to help clean up when the others left at midnight. Emmett washed; they dried. He was uncharacteristically quiet.

"What's on your mind?" Virginia asked.

"Nothing," Emmett said, then shook his head. "Actually, there's a lot on my mind. I just realized everything that's happened in my life has been the result of some effort on my part. For good or ill, I have pretty much run the show. Whether it was a good grade in school or a job, I've always made things happen. What happened tonight, though, had nothing to do with me. In fact, it was completely beyond me. You and the others forgave me. I didn't deserve it, but you forgave me anyway."

"You're right," said Virginia, putting the glass down on the counter and looking directly at Emmett. "You didn't deserve it, but isn't that the point?"

"Isn't that what the church is supposed to do?" Sara added. "It seems to me that's what this thing called grace is all about."

"We've all been forgiven, and none of us deserved it," Virginia added. "That's what I've heard you preach, anyway."

"I know," said Emmett as he resumed cleaning. "It's just different when you experience it firsthand."

— 5 —

CHAPTER

Church At Home

Emmett stared out the window the next morning as if
meditating on an icon. His mind wandered from what
had happened the day before to what needed to happen now. The
words he used in his letter of resignation echoed in his heart. "It
has been my profound honor…41 years…never wanted to leave
under such circumstances…always hoped to leave a legacy." The
vestry had given him a wonderful gift, but as he sipped his coffee,
he realized he had no idea what to do with it.

Emmett looked across the common at the church ruins.
Only portions of the walls remained, that and the granite steps,
the Revere Bell on its side, and remnants of Cutter Hall. Quite a
legacy, he sighed in disgust.

He had awakened determined to see the parish through this crisis, but his plans melted like the snow when he saw the vacant lot that used to be his church. Whatever was to come, he thought as he looked at his to-do list, would need to be completely new. The blank canvas scared Emmett more than the fire.

The finance committee had scheduled a meeting for tomorrow morning, and the committee charged with finding a temporary place to worship was beginning their work later that day. Virginia and Sara were coming over later in the afternoon to discuss what the parish could do between now and finding a new space.

In the meantime, Emmett had to occupy himself. He went into the front hall and wound the grandfather clock he and Abby had purchased. The card she wrote, which read "Let's not waste a second," was taped inside the clock behind the chimes. He watered the plants and straightened up the living room from last night's spontaneous gathering.

Emmett decided to go into his study and do something he hadn't in a long time: say the prayers of the Morning Office. When he was in seminary, he began each day with Morning Prayer. He continued when he arrived at St. John's, and Abby often joined him, but after she died, he stopped.

A bookmark was wedged between the pages of Acts, the book about the early church. Before turning to the assigned readings for the day, Emmett read about how the early church went to one another's houses and shared meals, said prayers, told stories about Jesus, and sang songs. They also imitated the last supper by breaking bread and drinking wine. The church was simpler then, Emmett thought.

Virginia and Sara arrived late, but Emmett welcomed them like old friends and ushered them into the kitchen. Gathered around the table, Virginia asked Emmett to begin their meeting with prayer. He began to stand and get his prayer book from his study, but Sara reached over and touched his arm, encouraging him to offer a more informal prayer. Emmett bowed his head and offered the prayer.

"Almighty God, we give you thanks for this new day. Although the mountain before us is great, and we don't know why, you have given it to us in the first place. We pray for you to guide us on our way. Be with us as we take this first step and remain with us until we take our last. All of this we ask in Christ's holy name. Amen."

The conversation began with Virginia suggesting St. John's rent a tent that could be placed on the lawn in front of the church.

"But it's winter," Sara pointed out. "There's snow, and it gets really cold."

"I know," Virginia replied, "but I thought with some space heaters, it could work."

Sara suggested meeting at Maria's. "It's not open on Sundays, and we could set up the table and chairs in a church-like way. We could make it feel like home."

When Emmett heard the word home, he remembered the passage from the Bible that he had read earlier.

"What?" Virginia asked, as she saw Emmett turn thoughtfully to the window.

"Nothing," he said at first, then added, "well, maybe it's something. This morning when I was reading from the Book of Acts, I was reminded that the early church used to meet in people's houses. There were no church buildings. They'd meet informally, and what they did then eventually led to the services we know today."

"What did they do?" Sara asked.

"They met in small groups, told stories about Jesus, sang hymns, and shared communion. I'm wondering if we should follow their example. It's not what we're used to, but it might be worth a try.

"I love the idea," Virginia said, "but I don't think we could fit everyone in the rectory."

"We can't," Emmett agreed. "We'll have to host small gatherings in parishioners' homes."

"Home churches?" Sara asked.

"Exactly," Emmett said with delight.

"Todd and I would love to host a group," Virginia offered.

"My place isn't big enough," said Sara, "but I'd be happy to help find other hosts."

"Could you work up a simple service that each home church could follow?" Virginia asked. Emmett nodded.

"How will you be able to be at each house?" Sara asked Emmett.

"I won't," he said. "People will need to take turns leading."

With a look of fear on her face, Sara continued, "What about sermons?"

"Someone will have to be appointed to deliver a homily, which is just a short sermon," Emmett explained. "There are plenty in the congregation who could do it."

"Not me!" Sara stated adamantly as she shook her head from side to side.

"What about communion?" Virginia asked. "Aren't there rules about how that's done?"

"Yes, a priest needs to consecrate the bread and wine, but I could do that and have it delivered to each house before the services," Emmett explained.

Although it sounded unconventional, the three decided home churches were worth a try, at least until a temporary worship space was found.

The finance meeting did not go as well.

"How much does it cost to build a church?" someone asked.

"More than we have," Terrance said, then added, "and more than we have ever had." He explained that the church currently had enough money to continue operating through the spring, especially now that there were no building maintenance costs for the church building. "After that, well, I'm not sure what we're going to do."

As the group discussed the costs associated with renting a temporary worship space, they realized the church was facing a major financial crisis.

"We're not even talking about the costs associated with rebuilding," Terrance pointed out. "It's clear we will need a capital campaign if we ever plan to rebuild. Right now, we need to focus on surviving."

Other committee members looked away and didn't respond. They needed time to let the news sink in. Emmett shared that the Christmas Eve collection had been left on a pew and destroyed with the rest of the church.

"One thing we could do," he said, "is ask everyone who wrote a check for the Christmas Eve collection to write another since the collection burned with the church. There were lots of checks. Although I didn't take an accurate count, it looked like something close to $10,000."

"That would be a big help," Terrance said.

Someone brought up the need to begin thinking about a capital campaign, but everyone agreed it was too soon. Right now, they needed to find a temporary home and a way to afford it.

"I have one more idea," Emmett said raising his hand. "As you all know, the financial crisis we face is because of me. If I had paid the insurance, we wouldn't be in this situation."

"The insurance probably wouldn't have covered the full cost of rebuilding," Terrance pointed out.

"No, but it would certainly have provided resources we dearly need to start. I feel responsible for this and want to suggest I work for half salary for the year. I have savings to cover the rest of what I need."

Everyone but Robert refused Emmett's offer. "We'll find a way without you taking a pay cut," Terrance said. "We'll find the money somehow."

Mac came to the rectory that evening for dinner. He was eager to hear about the various meetings, but he could tell from the look on Emmett's face that things had not gone well.

"You look awful," said Mac.

"Good to see you, too."

"Were the meetings that bad?"

"They weren't great. I think we have a solution to get us through until we find a temporary space, but the money's bad."

"How bad?"

"Let's just say unless we find some big-time money, this rectory will be up for sale in June."

"That bad?"

Emmett nodded and handed Mac a beer. The two had no sooner taken their seats by the fire than Emmett saw a curious look on Mac's face.

"What?" Emmett asked.

"You know what," Mac said.

"I'm afraid I don't."

"You need to go see him."

"Who?" Emmett asked, but Mac didn't need to answer. "I know. I just don't want to." Emmett said, sounding like a child told to eat his vegetables.

"He's the bishop, for God's sake, and St. John's is one of his parishes. It makes sense that we reach out and ask for help."

"You're right, but it doesn't make it any easier. I guess I was hoping..."

"That you could do it without him. I know. I don't blame you. I can't stand the guy, but he's also the bishop, the head of the diocese, and we lost our church. It's only right that he helps us."

"When I called to tell him about the fire, all he said was he was sorry and that we would be in his thoughts and prayers."

"Thoughts and prayers?" Mac said, almost spitting out his beer. "You clergy throw that line around like spiritual air freshener."

"He sent a note the next day, but that's it."

"A note? Really? Like that's going to make it all better. Did he send some chocolates, too, maybe some flowers?" Mac took a deep breath and looked directly at Emmett. "You and I know you're dancing around the real issue. It's time to put on your big-boy pants, Emmett, and go see him. Grovel if you must, but we need the diocese's help if we're going to have any hope of rebuilding. Your ego and personal history with Michael Phillips have to be put aside, just this once."

"You're right," Emmett said, "but what am I going to tell him about the insurance?"

"The truth," Mac said bluntly. "You screwed up. The vestry forgave you. He needs to do the same."

Emmett groaned. "I'm afraid it won't be that simple."

"Perhaps not," said Mac, "but you need to go see him either way."

6

CHAPTER

On Our Own

Emmett and the bishop had history. It began when they met the first day of seminary. Emmett arrived early, but Michael Phillips had already unpacked and set up his room by the time he offered to help Emmett carry his things into the dorm.

"Nice to meet you, Mike," Emmett said as he shook his classmate's hand.

"Michael."

"Excuse me?" Emmett asked.

"I go by Michael."

Michael was dressed as if heading to class. Khakis, button-down shirt, and loafers were soon to become their daily uniform. Michael started a day early. Emmett was dressed in shorts and a T-shirt. He defied his father's request that he be "presentable," as he put it. "You represent me," his father had said before Emmett departed.

"So, you're Bishop Hodges's son," Michael said with renewed interest in his classmate. Emmett was used to it. People often liked him because of his father. A father who was a bishop paved a smoother road for the son. Whether getting out of a speeding ticket or getting into seminary, having a father who was a bishop had its advantages.

Michael invited Emmett across the hall to his room for some water after they unloaded his car. Michael's room looked as if he'd been there for months. His bed was made, books arranged by subject on his desk, and a cross hung on the wall, surrounded by photographs of Michael and his family. Beside his bed was a Bible that looked untouched.

"It's new," Michael said, reading Emmett's thoughts. "I wanted to start fresh."

In one of the boxes across the hall was Emmett's father's Bible, the one he had used when he was a student. Twisting the family crest ring on his finger, a gift for his twenty-first birthday, Emmett tried to appear comfortable in his new surroundings.

Unlike Emmett, Michael hadn't grown up in the Episcopal Church. He was raised in the Baptist tradition but became an Episcopalian in college. Like many converts, Michael became a zealot about the canons, or rules, of the Episcopal Church and militant about liturgical practices. "People who come into the church later in life," his father once pointed out, "always seem bent on becoming more Episcopalian than those born into it. I guess they feel like they have something to prove."

Michael paraded, more than walked, around campus. Emmett often joked Michael seemed to have a sixth sense about when a bishop was on campus. He dubbed Michael the charter member of a group he called the "purple-shirt sniffers." They were the ones determined to suck up to any bishop and to one day wear a bishop's purple shirt of their own.

The friendship between Emmett and Michael became a competition before the first semester ended. First, it was grades, then elected positions. By the time the first-year students had to find a local parish in which to train for ministry, their competition became an all-out war. The more prestigious their parish, the more likely they were to stand out among the other classmates, or so they thought.

By senior year, the two hardly spoke. That is, until they stood beside each other on stage as finalists for the prestigious Cranmer Debates. The question for the debate was: "Justice or Mercy: which matters more to God?" The entire seminary attended, and the debate went on for two hours. Emmett was assigned justice. "Justice is the bedrock of faith," he argued. "Without it, our faith is but sand and God a fickle bystander. Actions have consequences. Justice is the backbone of the body, which is the church." Michael's response was more poetry than rhetoric. His call for mercy won the debate. Emmett did his best to graciously shake Michael's hand, but it wasn't until graduation, when Emmett won the Aspinwall Preaching Prize, that Emmett felt vindicated.

Their competition continued when searching for their first appointments after seminary. Michael was the first to receive a call, a position as assistant dean at St. Matthew's Cathedral in Texas. It was a major appointment, and Michael walked around campus as if he had half-expected it.

Emmett tried to act excited for Michael. Although he had been offered an assistant rector position, no one knew he was also being considered for the rectorship at St. John's, a renowned parish in New England. It was highly unusual for someone right out of seminary to become a rector, particularly at a church as well-known as St. John's, but the vestry was drawn to Emmett's innate talent and Episcopal pedigree. His appointment to the church was significant enough for the dean of the seminary to congratulate Emmett at lunch. That Michael Phillips was sitting two seats away was a bonus.

The two kept a watchful eye on each other after seminary. It wasn't until years later that their paths crossed again, and it proved to be a dramatic climax to an already spiteful relationship.

When the bishop of New Hampshire announced his retirement, everyone in the diocese thought Emmett was sure to be his successor. Given he was the senior priest in the diocese, many clergy joked the election was an unnecessary formality. When the nominations were announced, however, Emmett groaned. Michael Phillips's name was among the other finalists.

"I don't believe it!" he said, slamming the paper on the kitchen table.

"Don't believe what?" Abby asked.

"This," he said, looking up at his wife with the eyes of a wounded child. "Guess who's also a finalist?"

"Oh no," Abby said as she saw the familiar name.

"Game on," Emmett growled as he wiped his mouth and stormed toward his study. "I'll be damned if I'm going to lose this battle!" Abby knew better than to reason with her husband right away. She knew how much the position meant to him and wished there was something she could do to assure his success. She also knew this was not only a competition with Michael Phillips but also with Emmett's father.

Emmett always spoke with disdain about clergy who lobbied for positions and ran for them like they were political posts.

He joked that it was only a matter of time before clergy started putting yard signs around the diocese when seeking an elected position, but seeing Michael's name on the list of finalists flipped a switch inside Emmett. He started making calls to other clergy and shoring up what he felt was an overwhelming base of support before the diocesan convention that February. He was encouraged when he received the most votes on the first ballot and remained in first place on the second. Such elections often take between seven and ten ballots, he knew, but when one of the candidates withdrew, Michael Phillips took the lead. After the fifth ballot, the clerk of convention stood and announced the name of the next bishop of New Hampshire: Michael S. Phillips. Abby squeezed his hand under the table, and Emmett tried to hide his devastation. He stood to congratulate the bishop-elect. For the second time, Emmett struggled to shake Michael's hand.

"That's it," he said to Abby as they drove home. "We're leaving. I'm not going to serve under that detestable, egotistical charlatan."

Abby was as distraught as her husband but said nothing. Many parishioners reached out to Emmett and encouraged him to stay at St. John's, but it was Mac who finally convinced him.

"Look at it this way," he said to Emmett over breakfast at Maria's soon after the election. "You're the rector of one of the most historic parishes in the diocese. Why not hang around and make life difficult for the bastard?"

Emmett smiled for the first time in a week. He usually cringed when Mac used such language but not that morning. Reluctantly, Emmett decided to stay at St. John's. "I'll do my work, and let him do his," he told Abby, who nodded as if she believed him.

Whenever the bishop came to St. John's for his annual visitations, Emmett was civil, but he avoided his nemesis at other diocesan events. When the bishop proposed diocesan initiatives and asked parishes for support, Emmett did his best to convince St. John's to refuse or send a token contribution. The same was true each year when the diocese determined St. John's annual contribution. Emmett made sure they sent less than what was suggested and waited for the bishop to call and personally request a larger sum.

Emmett drove into the diocesan parking lot slowly, not out of reverence but disdain. It was empty, except for the bishop's recently washed Mercedes sitting in its reserved spot. Emmett parked his salt-covered Subaru two spots over and sat in his car to brace himself. "The bishop does not like to meet on Friday afternoons," his assistant had informed Emmett when he called to make an appointment. "But, given the circumstances, he will make an exception." Sitting in the parking lot, Emmett wanted to reschedule.

The diocesan center was a large Victorian home given to the church years ago. Like Cutter Hall, the rooms were adapted to serve as offices. Emmett pushed the front door and entered the stately front hall. The sound of the door announced his arrival, and the bishop called out from his office that he'd be right there. Emmett knew to sit in the reception area across the hall from the bishop's office and wait, like an obedient dog. The two mahogany pocket doors leading to the bishop's office were closed. Emmett sat, knowing the bishop would announce his availability by sliding the doors open and extending his arms as if to say, "Behold, your bishop!"

"Emmett, my dear fellow," the bishop bellowed like an English squire. In his pressed purple shirt, he waited for Emmett to cross the lobby. Emmett begrudgingly complied.

"I can't tell you how heartbroken I was to hear of the fire. We all were," the bishop said, sounding as if reading a script.

"Hello Michael," Emmett said as he extended his hand to his seminary classmate. Emmett knew calling him by his first name would irk the bishop.

"I wanted to come right over and see you," the bishop said, "but my schedule's been particularly hectic. I'm sure you understand. I hope you received my note."

"I did. Very kind of you," Emmett said, trying to hide his sarcasm.

There was a day, particularly in other denominations, when priests were expected to kiss the ring of the bishop when arriving or departing. Fortunately, those days were past, but Emmett smiled as he thought about Mac's last words before leaving Webster. "If the bishop asks you to kiss his ring, tell him to kiss your ass."

"It does me well to see you face to face," the bishop said as if they were friends. "I can't begin to tell you how upset we all were to lose our oldest and most revered church. It's still too much to comprehend."

"For us, too," Emmett replied.

"I hope you're holding up as well as can be expected."

"We're doing our best," Emmett replied, following the bishop's invitation to sit in one of the seats in front of his desk. "But it's tough."

"I'm confident, with the Lord's help, you'll rise from the ashes and become an even better parish in the end."

Emmett nodded, wondering if that was a line the bishop had used before. "Right now, the situation feels like the church looks—a dismal pile of ash," Emmett said as he twisted his signet ring.

"Indeed," the bishop said as he took his seat behind his desk and pressed his fingertips against each other. Emmett noticed the bishop's cufflinks were in the shape of the diocesan shield. Theirs had always been an understated diocese, but Michael had never understood that.

"We're praying for you."

"I appreciate that."

"If there is anything we can do, don't hesitate to ask."

"I'm glad to hear you say that because that's why I'm here. We need your help."

"Certainly, what can I do?"

"Well, we need just about everything, but, most of all, we need financial assistance."

The bishop's eyes widened as he sat back. "I see."

"The fire destroyed everything. We're going to have to start from scratch, and there's no way we'll be able to do it without help."

"The insurance will certainly help," the bishop pointed out. "How long until you receive your settlement?"

Emmett looked down to gather whatever strength he could before looking back across the desk. "There's not going to be any settlement," Emmett said.

"Excuse me?" the bishop responded.

"It seems the required premium payment was not made in time. The fire occurred when the church was no longer insured.

I was the one who made the decision to hold off paying it until the end-of-year gifts arrived, and it seems I waited too late."

"You must be joking," the bishop said as he sat up in his chair that was noticeably higher than Emmett's.

"I wish I were," Emmett muttered.

"But every parish is required to carry insurance. It's a diocesan rule."

"And we did, but our policy was terminated."

"When, exactly?"

"Before the fire."

"I don't believe this," the bishop said, looking away. Placing his hands flatly on his spacious desk, the bishop took a deep breath. "Frankly, I'm at a loss as to what to say. Clearly, this is horrible news, not only for St. John's but for the diocese as well."

"That's why I came as quickly as I could."

"Yes, but I'm not sure there's much we can do. In the best of circumstances, parishes are to look out for their own particular needs. The diocese cannot be expected to jump in whenever a parish has a crisis. Having insurance is one of the ways we make sure things like this don't happen."

"But isn't helping the parishes of the diocese what this office is supposed to do?" Emmett asked and regretted the question the minute he asked it.

"Please don't try to turn this around and blame us," the bishop said. "You are the ones who brought this upon yourselves. We require parishes have insurance to avoid this very thing. There simply aren't the resources needed to bail out every struggling parish."

Emmett was tempted to mention the bishop's recent pay raise and the renovation of the bishop's house approved at the last diocesan convention but didn't.

"Even if there were enough resources, we wouldn't help," the bishop continued. "Your church is faced with a financial crisis because you chose to ignore a clearly stated diocesan requirement. Surely, the diocese can't be expected to step in and save you."

"Actually," Emmett began, but decided any argument or plea would be futile.

"We're not a bank, Emmett," the bishop sputtered while adjusting one of his cufflinks. "You know that."

"I know," Emmett replied in disgust, "but we lost our church. We need help."

"You must accept responsibilities for your actions, Emmett," the bishop said, sounding like Emmett's father. "As you once pointed out, actions have consequences."

"You're not going to bring up our debate after all these years, are you?" Emmett asked.

"Just reminding you of your words. All of this is the consequence of your negligence."

"What about mercy, the topic about which you spoke so poetically? I made a colossal mistake, and I take full responsibility..."

"Do you?" The bishop interrupted.

"Do I what?"

"Take full responsibility? Is coming here and asking for help what full responsibility looks like?"

"I told the vestry what I had done. I even offered my resignation, which they refused. Now, together, we are trying to walk through this crisis. I came here to ask the diocese to join us."

"There's nothing the diocese can or will do to help. You caused this crisis; you must solve it."

"Our church burned to the ground, and now you sit behind your fancy bishop's desk and refuse to help."

The bishop started to say more, then stopped. He stood up and waved his arm toward the door. "I think we are done here."

"Can't you rise above our past and be a bishop?" Emmett said as if throwing darts across the bishop's desk.

"Careful," said the bishop. "The fact that you came here expecting me to save your skin is more than I can fathom. Our past has nothing to do with it."

"Really?" Emmett snorted.

"The fact that I became bishop, and you did not, has nothing to do with my decision. I would make the same decision with any of my parishes."

"They're not yours," Emmett said, stepping closer to the desk. "They belong to the diocese, to God, actually, and I didn't come here to have you save my skin or bail me out, as you put it so pastorally. I came because a parish is in trouble and needs the help of its bishop."

"If you had followed our clearly stated policies, we wouldn't be having this conversation. I must tell you, this is such a serious matter, far beyond a fire destroying a church. The diocesan attorney might well need to get involved."

"Now you're threatening legal action?"

"I said nothing of the kind, but you've clearly broken diocesan protocols. By doing so, you've put not only St. John's but also the diocese in a precarious position. This is serious, Emmett, serious indeed."

Emmett stood up. "This has been illuminating, to say the least. How silly of me to think... "

"Don't you dare go playing the victim card, Emmett," the bishop interrupted. "You know as well as I that you're the one to blame for this mess. Maybe the vestry should have accepted your resignation."

Emmett didn't stay to hear anymore. Back in his car, he slammed the steering wheel and screamed as loud as he could. A woman walking her dog on the sidewalk turned around, and Emmett tried unsuccessfully to assure her everything was all right with a smile and wave. She shook her head and walked away.

On the way home, Emmett was tempted to turn north. Never had he wanted to escape to the cabin more, but it was closed for the winter. Instead, he took the long way home in hopes of calming down. It didn't work. When he returned to the rectory, he was surprised, and grateful, to see Mac in the driveway, leaning against his beat-up truck.

"Thought I'd check up on you," he said as Emmett climbed out of the car. "How'd it go?"

Emmett shook his head in disgust.

"That good, eh? Well, it's not like you lost a friend or anything. Maybe it's for the best."

"Best?" Emmett asked as he stopped to look at his friend in disbelief. "How could it be for the best?"

"There's no diocese to get in our way."

"Well, that's one way to look at it," Emmett said, looking over at where the church once stood. "All I know is, we're on our own."

Mac placed his hand on Emmett's shoulder as the two walked into the rectory. "That sounds funny coming from a minister."

—— 7 ——
CHAPTER

Communion

The plastic containers were lined up along the edge of the linoleum kitchen counter, as they had been for each week the last month since the home churches began. Emmett tried not to look at them. Even though he was the one who suggested the short-term solution of meeting in parishioners' homes, he missed the way things used to be.

Each Saturday, he blessed the elements of bread and wine for the home churches and placed them in plastic containers so they could be delivered to the homes for Sunday services. The ritual was a painful reminder of all that was lost in the fire. Convenience usurped sacredness, silver gave way to plastic, and Emmett felt communion had become like fast food—easy but lacking nourishment. His ministry was beginning to feel plastic, too.

Determined to bring some dignity to his weekly ritual, Emmett used an old stole he had in his study and a silver punch bowl that Abby's parents had given them as a wedding present. He unwrapped the wafers, opened the wine, and recited the traditional eucharistic language in hopes of making the kitchen ritual sacred.

He knew he should celebrate the success of the home churches. In just three weeks, the services had become a routine people enjoyed. Overall, attendance was almost back to pre-fire level. Although Emmett had created a service each house could use, hosts added their own, unique touches. Virginia and Todd had people sit around their dining room table; at another home, people met in the living room. One group even had people gather outside around a fire pit. Some played music; others used silence in ways that would make the Quakers proud. Emmett attended a different home church each week, and he was beginning to feel dizzy from all the variations. Communion was the one constant.

In seminary, he learned communion was a sacrament, an outward and visible sign of an inward and spiritual grace. Ever since the Last Supper, communion was a way the church experienced Christ's presence. Looking at the plastic containers spread out across the counter, Emmett had a hard time seeing them as such. Never had he imagined celebrating the eucharist in such a way when he was in seminary.

"Almighty God, to you all hearts are open, all desires known, and from you no secrets are hid: Cleanse the thoughts of our hearts by the inspiration of your Holy Spirit, that we may perfectly love you, and worthily magnify your holy Name; through Christ our Lord."

The words echoed off the cabinets.

"In your infinite love you made us for yourself; and, when we had fallen into sin and become subject to evil and death, you, in your mercy, sent Jesus Christ, your only and eternal Son, to share our human nature, to live and die as one of us, to reconcile us to you, the God and Father of all."

Emmett wondered what people would say if they caught him celebrating the eucharist alone in his kitchen. "Look who's playing church," he could hear Mac joke, but he lifted the wafers and continued anyway.

"On the night he was handed over to suffering and death, our Lord Jesus Christ took bread; and when he had given thanks to you, he broke it, and gave it to his disciples, and said, 'Take, eat: This is my Body, which is given for you. Do this for the remembrance of me.'"

Lifting the wine, he poured it into the silver punch bowl as he said, "After supper he took the cup of wine; and when he had given thanks, he gave it to them, and said, 'Drink this, all of you: This is my Blood of the new Covenant, which is shed for you and for many for the forgiveness of sins. Whenever you drink it, do this for the remembrance of me.'"

Emmett took the ladle and began filling each of the plastic containers. He cringed as he listened to the wine splash into the containers. He realized how insufficient his efforts were to bring dignity to this ritual.

"The small groups were your idea," Mac pointed out when Emmett complained one day.

"I know. I just miss being in church."

"What you miss is all the pomp and circumstance, the candles, robes, and standing up front." Emmett waved Mac off but knew his friend had a point.

Once all the containers were filled, Emmett laid them in cardboard boxes and placed them on the stoop by the kitchen door. Volunteers would be by soon to pick them up and deliver to each home. Before going back inside, he touched each container with his hand and said, "The gifts of God for the people of God. Feed our bodies; nourish our souls."

Emmett heard an abrupt knock on the kitchen door while washing the silver punch bowl. He leaned over to see out the window and tried to hide his displeasure when Marty Starnes looked at him and waved.

"Morning, Emmett," said the woman responsible for the church's outreach ministries.

"Morning, Marty. I've been meaning to call you," Emmett said as Marty stomped her boots on the porch, slipped them off, and entered the kitchen in her socks.

"You've had your hands full, but it's time we figure out what to do about the food pantry and Wednesday night dinners."

Emmett invited Marty to sit at the kitchen table. "I've been distracted by everything that's gone on. I know we need to decide how to handle things now that we've lost our church."

"We've lost our building, not the church," Marty interrupted.

"You know what I mean," Emmett said, looking down and rubbing his hand on the table.

"The needs are still out there," Marty said, gesturing toward town, "It's our job to figure out how to carry on our ministries without the building."

"You're right," Emmett conceded. "We should get some folks together and…"

"I hope you're not going to suggest forming a committee," Marty interrupted. "You know what they say, 'God so loved the world he sent not a committee.' We don't have time to sit around and talk about things. You and I can decide what needs to be done right now."

"I appreciate your sense of urgency, Marty, but if you look across the common, you'll see we have more pressing matters."

"More pressing than feeding the poor?" she asked. "I am sorry about the fire. I'm sure you will find a way to rebuild the church. In the meantime, we need to remember to do the work of the church."

"It's not that simple," Emmett replied.

"No, but it shouldn't be that hard to feed people while we figure out all the rest. The fire didn't take away people's hunger or their other needs."

"I appreciate your passion and the importance of your ministry."

"Our," Marty interrupted.

"Excuse me?"

"Our ministry. It isn't my ministry or the people who work with me. The ministry belongs to all of us."

"Yes, I know, but the fact is we don't have a building, and we're all but out of money. Maybe others in the community can serve the poor until we're back on our feet."

Marty stared at Emmett until he shifted in his seat and looked away. Marty always looked for a fight, he felt, and he wasn't in the mood this morning.

"What's the silver punch bowl for?" she asked.

"Communion. We've started home churches, and it's my job to prepare communion for each group."

"Glad you pulled out the silver," Marty said with a smirk.

"Communion's important."

"So is feeding people real food. Surely, the Lord wants that, too."

"The world is not black or white, Marty," Emmett began, sounding defensive. "It's not either/or. We need to feed the parishioners with the food they need while also feeding others. We'll resume our work with the poor but just not now."

"I see," Marty said, reaching for her gloves.

"You see what? We need time to take care of a congregation that has lost its church building before we think about taking care of others."

"So, you're saying the hungry matter less?"

"Don't twist my words, Marty," said Emmett.

"You want me to wait, to be patient. Sorry, that's not my thing. I can't sit around. I need to do something."

"Just until we find a home. Then, I promise, we'll find a way to begin your ministries again."

"Our?"

"Yes, our," Emmett said.

In a rare moment of restraint, Marty said nothing more. She got up from the table, apologized for the interruption, and saw herself out the door.

Emmett stood and leaned against the counter. Marty had a point, but why did she have to be so condescending and self-righteous, he wondered. Marty appeared one day, asking if she could start a food ministry at St. John's. Emmett was delighted to give such work to Marty and her team of volunteers. The ministry grew over time, and some of the parishioners joined Marty and her team. The ministry became a model for other parishes, and Emmett was proud of the work, but it was as if there were two churches: those who served and those who worshiped. Marty and her team were so good that others sat back and watched. Marty and most of her volunteers never came to worship services. "I can't stand all the religious hocus pocus. This is my church," Marty told Emmett one night in the parish kitchen after a Wednesday meal.

Emmett was headed to his study when he heard another knock on the kitchen door. "What is it now?" he sighed. Sara Pierce and Simon Jackson were standing on the doorstep. Sara was hopping from one side to the other, with her hands wrapped around herself. She was clearly cold, Emmett could see, but she appeared excited, too. There was a childlike grin on her face. "We found it," she exclaimed as Emmett opened the door.

"Found what?" Emmett asked.

"Our new place," said Simon as Emmett invited them inside.

"The church's temporary home," Sara clarified.

"You did!" Emmett said with delight. "Where?" He gestured toward the kitchen table and went to the pantry to find some cookies.

"I was at work in the library when a woman with bright pink hair came in looking for a book on some obscure artist. I helped her find it, and we started talking about her work. She mentioned she has a studio with a bunch of other artists at the old Hampstead Grist Mill. Seems they have a sort of artist colony on the second floor."

Emmett came to the table and offered the two something to eat. The confused look on his face let his guests know he wasn't connecting the dots.

Sara continued. "Anyway, she said the whole first floor of the mill was empty and that the owner was looking for someone to rent. It's huge, she told me, and she thought the owner would make whoever rents it a good deal."

"We could use a good deal," Emmett muttered as he took a bite of a cookie. The idea of housing the church in a grist mill was going to take some getting used to, Emmett told the two, but the possibility of having a space for the church filled him with hope. "Have you seen it?" he asked.

"This morning," said Simon. "I've driven by the place for years but never been inside. It's large and open. It'll need some work, but it's the best of all the places we've seen. Looks out on Webster River and has real character. But it hasn't been used in some time, and I'm not sure how the older members of the parish will respond to such a solution."

"Don't listen to him," Sara said, dismissing Simon with a wave of her hand. "It's perfect. It's big enough for the entire congregation, and there's a small kitchen and two rooms in the back that could be used as offices."

"The grist mill," Emmett said trying to imagine it.

"It's not exactly your typical church space," Simon added, "but we think it might work. I had my doubts, but Sara's convinced me it could work."

"I need to see it," Emmett said.

"Glad to hear you say that," Sara said like a child at Christmas, "because I told the owner we'd be back this afternoon."

"Any idea when we could move in, or how much rent he wants?" Emmett asked.

"No. We thought you and the other higher-ups could handle that," said Simon.

Emmett agreed to meet at the mill later that afternoon. When he finally made it to his study, all he could do was sit and think about this recent development.

"A grist mill," Emmett sighed as he closed his eyes and leaned his head back on the chair. It was the last place he'd imagined for the church.

— 8 —

CHAPTER

New Wineskins

Emmett arrived early for the tour of the mill. Like Simon, he had driven past the mill for years but never pulled into the driveway. From the parking lot, you could see down a long, steep embankment to Webster River. Upstream were the falls that had supplied water for the paddle wheel when it was still an active grist mill. The wheel remained on the side of the mill, but it no longer moved. The building was three stories, not two as it appeared from the road. There was a lower floor that went to the water's edge. The windows on the top floor were decorated with colorful flags and plants. Those must be the artist studios, Emmett thought as he walked toward the front doors to see if they were unlocked. They weren't.

Virginia was the first to arrive, then Simon and Sara. Terrance drove in next, followed by Mac.

"Did you think we were incapable of making this decision without you?" Emmett joked as Mac walked over.

"Figured since I was going to have to take care of the place, I'd better see what you're thinking of getting us into."

"Glad to have another set of eyes," said Emmett, "but the good thing is we're only renting. You won't have to do any maintenance or repair."

"Yeah, yeah, that's what you think. Never turns out that way."

The group stood in the parking lot waiting for the owner when a dilapidated VW bug pulled in. The driver was a short woman with bright pink hair, and the passenger, a tall lanky man with a ponytail and a few days' growth on his chin.

"Namaste," the woman said with a welcoming voice. "Can we help you?"

"Remember me?" Sara asked as she walked toward the woman. "From the library."

"Oh yes," the woman said with delight. She hugged Sara as if they were long-lost friends.

Chuckling over the effusive greeting, Sara turned toward the others. "Everyone, this is Jewell. She's the artist I told you about, the one who told me about the mill."

"And this is Raj," said Jewell. "Another one of The Wackos."

"The Wackos?" Mac asked.

"That's what we call ourselves. We're a group of artists who use the studios upstairs." Jewell pointed to the colorful windows on the second floor. "I'm a fabric and mosaic artist. Raj, here, is our resident woodworker. We also have a painter, sculptor, and potter."

"We're here to look at the first floor you told Sara about," Virginia said.

"Awesome," said Jewell. "What do you people do?"

"Oh, we don't do anything," Virginia replied. "We're a church."

Mac bellowed. "Well, if that isn't the frickin' truth."

"I mean, we're a church. We're interested in the first-floor space. Our church burned, and we need a home until we can rebuild."

"The church on the town common?" Raj asked. "I read about that. Sucks, especially on Christmas." Looking at Jewell, he added, "It'd be cool to have a church here, don't you think?"

"Never imagined it," Jewell replied, "but, yeah, it would be great."

"We'll be good neighbors, I promise," said Sara.

"No speaking in tongues or loud revivals," Mac joked.

"It's all good. We're not all that religious upstairs. Spiritual, maybe. Just not churchy." Raj said. "Hope the space works for you."

"The more the merrier," Jewell added before Thomas Barkley, the owner, arrived. The two artists excused themselves and said they hoped it worked out. Thomas apologized for being the last to arrive and began with a brief history of the mill as he ushered the group into the building.

"The grist mill was the focal point of the Webster community years ago," he explained. "Farmers would bring their wheat for grinding and talk for hours until their sacks were full. Legend has it, during prohibition, thirsty residents would come and ask if Elijah was there, which was code for alcohol. Authorities turned a blind eye, but the mill was eventually abandoned. Someone once suggested making it into a shopping center, then condos, but that never happened. It needs work, as you'll see," he said while fumbling with the keys, "but it could work for a church. It has big windows overlooking Webster River, which, at the time the place was built, was known as the Ashuelot River."

"What does that mean?" asked Sara.

"It's a Native American name," Simon answered. He taught a unit on Webster history in his high school social studies class. "Means 'place between,' or something close to that."

"Sounds about right," Mac said with a smile.

The wide wooden planks creaked as the group walked across to the large windows. It wasn't anything like their old church, but the weathered brick walls and high ceilings had a charm of their own.

"It's got character," Mac said to Emmett. "I'll give you that."

"Just like you," Emmett whispered as he walked.

"You're no shrinking violet yourself, rector," Mac responded.

At the far end of the room was the door leading to the small kitchen and storage rooms. In the corner, on the river side, were two enormous granite stones that had been used to grind the wheat. Outside, the large rusty paddle wheel sat dormant. The paddle wheel was familiar because it was featured on almost as many Webster postcards as St. John's steeple.

"Water from the river would flow down that shoot," Thomas explained, "into those chambers in the paddle wheel, which made it turn. The wheel then turned the grinding stones."

"Does it still work?" Mac asked.

"The wheel might, but it's been disconnected from the stones. Back in the day, the lever over there opened the water shoot."

"What's below us?" Mac asked, looking down at the river.

"There's a lower level, a basement I guess you could call it. Opens to the river. It's about the same size as this room but sits at water level, which means it's susceptible to flooding."

"Does that happen often?" Terrance asked.

"Not in 50 years, but I'm required to disclose that. It's a mess down there. Mostly storage."

"Could we see it?" asked Emmett.

"Sure, but I can't rent it. If you're willing to clean it out, though, you could use it for free."

"Free's good," Terrance said to no one in particular.

After showing them the space, the owner excused himself so the church members could talk among themselves. Sara pointed out the rustic charm, Simon mentioned the wonderful connection to Webster history, and Mac said he just wanted to find a space and "get on with it," as he put it. Emmett was intimidated by the amount of work the place needed, but Virginia assured him they could do it, if everyone helped.

"But it doesn't look like a church," Emmett protested.

"Neither do we, these days," said Mac as he came and stood beside his friend. "Maybe that's a good thing. People won't be tempted to compare it to the church we lost. Think of it as a fresh start."

"A new wineskin," Emmett said softly.

"A what?" Sara asked.

"Nothing," he said. "Just agreeing with Mac."

"What about all the things we'll need? Pews, altar, pulpit?" Virginia asked.

"We'll need to beg, borrow, and steal," Emmett said. "We're going to need to be creative."

CHAPTER 8

"Excuse me?" Mac interrupted. "Who are you, and where did you take our rector? I never thought I'd hear the word 'creative' come from your mouth." Everyone laughed.

Ignoring Mac, Emmett continued. "We'll need to go to the local churches and businesses and see if they'll give us some items." Emmett felt a surge of unfamiliar excitement.

Thomas returned from visiting the artists upstairs.

"I'll tell you what I'll do," he said, looking at Emmett. "Given you've lost your church, I'll rent this to you for half the price and throw in the basement for free."

Virginia said she'd bring the offer to the vestry but was certain they'd approve. In the parking lot, she began handing out assignments as if it was already official.

"I'll get the vestry to sign off. Emmett, you approach the local churches to see what they might lend us. Simon, canvas businesses in the community and see if you can find a whole bunch of folding chairs, and, Sara, coordinate with Gladys Fitzpatrick to see what other things we're going to need. Mac, your job is to figure out what the building needs. I'll find the volunteers to help when you're ready."

"I don't need volunteers," Mac protested.

"Yes, you do," Virginia argued. "It's time you let others help."

"What about the space downstairs?" Sara asked.

Emmett looked as if he just came up with an idea. "Don't worry about that," he said. "I know just what we can do with it."

Virginia called each member of the vestry instead of waiting for the next meeting. The decision to rent the building was unanimous. The fact that they would be gathering in a grist mill caught everyone by surprise, but once they saw the space, they signed up to help.

On the morning they signed the lease, Emmett received a call from the fire marshal. His report was finished, and he wanted to discuss it with Emmett and Mac before filing it.

"Did you find the cause?" Emmett asked.

"It's better if we talk in person."

Emmett wished he knew what they found, but he was relieved the report was completed, regardless of its findings. Robert Prescott had asked about the report every day since the fire.

Emmett was surprised to find Mac at work when he arrived after signing the lease.

"You certainly didn't waste any time," he said to his friend who was high on a ladder. "The ink on this lease isn't even dry."

"No time to lose," Mac replied without looking down from the ladder, "but downstairs is a disaster. Storage is all it could be used for."

"Exactly," said Emmett sounding proud of himself. Mac turned as Marty Starnes and a group of her friends arrived.

"You focus on the first floor," Emmett said with a grin. "I think these folks can help with the lower level."

"Aye, aye, Captain," Mac said with a sarcastic salute.

The two weeks were better than any community workday Emmett had experienced in 41 years as rector. Folks from town and even the artists from upstairs pitched in to help. Mac built a stage at the far end, while Simon and Sara led the painting crew in touching up the trim around the windows. Gladys and the altar guild dusted and polished every conceivable surface while Emmett and others created offices in the two large storage rooms next to the kitchen. Virginia and Todd worked on the kitchen, transforming it into a space the church could use.

"You know," Sara said as she dipped her brush in the paint, "we should get the youth involved."

"Sounds good, in theory," Emmett replied, "but don't you think they'll just get in the way? We're pressed for time as it is if we hope to have our first service in time for Lent."

"I know the youth are not your thing," Sara said, "but I'll take care of them. I'll get them to clean the windows or something. It'd be great to get them involved."

Emmett focused on the local churches. He visited each church as well as the local synagogue to ask for whatever help they could give. The Congregational Church gave a set of candlesticks and a wooden cross for the front of the worship space. The Methodists said they might be able to scrounge up some hymnals—but not enough for the whole congregation. The Presbyterians offered a lectern on wheels, which, they pointed out, could also serve as the pulpit. The local Roman Catholic Church donated some black robes for the acolytes and crucifers.

Simon convinced the high school to donate the folding chairs they had just replaced in the band room. The Rotary and Kiwanis clubs donated chairs as well. The altar guild polished each chair regardless of its condition. In the end, the church had many shiny, dented chairs. "Just like us," Mac joked to Emmett.

Emmett had unexpected visitors at the rectory one afternoon. Clustered on the front stoop, three members from the local synagogue said they wanted to help. Rabbi Kaplan handed Emmett a large black book he'd been clutching like a baby. "We met and decided we would like to loan you this English translation of the Torah. You may use it for as long as you need."

Emmett took the book from the rabbi with reverence and struggled for fitting words. He looked down at the weathered cover and rubbed his hand across the gold Hebrew letters.

"Your Jesus was a Jew, after all," said the rabbi.

"He was," Emmett replied.

"So, this was his Bible. We thought you might be able to use the scriptures we have in common."

"I'm touched beyond words," said Emmett, "and accept your generosity on behalf of the people of St. John's with deep appreciation. We'll use it at our first service and many times after that. In fact, would you do us the honor of joining us at the opening service and reading the first lesson from this extraordinary book?"

The three guests looked at each other, then back at Emmett.

"It would be our honor," said the rabbi.

Emmett invited them in for tea, but they politely declined.

"Perhaps another time," the rabbi said. "I've always regretted not making the time to get to know each other better. Maybe the fire has given us the chance."

"I certainly hope so," said Emmett.

In a rare moment of having the mill to himself, Emmett walked over and stared out the window. While the work had been exciting and the participation inspiring, he felt overwhelmed by all the challenges ahead. Watching the water navigate between the frozen patches, he knew spring was still a long way off. "Always winter, never spring," he said, quoting a favorite book from his childhood, and the sound echoed through the empty space. The acoustics of the grist mill were better than in the church.

Sara and several of the youth came after school on the Thursday before the opening service and cleaned every windowpane. The altar guild also worked to put the finishing touches on the makeshift altar. Mac had heard them complain that there was no altar and offered to construct one out of two sawhorses and three planks of lumber. Gladys and the others reluctantly accepted Mac's offer. They wondered if they could find a sheet or something to make it look more official, which is when Jewell said she might have just the thing. She went up to her studio and returned with a beautiful cloth big enough to cover the altar.

"I know," Emmett said when he noticed Gladys's sadness. "It's just a cloth, but at least it covers the sawhorses."

"I'll iron it," Gladys said. "Maybe that will help."

Emmett had regrets of his own. Because the prayer books and hymnals were destroyed in the fire, they had to make handouts for the congregation. It makes worship feel like a workshop, he said to Alma when he saw the packet.

A few days before the first service, the core group sat in a circle in the mill. The metal chairs were cold, but the sound of the river outside was soothing. Emmett paused before going through the service and encouraged everyone to look around. The stage Mac built was big enough for the altar, piano, and choir. One of the altar guild members was placing a vase of flowers on a table in front of the altar when Gladys Fitzpatrick arrived with something draped over her arm.

"You're not going to believe this," she said between gasps. "You're simply NOT going to believe this!"

Gladys came over to the group and lifted the cloth in her arms as if it was a holy relic.

"I was dropping off our dry cleaning yesterday, and they asked me if I also wanted to pick up the church linens."

"The what?" asked Emmett.

"That's what I said. Seems I dropped the Easter linens off to have them cleaned and forgot all about them. So, here they are!" she said, unfolding them with tears in her eyes. "They may not be the right liturgical season, but they're a piece of our old church."

The group stood and applauded. Emmett reached over and touched the church linens before hugging Gladys. The two walked up to the altar and placed St. John's Easter linens on top of Jewell's altar cover. Neither cared about the embroidered words "He Is Risen." Having a piece of the old church more than made up for the wrong liturgical season.

Jason Abrams, a potter from the artist's loft, came downstairs with a goblet and plate he'd made for the church. "They're called a chalice and patten, in churchy lingo," Emmett informed him as he handed them to Gladys. "They're wonderful," said Gladys as she placed them ceremonially on the altar.

When they were through going over the service, Alma asked to be excused so she could get to the printer before they closed. "It takes time to print and staple so many bulletins," she said. Mac entered just as Alma was starting to leave. "Did somebody order something?" he asked. "There are a bunch of boxes out here with your name on them, Emmett."

"Mine?" Emmett responded.

Simon offered to help Mac bring them in and handed Emmett the envelope attached to one of the boxes. The boxes were from St. Barnabas Church in Maine, a church no one in the group had heard of. Inside the envelope was a note to Emmett:

Dear St. John's,

A mutual friend, Jake Davidson, told us about the fire. We thought you might be able to use the enclosed prayer books and hymnals. They've been in our basement for years doing no good. Maybe you can bring them to life again, and they you.

May God bless you,
St. Barnabas Episcopal Church

"Guess we won't need to make all those copies after all," Emmett said to Alma. They both looked like they were holding back tears. The group quickly unpacked the boxes and placed a prayer book and hymnal on each seat. David Livingston went up to the piano and began playing "Joyful, Joyful We Adore Thee" from one of the hymnals and everyone sang along. The singing filled the rafters. "I think we're ready," he whispered to Virginia, who reached over and squeezed Emmett's arm.

A Companion

T he transformed supply closet was a far cry from the church office Emmett once enjoyed. With only enough room for a donated metal desk and chair, dented file cabinet, and hook for his vestments, Emmett tried to remain grateful. In less than an hour, his church would be worshipping together for the first time in more than two months. Never had his parishioners worked as hard as they had in getting the space in the mill ready. Walking over to one of the large windows and looking at the river below, Emmett let his mind wander. None of this is what he expected, but he knew he had to do his best to make the space a church.

The front door slammed shut as Mac and Simon entered. "Here goes," Emmett whispered. "Please, be with us."

"OK, it's showtime," Mac announced with arms opened wide.

"Good morning, you two," said Emmett with a smile. "If I don't get a chance to say it later, thank you for all you've done to get us here this morning."

"Not at all," Simon replied, checking to make sure all the chairs were in place and ready.

"Piece of cake," Mac added as he joined Emmett by the window. "That's quite a sound. Never thought I'd hear a river while going to church. Isn't there some hymn about an ever-rolling stream?"

"Yes," said Emmett. "O God, Our Help in Ages Past."

"I've always liked that one. Anyway, now we have that ever-flowing stream right outside our windows!"

"Indeed," Emmett said. Soon, he was dressed in borrowed liturgical garb and standing in the back of the mill with the choir as they waited for the service to begin. Some choir members wore red robes, donated by the Presbyterians down the street; others were in blue robes, given by the Methodists. Three were in yellow robes, two in green. The black robes, given by the Roman Catholics, were saved for the acolytes. Fortunately, they had white surplices to drape over the colorful robes.

It was a good crowd. Emmett looked out at the large assembly and was glad to see many familiar faces. It felt like a homecoming, but there were new faces, too. Rabbi Kaplan and others from the synagogue were in the first row, alongside people from some of the local congregations who had made donations to help St. John's get re-started. Maria and some of her staff were there, which was a surprise, and Jewell's presence—with her pink hair, two rows back from Maria—was unmistakable. Beside her were other artists from upstairs who had worked with the parishioners to get the space ready. It was as if the church had grown since the fire.

"I don't like change," was the opening line of Emmett's sermon. "Maybe I'm just old or too set in my ways but whether I like it or not, change comes. It comes to us all, and it comes to churches as much as it does to individuals. If the fire taught us anything, it is that nothing lasts forever. The question is, what, then, shall we do? And I might add a second question: and who then, shall we be?"

He spoke of the Hebrew people wandering in the wilderness, feeling lost during the exile, and the disciples huddled together in an upper room. "Seems like change and uncertainty are recurring themes in the Bible. That, and perpetual homelessness. Jesus wasn't the only one who didn't have a place to lay his head. Lots of people were homeless in the Bible, and in their homelessness, God seems to have taught them important lessons. Like all those who came before, maybe God has something to teach us. Maybe taking away what we love most was the only way to get our attention. I don't know. Whether losing a church, possession, parent, or spouse, we're sometimes forced to hold fast to the one who never changes, never leaves. Saint Augustine once said, 'We'll never rest until we rest in God.' With everything being taken away, perhaps it's time we rest, and trust, in God." After a pause, he added, "It all sounds good, but it's easier said than done, I'm afraid."

Emmett looked out and saw smiles and heads nodding before returning to his seat. It was then that he spotted a familiar red-and-black-checkered jacket. Jake Davidson's broad grin caused Emmett to almost forget to say the offering sentences. While the ushers passed the offering plates, the choir stood and sang their anthem.

The line to greet Emmett after the service was long, but Jake waited to see Emmett. During coffee hour in the back of the worship space, Jake caught up with those he had met at the Christmas breakfast at Maria's. He also met Jewell and the other artists and asked if he could see their studios one day.

"You came back!" Emmett said, shaking Jake's hand and not letting go. "And thank you so much for the hymnals and prayer books."

"A church down the street from my parents' place wanted to do something to encourage you. Glad you could use them. You must be pleased with the turnout this morning."

"It went well," Emmett admitted. "But I can't say this is exactly what I had in mind when I thought about a temporary home."

"Temporary homes may not be what we expect, but sometimes they're just what we need," Jake said with a smile as he patted Emmett on the back. "I think this place is perfect. The floors, brick walls, and high ceilings, and look at those millstones! If you ever run out of sermons, you can preach about them."

"To warn people what happens if they misbehave?" Emmett asked.

"No, to illustrate what's needed to make bread," Jake said.

"I suppose," Emmett replied, as he looked out the window for a moment. "Listen, I'd love to catch up. Is there any way I could convince you to stay the night and head back tomorrow?"

"Sure," said Jake, which seemed to catch Emmett by surprise.

"Let me get out of my robes, and I'll meet you over at the rectory for lunch."

"You must be amazed," Jake said as the two had lunch in the kitchen. "Looks like things are going so well."

"What do you mean?" Emmett asked, unable to hide his confusion. "Not much has gone well: there's no insurance, the bishop washed his hands of us, and many parishioners left for other churches after the fire."

"The place looked full to me this morning," Jake said. "You have a space. People are excited. That's more than half the battle. The money stuff will work itself out."

"I wish I shared your optimism. We only have enough money to get us through the summer. We're thinking about a capital campaign and even approached a few of our wealthier families. But the response has been lukewarm, at best."

"Give it time," Jake said. Emmett looked at him quizzically, wondering if Jake had heard anything he said.

"Take Robert Prescott," Emmett explained. "I went and saw him personally. I explained how we needed someone to step up and make a lead gift, which we could then use to inspire others to give, but all he said was that he'd think about it. A few days later, I got a letter and a check for $1,000."

"That's something," Jake offered.

"It's a joke, that's what it is. I don't mean to sound ungrateful, but we need a lot more than that if we ever hope to rebuild." Jake looked out the window, trying to think of something to say. He knew Emmett was right. Emmett continued: "Plus, I have to meet with the fire marshal on Wednesday and hear what they found. Robert and the vestry have been all over me about the report."

"What do they think it will say?"

"Who knows? And what difference will it make? It's not like we have an insurance claim to file."

Jake gave a slow nod.

Emmett decided to shift topics. "Listen, I know this isn't exactly your line of work, and I know we've only known each other since the fire, but I was wondering if you might be willing to come work with us."

"Work with you in what way?"

"I'm not sure, exactly. In fact, I hadn't even thought about what I am asking until just now, but you said you were between jobs. We're between churches. I know we're nowhere near rebuilding, but I wondered if you might come and work with us to get us ready for when that day comes."

"What do you have in mind?"

"I'm don't know exactly," Emmett conceded. "I just know there's work we need to do as a parish to prepare ourselves. I'd do it, but I need to focus on finding the money, not to mention running the parish. Seems to me someone like you, with your background, could make sure we're doing whatever it is we need so that we're ready to rebuild once we have the money."

Jake looked away again, then back at Emmett. "People usually come to me with plans in hand. They ask for my help but usually aren't prepared for what that means. Not all the work is fun. At times, it'll be uncomfortable and hard."

"We can handle it."

"I believe the parish can. I'm more worried about you."

"Me?"

"The kind of work needed can be particularly hard for the person in charge. St. John's matters to the parishioners, but it clearly means a lot to you, too. In many ways, the parish had become an extension of you and your ministry. The kind of work that's needed might be particularly hard for you."

Emmett paused. "It hasn't been easy so far."

"No," Jake said with a smile, "It hasn't, but it's going to get harder. The work will be like preparing soil. We'll need to dig and turn over the soil so seeds can be planted. People often think about the seeds and not what needs to happen to prepare the soil."

"I used to help my mother get her rose garden ready every year when I was a boy," Emmett shared. "She'd hand me a hoe and tell me to get going. It was hard work breaking the crusty soil and pulling weeds. It took days, but I got it done."

"Well, you'll need to summon that little boy," said Jake, "and you're going to need a lot more than a hoe. You'll hear people say critical things about the church. They'll also tell you how they wish things would be done. It'll be hard not to take it personally. I guess what I'm asking is, are you up for the challenge?"

"I am," said Emmett, trying to sound confident. "We don't have much money, but you could stay at the rectory and your meals..."

"Room and board are enough, for now," said Jake. "When would you like me to start?"

"Right away," said Emmett. "In fact, I'd love if you could join Mac and me when we meet with the fire marshal on Wednesday afternoon. Could you do that?"

Jake stood. "See you Wednesday."

—10—

CHAPTER

A Surprise Challenge

Walking to the church site felt like the time Emmett had to trudge to the principal's office after lighting firecrackers in the girls' high school locker room. He had avoided the meeting with the fire marshal for over a week, claiming a schedule too busy because of opening the new space in the mill. Now there were no more excuses. Time to face the truth, he told himself.

Seeing Mac leaning on his truck across the common gave him a bit of comfort. Mac was still incensed when someone suggested mechanical failure as one of the possible causes. He was there to defend his kingdom.

The fire marshal arrived and the three walked up the pavement toward the granite steps just as Jake pulled up and honked his horn.

The fire marshal began. "We always begin by eliminating things that didn't cause the fire. In this case, we looked at the boiler, then the wiring. Both were exceedingly out of date. It's remarkable the boiler was still working." Mac stood with pride as he listened. "But neither caused the fire."

"I told you," Mac muttered. Emmett tried to ignore him.

"We then looked at the building itself, or what's left of it," the marshal said, walking past the steps to the tarp-covered debris. "The key is to determine where things burned the longest. That usually indicates where the fire started." Leading the group forward, he continued. "Which is why we were led in this direction."

"The chancel," Emmett said.

"Is that what it's called?" the fire marshal asked. "We're pretty sure the fire started here in the chancel." Lifting the tarp delicately, like a sheet over a corpse, he continued. "Tell me what was up here."

"The organ was there, and the choir sat on either side." Emmett explained. "Up there, where you're pointing, was the altar."

"Anything else?"

"Just seats for the participants: the crucifer, acolytes, and me."

The fire marshal stared at Emmett. "I'm not well-versed in church terms."

"The crucifer carries the cross, and acolytes carry candles."

"Candles?" the fire marshal asked, staring harder at Emmett.

"Yes. Each acolyte carries a candle. There were also two candles on the altar. The acolytes walk in on either side of the cross during the procession, then place their candles in stands along this wall.

"Against the wall?"

"Yes," Emmett replied. "Wait. You're not suggesting the acolytes' candles were responsible for the fire, are you?"

"Well, the fire started in this area, and now you're telling me there were candles here. Anything on the walls?"

"Just the two antique tapestries given to the church... " Emmett stopped mid-sentence as he connected the dots. "Oh no," he said, looking at Mac.

"All I'm saying, and what's in the report, is that the fire most likely started in this area. Given what you've just told me, it's likely a candle in this area started the fire. To be more specific, it was the candle on this side," he said pointing to the right, which was where Emmett and one of the acolytes always sat during services. Emmett heard very little else the fire marshal said. He took the report, thanked him for his work, and waited until the marshal returned to his truck.

"Who was sitting there?" Mac asked, trying to recall the Christmas Eve service. "Do you remember?"

"Well, I was there," Emmett said, pointing to the place he always sat. "Jackie Woodland was the crucifer, and she sat over there. The Johnston girl was the acolyte beside her. I remember because I had to tell them to stop talking during the choir's anthem. Over here, beside me was...oh, no."

"Who is it?" Jake asked, seeing the stunned look on Emmett's face.

"It was Trey Prescott," Mac answered for Emmett. "Wasn't it?"

"I need a moment," Emmett sighed, as he walked away from Jake and Mac.

Mac reminded Jake that Trey was the son of one of St. John's most influential families. "His father's been determined to find out the cause of the fire. He was desperate to find some thing or someone to blame for the fire."

"If what the fire marshal said is true, it was Trey's candle that caused the fire." Emmett said, squeezing the report in his hand. "How am I ever going to share this news?"

"Robert's gonna go ballistic," Mac said, looking down at his feet and shaking his head.

"That's an understatement," said Emmett.

"Maybe he won't figure it out," Jake suggested.

"He asks about the report at every vestry meeting," Emmett pointed out. "He's been looking for someone to blame, particularly after he found out there was no insurance. But this, this is beyond anything I imagined."

"Forgive me," said Jake, "but the fire marshal only said it started in this area. He didn't say whose candle caused the fire."

"It had to be Trey Prescott's," Mac grumbled.

"But he said they didn't know for sure. Why not leave it at that? Surely there's no need to share whose candle caused the fire. The church burned. That's all that matters. Anything else would only devastate a young boy and embarrass his family."

"Robert will put two and two together," Emmett said.

"Maybe," said Jake. "Maybe not."

"I need to present the report to the vestry on Friday. I can try to keep it as general as possible, but I'm not sure Robert will let it rest," Emmett said. "For now, let's keep all of this between us."

The vestry members began assembling at the mill a half hour before the meeting. Emmett used that time to introduce Jake to those who had not met him and explain what he hoped Jake would do to help the congregation prepare for the future. Virginia called the meeting to order at the head of the two folding tables in the middle of the room. After commenting about how nice the opening service had been and how grateful she was to Simon and Sara for finding such a special space, Virginia turned the meeting over to Terrance Adler to present the financials. "We've weathered the immediate storm," he said at the end of his report, "but there's no doubt that we are going to need a capital campaign if we are to do anything more than survive."

Emmett followed with an update on the initial fundraising efforts. "We've raised just over $76,000, so far," he said, "which includes gifts from every vestry member."

"That's promising," said Sara.

"I suppose it is," Emmett lied, "but the amount of money we have to raise is significant. I'm not sure we have the means to raise the kind of money we'll need if we ever hope to rebuild. We'll need a lead gift or something to challenge the parishioners to dig deep. Right now, with the responses we've had, I don't see it."

There were some follow-up questions, but when Virginia moved to the next agenda item, Robert interrupted. "What about the fire marshal's report?"

Emmett looked at Virginia for permission to proceed. Alma had prepared copies of the fire marshal's report for each member of the vestry, and Emmett kept his presentation as general as possible. "Just tell 'em the place caught fire because of a candle and leave it at that," Mac had advised him. "There were certainly plenty of candles that night, plus lights on the Christmas tree. Any one of them could have caused the fire."

Emmett explained that he had met with the fire marshal and determined there was no mechanical error, no sign of foul play. "The fire was most likely from a candle, or something like that," Emmett said, trying to dismiss any specifics. "As we all know, the place was full of candles. The thinking is, one must have remained lit and started the fire."

There were a few questions, and Emmett took his seat feeling relieved. After the meeting, Robert remained behind, thumbing through his copy of the lengthy report.

"You coming?" Emmett asked.

"Not yet," he said. "I'll turn off the lights when I'm done."

Mac joined Emmett and Jake for a lasagna dinner at the rectory after the meeting. "How did it go?" Mac asked before even taking off his jacket.

"Emmett did great," Jake said. "People accepted the explanation that the fire came from a candle and were willing to leave it at that."

"Robert, too?" Mac asked.

"He didn't say anything, but he was busy reading the report when we left," Emmett said.

"What do we do now?" Mac asked as he poured himself a beer. "There's no insurance. Robert doesn't have anyone to sue. The church is lying in ruins, and St. John's is now meeting in a grist mill."

"Please," said Emmett, waving both hands. "Don't sugarcoat it, Mac."

"I can keep going. We're also all but out of money!"

"Thank you, my blunt friend," Emmett said as he took a sip of wine.

"Trust me," said Jake, "this story's just beginning."

"Maybe," said Mac, "but the first chapter's a doozy."

"There are challenges," Jake conceded, "but it's only a chapter, not the story."

When Emmett arrived for work the next morning, Robert was standing in the parking lot, holding his copy of the report.

"Is the door locked?" Emmett asked.

"No," Robert replied as he stomped his feet to keep them from going numb. "I just wanted a word before you went inside."

"Of course. What is it?"

"I read the fire marshal's report. In fact, I read it many times, and I've been up all night thinking about what it says—and what it doesn't. No concrete cause was given, as you pointed out in the meeting, but it's pretty clear the fire came from somewhere by the altar. You said it came from a candle. I can't help but wonder which candle. You know Trey was one of the acolytes that night. Was it his candle, Emmett?"

Emmett was unprepared for such a direct question and looked over toward the river as he struggled to find the right words.

"It was," Robert said, seeing the look on Emmett's face.

"We don't know anything for certain," Emmett said, looking back at Robert. "It could have been one of many candles."

"But it wasn't. It was Trey's," said Robert. "I'm not stupid. I can put two and two together, but I certainly appreciate your efforts to soften the truth and protect my son, which is why I've decided to give you this." Robert reached into his coat and pulled out an envelope.

"What's this?" Emmett asked.

"I'm sure you noticed our recent gift was, how do I say it, modest."

"You were very generous," Emmett lied.

"No, we weren't, but now I'm giving you a pledge. It's a challenge, actually, and it needs to remain anonymous. I must insist on that. Millie can't know about it. Neither can our sons, or anyone else for that matter. I don't want it to look like we're trying to pay for Trey's mistake. The money is coming from our family foundation. That should keep Millie from finding out.

"What's the challenge?" Emmett asked.

"I'll match every gift on a one-to-one basis up to the amount in that envelope, but you only have until next Christmas to do it. No extensions." Robert patted Emmett on the shoulder. Before turning toward his car, he added, "You're a good man, Emmett."

Robert was gone before Emmett had the nerve to open the envelope. Inside was a pledge of $1 million, the largest single gift in parish history.

PREPARATION

Ashes

"I guess it's time to start," Jake said as he entered the kitchen.

"We just received the challenge a couple of weeks ago. I had to wait until the papers were signed," Emmett said, hoping to enjoy his coffee in peace. "I'll announce it on Sunday and start fundraising right away."

"I wasn't talking about fundraising," said Jake. "It's time to get started on the preparation."

"The preparation?"

"What you hired me for. We need to begin the work so that once you've raised the money, you and the congregation are ready."

"You talk like raising a million dollars is a done deal. I'm not sure we can do it, let alone by the end of the year, but right now, I've got to figure out what we're going to do about Lent."

"Lent? Isn't that when people give up chocolate?" Jake asked as he poured himself a cup of coffee. "I've never understood what chocolate has to do with one's faith. Seems to me that's more about losing weight."

"I suppose you're right, but the intention is to clear away stuff that's getting in the way spiritually. Lent lasts forty days, forty-six if you count Sundays. It begins on Ash Wednesday, which is next Wednesday and goes until Easter. Some people give up bad habits; others give up things they love as a way to challenge themselves and make them mindful of the season. Some use it to take on things, like reading or performing acts of service. However people choose to keep Lent, the point is to awaken, spiritually."

"Why forty days?"

"It's modeled after Jesus going into the wilderness for forty days after his baptism. It was where he was tempted to be someone he wasn't. The church thought we should follow his example and confront those things that aren't our true selves."

"What are you going to do?" Jake asked.

"Me?" Emmett asked, suddenly flustered. No one had ever asked him about his Lenten practice. "Not sure. With all that's been going on, I haven't been able to give it a thought."

"Tell me about the Ash Wednesday service."

"I keep forgetting you're not an Episcopalian."

"I'm not much into organized religion, but Lent sounds interesting."

"That's one way to put it," said Emmett. "Ash Wednesday is the service when people begin their Lenten pilgrimages by coming forward and having ashes put on their foreheads. It's intended to remind us of our mortality."

"Is that where 'ashes to ashes, dust to dust' comes from?" Jake asked.

"Listen to you," Emmett said with delight.

"My mother used to say it when I was growing up."

"Anyway, I've got to figure out how to do the service now that we're in the mill."

"Why there?" Jake asked, raising his eyebrows with a grin as he looked across the common.

"You think we should have the service over at the church?"

"Why not? We both know where there is a whole bunch of ashes."

"But the ashes used on Ash Wednesday normally come from burning the palms that were used on Palm Sunday the year before," Emmett explained.

"And where are those ashes?" Jake asked.

A chill spread over Emmett's body as he shifted in his seat. "If ashes are used to remind us of our mortality, I can't think of a more vivid reminder of life's impermanence than the church's ashes." When he mentioned the idea to the vestry, they were ecstatic, so Emmett began planning the service.

"I have another idea," Jake announced at dinner later in the week.

"You've had your quota for the week," Emmett joked.

"I'm just getting started," Jake said with a smile. "I'd like to follow up the Ash Wednesday service with another kind of service on Saturday."

"What kind of service?" Emmett asked.

"You'll see. You take care of Wednesday. I'll take care of Saturday."

"I've created a monster," Emmett said.

"Trust me," Jake said. "You promised to do whatever was needed to prepare the congregation. Lent begins with ashes. So does rebuilding a church." Before Emmett had a chance to ask what Jake had in mind, his houseguest was off to his room to do planning of his own.

When Emmett made the two announcements on Sunday, people were as excited about the Ash Wednesday service as they were about the $1 million challenge.

"What's going on around here?" Gladys Fitzpatrick muttered as she began cleaning the coffee pot in the small kitchen. "Sure doesn't sound like the St. John's I've known."

"Maybe that's the point," Sara replied as she carried a tray of dirty coffee mugs.

Turnout for the Ash Wednesday service was the largest Emmett could remember. A reporter from the local newspaper attended the service when she heard about it. So did folks from town who had never been to St. John's. After they heard people talking about the service at Maria's diner, they wanted to come and see what all the fuss was about.

The blue plastic tarps over the church ashes looked like a funeral pall and rustled in the morning breeze. Virginia smiled as she looked at Emmett in his borrowed robes and Jake in his blue jeans and red-and-black-checkered jacket. "Someone looks out of his element," she whispered to her husband. "Guess business-as-usual is over," she said before walking over to encourage her rector.

When the service was about to begin, Mac pulled back a corner of a tarp to give Emmett access to the ashes. Emmett took that as his cue, climbed the steps, and faced the congregation. They hushed as Emmett extended his arms to begin. "Let us pray. Almighty and everlasting God, you hate nothing you have made and forgive the sins of all who are penitent: Create and make in us new and contrite hearts, that we, worthily lamenting our sins and acknowledging our wretchedness, may obtain of you, the God of all mercy, perfect remission and forgiveness; through Jesus Christ our Lord, who lives and reigns with you and the Holy Spirit, one God, for ever and ever."

"Amen," the congregation responded.

Virginia came forward in bright yellow rubber boots she had bought for the occasion and read the appointed lesson from Matthew. Emmett then gave an informal sermon.

"I must say, this is an Ash Wednesday service I'll not soon forget. Never did I imagine standing here with the church in ruins behind me. Yet, when Jake Davidson—that fellow over there—suggested we hold our Ash Wednesday service here, I felt surprisingly drawn to the idea. Jake pointed out that Lent begins with ashes, so why not receive this year's ashes right here?"

"Lent's never been a season for the spiritual amateur, and never has that been more apparent than this year. Standing here in the cold, outside of what used to be our beautiful church, is as challenging as it is profound. Lent requires a willingness to go beneath the surface and face things we'd rather hide, so in the name of the church, I invite you to draw close and observe a holy Lent—not just by having ashes put on your foreheads but also by having them placed upon your hearts."

"This is a hard and messy journey, a journey that begins in ashes but doesn't end with them. Easter and the promise of new life awaits us at the end of these forty days, but we need to go through the ashes to get there. May today be not only an Ash Wednesday we never forget but also a memorable Lenten journey as well. In Christ's name, we pray."

"Amen," the congregation replied.

The captivated congregation watched as Emmett climbed down the steps and turned to the pile of ash beside the steps. He knelt and used a spade to scoop a large clump of ash. Suddenly, Emmett remembered the day he opened the cardboard box and spread Abby's ashes in the lake below their cabin. The memory caused him to forget what he was supposed to do next. Jake came over and placed his hand on Emmett's back, bringing him back to the service. He stood and faced the congregation with a spade full of ashes. His hands were covered, his vestments smudged.

"Let us pray," he said to the congregation. "Almighty God, you have created us out of the dust of the earth: Grant that these ashes may be to us a sign of our mortality and penitence, that we may remember that it is only by your gracious gift that we are given everlasting life; through Jesus Christ our Savior. Amen."

Virginia and Simon served as ushers and led the congregation forward. Emmett dipped his thumb into the ashes and spread them on each forehead in the shape of a cross, saying, "Remember that you are dust, and to dust you shall return."

He took his time this year. When everyone had come forward, Emmett realized he hadn't received his ashes. He motioned for Jake to help.

"I'm not qualified," Jake whispered as Emmett handed him the ashes.

"I thought you said you weren't into rules," Emmett grinned as he handed Jake the ashes.

"Remember that you're ash," Jake said, forgetting the next part.

"And to dust you shall return," Emmett whispered to his impromptu assistant.

"And to dust you shall return," Jake repeated.

After the service, Virginia came forward, waving for Jake to join her at the base of the steps. "The vestry would like to invite you to another special service, I guess you could call it. Jake Davidson, whom we have asked to work with us as we prepare ourselves for rebuilding our church, has come up with an idea that I hope you will find intriguing." Virginia stepped aside as Jake stuck his hands in the pockets of his blue jeans and cleared his throat.

"The vestry and I would like to invite each of you back on Saturday morning for a special moment in the life of the church. Like this one, it will involve ashes. It won't be a service, but I believe it will be meaningful."

"Today, ashes were put on your foreheads. On Saturday, they'll be put on your hands, feet, and probably every other part of your body." The congregation looked at one another, confused. "It's time we lift away the tarps and see what we can find in the ashes. So, we'll climb these steps and jump into the ashes. Beneath the surfaces are bits and pieces of the church. It's up to us to find them. It will be hard and messy work, just as Emmett said of Lent, but it's the first step on our journey to a new church. So, please join us. You won't regret it."

The youth practically ran home once Sara told them they were responsible for bringing the shovels, spades, and buckets. Mac and Simon prepared the staging area for what would be found, and a separate group organized the refreshments. Emmett found the congregation's excitement unnerving, but he didn't tell anyone but Mac. "It feels like we've opened a gate, and all the chicks are suddenly scurrying in every direction."

"At least they're scurrying," said Mac in his typical mumble.

CHAPTER 11

The turnout on Saturday morning was larger than on Ash Wednesday. Several of the youth brought friends, and Maria's sign in the diner drew some new faces as well. "Be sure to dress for the mess," the sign read.

By the time Emmett and Jake arrived, fifty people had assembled, and more were arriving. "They're here early," he pointed out. "This never happens. People are usually late to parish events."

After the opening prayer, Jake stepped forward and explained what would happen. "Behind us is what's left of your church. To an outsider, it looks like a pile of ash, but to most of you, it's your church. It's where many of you were baptized and married. It's where you said goodbye to loved ones. The fire turned your church to ash, but beneath the ashes are pieces of your church. I now invite you to come find what you can."

"On Wednesday, Emmett spoke of Lent as a journey. Think of today as an important step of that journey—not just the Lenten journey but the journey toward a new church. Both journeys begin in ashes, but, as Emmett pointed out, neither ends there."

"I want to caution you, though. When you begin digging, you'll be stirring more than the ashes. You'll likely stir up some powerful emotions, too. They can be scary. You might be tempted to stop or question why we're doing this in the first place. That's always how it is when you do this kind of work, but look around and remember that you're not doing this alone. When you become overwhelmed by what's been lost, reach deeper, and see what's being found. Whether it's a prayer book or hymnal, a piece of a pew or pulpit, there are treasures beneath the surface. They may be dented or burned, but they're treasures nevertheless. No item is insignificant."

"When you climb these steps, Emmett and I will be there to assist you into the ashes. From there, you can head in any direction. Sift through the ashes and bring whatever you find to one of the tarps off to the side."

Jake and Emmett climbed the steps and invited people forward. The congregation was hesitant initially, but Trey Prescott and some of his classmates decided to go first. They leaped into the ashes as if they were jumping into Webster Lake. The adults were more reticent and pulled their gloves tighter before following the youth.

When it was finally his turn, Emmett took off his signet ring and put it in his pocket.

"God forbid that gets dirty," Mac said. He always made fun of Emmett's attachment to his ring. A few minutes later, they noticed a man coming down the path late.

"Sam Tucker," Emmett said. "I'm delighted to see you."

"Good to see you too, Emmett," said the young man with wavy blond hair who used to be a regular at St. John's. On either side of Sam were his son and daughter. "It's been a while."

"Where've ya been?" Emmett said in as lighthearted way as he could.

"Keeping out of sight, I guess. The path seemed long," Sam said, pointing behind him, "and the doors thick after what happened."

"I'm sorry for that," Emmett responded, "but, as you can see, there aren't any doors now."

"That's true," Sam said with a smile. "Figured the time was right to come back." He looked around, and then added, "Not much to come back to."

"I don't know; the church's still here," Emmett said. "The trick's finding it."

Emmett held out his hand to Sam and his children, inviting them to join him at the top of the stairs. "Shall we? Ready? One, two, three!" Everyone stopped what they were doing to watch their rector jump into the ashes.

Walking through the ashes was more difficult than Emmett expected. It was like walking through wet sand at the beach. On top, the ashes were light. Underneath, it was all Emmett could do to move his legs. Like the others, he stumbled as he got used to the terrain. More than once, he had to pause to catch his breath.

The first thing people found were fragments of prayer books and hymnals. Jake told the youth to gather as many as they could and place them in a pile on one of the tarps. Emmett found a prayer book that was completely intact. Even with soot stains and water damage, the words were visible: "Cleanse the thoughts of our hearts by the inspiration of your Holy Spirit." Gladys found a hymnal with part of a hymn still legible. "O God, our help in ages past," she began out loud, "our hope for years to come, our shelter from the stormy blast, and our eternal home."

"Amen," Emmett whispered as he looked over at her with a smile.

Mac and Simon wandered to the far end of the church and began lifting large pieces of wood and placing them on a tarp. Why collect charred beams? Emmett wondered but he knew better than to question Mac Ellis.

Tom and Alice Jenkins were searching in one specific place. Emmett realized it was where they sat each Sunday. "You two look determined," he said as he walked by.

They both nodded.

"We met in pew 25 and have sat there ever since," Alice said. "We're trying to find the brass numbers that were on the end of the pew." Emmett wished them luck and continued toward the front of the church. He tried to encourage people he passed. Their initial excitement had morphed into something solemn. Like monks for whom work was prayer, people fell silent as they continued to dig.

Jake and Sara stood off to the side, beside what was left of the southern wall and the window Sara had given in memory of her parents. She was showing Jake something small in her hand. Emmett was curious, particularly when she leaned toward Jake and put her head on his shoulders in tears.

David Livingston and members of the choir trudged through what used to be the chancel, searching for remnants of the organ. The pipes they found were either melted or dented. They also found keys from the keyboard and placed them on the tarps next to the other discovered pieces.

"This is where you were baptized," Emmett heard Sam say to his son and daughter, Sam Jr. and Sophie, as they lifted pieces of the baptismal font. It was one thing to look across the common at the ruins but something else entirely to walk through them and hold them in your hands.

Emmett struggled to lift his legs through the muck as he moved further on to the front of the church. He was determined to reach where the altar once stood, but a loud crash caused him to look over at Mac, who angrily threw a large piece of wood onto the pile.

"What's gotten into him?" Emmett asked Jake, who was now standing nearby.

"People grieve in their own way," he said.

"The building's always been Mac's baby," Emmett said. "He spent hours working on the place and made so many repairs over the years. The place became personal. I'm sure this is tough on him."

"On everyone," Jake said as he got back to work.

Emmett put his lips together and tightened his face as he felt his congregation's pain. He walked up to where the altar had been and saw the members sifting through the ashes. Sadness overwhelmed him. They looked like children searching for their home. As he took a step forward, his foot hit something, almost causing him to trip. Reaching down, he grabbed the object and pulled it to the surface. Wiping away the ash, he recognized the processional cross. Half the staff was broken, and the cross was melted into an eerie, twisted shape.

"Look, everyone," he called out as he ceremoniously walked toward the tarps, the cross above his head. Some began singing "Lift High the Cross," a favorite hymn at St. John's, as he processed through the ashes and placed the cross reverently on a tarp.

With every piece found came another reminder of what had been lost. Emotions ran high, as Jake said they might, and Emmett wondered if the whole thing was a good idea. It might have been smarter to hire a company to clean up the mess, he thought, but Jake assured him that it was better if the people did the digging themselves. Emmett was grateful for the respite of lunch. He expected people would leave after the meal, but most stayed and continued working.

"I don't believe it," Virginia yelled. Everyone stopped what they were doing and looked at her. She and Todd had been searching around the lectern area.

"What is it?" Emmett asked.

"Look!" she exclaimed, lifting a black clump of ash. Todd brushed away the ash, and Virginia blew away what remained. They had found the parish Bible.

"A corner has been burned," she said, "but the rest is fine."

Emmett walked over. She handed it to Emmett like a sacred relic, and he received it as such. It was still opened to the last lesson read on Christmas Eve.

A few moments later, Alice shrieked and embraced Tom. They had found the brass numbers they were looking for. Emmett smiled and whispered, "Thank you."

Sara continued to work by herself. "She's collecting pieces of the stained-glass windows," Jake told Emmett.

"What will she do with them?" Emmett asked.

"Who knows? She wants to find as many pieces as she can. She has an impressive pile of shards on the tarp already."

"Seems like a waste of time to me," said Emmett.

"To you," Jake replied.

The tarps were covered with fragments of the church by mid-afternoon. It was a strange and eerie collage. People agreed to return in the coming days, but all they wanted now was a hot shower. Emmett watched as they made their way toward their cars. Their eyes and teeth were highlighted by the ash smeared everywhere else. "What a beautiful mess," Emmett said to Jake. "They've never looked more alive."

Mac and Jake began covering up what had been found, and Emmett decided to wander toward his old office where the chimney and other portions of the building remained. Emmett was curious about what he would find.

The shell of his reading chair stuck out above the pile of ash. So did a skeleton of his desk. The charred remains of his father's books lay scattered, and Emmett noticed a corner of a frame from one of Abby's paintings that had hung above the mantle. The canvas ripped as he lifted it, and something flipped inside Emmett. He threw the ruined painting as far as he could.

"How could you let this happen?" Emmett grumbled. He pushed the chair over and threw anything else he could reach. "I hope you're happy. It's not enough we tried to be your church. It's not enough we worshipped you every Sunday. Where did it get us? Nowhere. Only here, to a pile of ash. Serves us right for trusting in you."

Emmett continued to stomp throughout his office, a child throwing a temper tantrum.

"No wonder the pews are empty," he continued, getting louder with each word. He felt something and lifted a book underneath his foot. It was his father's prayer book.

"See!" he said, lifting it toward the clouds. He opened the prayer book and saw his father's elaborate signature on the cover page. *The Right Reverend William E. Hodges.* He slammed the book, which caused ashes to fly into his face. He kicked everything around him. "It was your church," he yelled. "Why did you do this?" With a final kick, Emmett lost his balance and fell into the ash. He sat up and shook his head like someone rising from a lake, spitting the ash from his mouth.

He looked up and saw Mac and Jake staring down at him. "Feel better?" Mac said with a smile as he walked over to help Emmett stand.

"Sorry you saw that," Emmett said as he brushed himself off. "I'm not sure what came over me. I shouldn't have said all that."

"I'm sure God can take it," Jake said.

— 12 —

CHAPTER

Debris

"**W**hy do you do that?" Jake asked as he approached the kitchen table.

"Do what?" said Emmett as he traced the water ring left by years of Abby setting her coffee mug on the spot.

"That!"

"Habit. Keeps her memory alive."

The kitchen smelled like a campfire. Showers and fresh clothes couldn't remove the ash smell. It was a reminder of a remarkable day, and neither minded.

"I think I've got a good idea who should be on the vision committee we spoke about," said Jake.

"You what?" Emmett said, putting the spoon on the table.

"I think I know the people we need to begin envisioning the new church."

"But we never discussed who should be on the committee."

"I'm not interested in who should be on the committee," Jake said. "People who *should* be on a committee always bring buckets of entitlement. They take up room without offering anything in return. No, I want people like those who showed up yesterday, the ones willing to get dirty and do the work."

"Yes, but…"

"Don't worry," Jake said as he reached over and touched Emmett's arm. "You're on it."

"I'm glad to hear it," he replied, amused.

"In fact, you'll know everyone, including Sam Tucker, the guy who came with his kids yesterday."

"Sam?" Emmett said.

"He seemed surprised when I asked, but he agreed."

"I'm delighted, but he's an unlikely choice. He's pretty much written St. John's off."

"And yet he was there yesterday." Jake pointed out as he freshened his coffee. "Who is he?"

"A parishioner, though he hasn't darkened the door of the church in years. Grew up in St. John's. I baptized him and married him and his wife, Jenny. They were high school sweethearts who married right after college. They have those two children who were with him yesterday, and Sam works for his father's construction firm here in town. The company also owns the Webster quarry."

"Why'd they stop coming to church?"

"Not they, just Sam. Jenny and the kids still attend church regularly. Sam had a spectacular meltdown a few years ago."

"What happened?"

Emmett leaned back in his chair and looked at the ceiling. "Sam's always been on the wilder side of life. He was popular in high school and known to accept any challenge put before him. He was always surrounded by friends, particularly girls who loved it when he played the guitar. I always thought he'd end up in a band or something, but his father roped him into working for the family business after college. Been there ever since."

"And?" Jake asked.

"At some point, his drinking got out of hand. Maybe it was the work or the pressures of family life, but one Christmas, Sam showed up at the annual tree lighting ceremony drunk as a skunk. The entire town was there, including Jenny and the kids. I was about to offer the prayer before they turned on the tree lights when Sam showed up, bellowing "Merry Christmas" like an exaggerated Santa. There was no ignoring him, and it devastated Jenny and the kids. I tried to pull him aside, but it was too late. The police found him the next morning lying in the manger, clinging to the doll we used as the baby Jesus."

Jake chuckled as he tried to imagine a grown man in the manger with Jesus.

"His father sent him off to rehab later that day, and he's been sober ever since."

"What about his family?"

"Jenny asked him to leave when he got back, but they've never divorced. He lives in an apartment. Jenny and the kids are still in the house. Sad."

Jake listened closely and waited to respond. "Sounds like he became a caged bird. I love imagining him in the manger, though."

"Why's that?" Emmett asked.

"He was clearly lost. Probably wanted something, or someone, to cling to. The bottle obviously didn't work. Maybe he thought it was time to try Jesus."

"It was a doll," Emmett reminded him.

"I know, but it's the hunger that moves me. I'll bet that same hunger brought him back yesterday. Either way, he sounds like the kind of person we need on the committee."

At church the next Sunday, Emmett was surprised to see Sam in the pews. After the service, Emmett went back to his office to remove his vestments, and Sam followed him.

"Twice in a week," Emmett said with delight. "Jake tells me you're going to serve on the vision committee."

"That's what I wanted to talk to you about."

Emmett offered Sam the only chair in the office and took a seat behind his desk.

"I'm happy to help in any way I can," Sam continued. "I'm not sure what I can bring to the committee, but our company has a bunch of dump trucks. How about we clear away all the debris once we've found whatever there is to be found in the ashes?"

"Really?" asked Emmett.

"I figure we could have it done quickly—if that would help."

"Let me talk to Jake and the vestry, but I'm sure they'll be delighted. It's exceedingly generous, Sam. Thank your father for me."

"He doesn't know," Sam said. "He doesn't care much for the church. I'm running the day-to-day operations now, so it's up to me what we do with our trucks."

After Sam left, Emmett knew he should be excited and grateful for the offer, but something about dump trucks carrying away the remains of the church felt final. He wasn't sure he was ready to let it go. It was like emptying Abby's dresser and closet; it took him more than a year to do it. Loss is one thing; letting go is another.

"That's huge!" Jake exclaimed when he heard Sam's offer later that night. "Clearing a site is often an enormous expense. What a gift."

Hearing Jake's enthusiasm helped Emmett come around. "So, I should tell him yes?" Emmett asked.

"Tell him hell yes!"

"I'll stick to yes, but I'm just as pleased by Sam's return as I am by his offer. I feel like I should kill the fatted calf."

"Not sure what that means, but I'll work with Sam to iron out the logistics. I'll also get the vision committee up and running so you can start raising the money."

"Could we switch?"

"Not a chance," Jake said, as he lifted his mug to toast Sam's generosity.

That night, Emmett knelt beside his bed and said his prayers before climbing into bed. It was something he always used to do but stopped once he started sleeping alone. He was grateful for all the good that was happening but felt each step forward was also a step away from the church he'd known. Guilt engulfed him each time he looked ahead.

CHAPTER 12

Four dump trucks lined up across the common at the end of the week.

"Can't we put it off a little while longer?" Emmett asked as he stood by the window like a child watching his parents leave for a trip.

"The place will be a mess if we wait much longer. There's new life at the other end of all this," Jake said. "Get your coffee and follow me."

"Where are we going?"

"To bless the fleet, of course."

They greeted the drivers, then walked up the path toward the steps to take one last look at the debris from the old church. Emmett reached over and tried to straighten a mangled railing.

"I know all of this is good," he said as he leaned over. "But I don't want them to take all this away. I know it's silly, but it feels like the church is being taken away from me. Marty Starnes and her gang have transformed the basement into a food pantry. Now, they want to use the sanctuary to serve meals. The finance committee is overseeing all the financial administration of the church, and you're taking over the rebuilding of the church."

"I haven't taken over anything. You asked me to get the parish ready. That's what I'm doing. There's still plenty for you to do."

"Like raise a million dollars," Emmett sighed.

"That'd be great," Jake said trying to bring some lightness to the morning, "but take your time. You have the rest of the year."

Emmett scowled at Jake.

"I'll also need you when the vision committee does its work. The conversations are likely to get uncomfortable. It'll help to have you there."

"Because it's been so comfortable so far?" Emmett said, rolling his eyes.

"Sassy," Jake said. "I like it. You're going to need some sass to make it through the days ahead."

The vision committee began meeting the next week and each one after that. Some familiar faces made up the committee, "the regulars" as Emmett liked to call them. But there were also Sam Tucker and Marty Starnes, who were unconventional choices, as was Trey Prescott. "We need the youth represented," Jake explained. Sam and Trey sat beside each other, looking nervous. Marty looked determined.

Jake began, "Thanks for being willing to serve on what we're calling the vision committee. To be clear from the start: we are not here to design the new church. That comes later. The first step is to discuss the church in general. What is it? What does it do? Depending on our answers, we then ask what kind of building we need. Such answers will be crucial when it comes time to build."

One of the dump trucks drove by the mill, shaking the road-side windows. The sound was so loud Jake needed to pause until it passed.

"As I was saying, this is important work. We need to discuss both what you loved about the church and what you didn't, what you want to be sure you keep and what you need to throw away. Such discussions are never easy, but they're essential."

"All we're going to do is talk?" Stanley Fitzpatrick grumbled.

"Yes. We can't move forward without having honest conversations."

Some longtime members shifted in their seats. The church had always valued keeping things the same. Change was tolerated, but only when absolutely necessary. Jake's description made them uncomfortable. They grasped onto the edge of the table as if to keep it in place.

"Can't we just get to work?" Stanley asked.

"This is the work," Jake said. "It's what needs to happen first."

"Can't we just rebuild the church like it was and be done with it?" Stanley muttered. Some nodded in agreement.

"St. John's was more than a building," Marty offered. "What Jake wants us to do is look at who we are and what we do as a church to see if there are ways to grow."

"I'm too old," Stanley growled.

"People and churches are never too old to grow," Jake said with a smile.

A second dump truck passed by.

"In architecture lingo," Jake explained, "when you build something, there's form *and* function. It's no different with a church. This committee's about the function. Form comes later."

"We're an Episcopal church, for God's sake," Stanley protested. "Our main function is to worship. What's so complicated about that?"

Marty was about to attack when Emmett stepped in. "Worship is certainly important, but we need to consider all the other things we do as a church, as well."

"Jesus didn't tell the disciples to go build churches," Marty said, gripping her notes in front of her. "In fact, he never said, 'Worship me.' Jesus said, 'Follow me...go feed the poor, love the unlovable.' He tried to point out that when someone serves somebody, they serve him. Remember the lost sheep? Jesus seemed more concerned about it than buildings. You'll have to forgive me, my biblical knowledge is rusty, but I can only remember him talking about a building once and it was about tearing it down."

"You need to remember, young lady, it's a church, not a building, and without the church, there is no ministry." Stanley said, his hands squeezing the edge of the table.

Marty let the "young lady" reference pass, and Jake redirected the growing conflict. He always ended each meeting reminding everyone what a special opportunity it was to envision a church and that disagreements would only make the final product better. Then he assigned homework. At first, the assignments were easy, but they grew more difficult. He wanted the committee members to move beyond their romantic views of the church and look at ways St. John's had not lived up to all it could be.

"I feel disloyal criticizing the church," Sara confessed.

"Disloyal? To whom," Jake asked.

"Emmett, for one" someone said.

"God," said another.

"I can't speak for Emmett," Jake replied, "but I know God can handle whatever you need to say. I'm sure God's heard it all before."

With each meeting, people grew more comfortable offering new ideas. Some suggestions were about the building, others focused on the ministries. If the conversation started to get heated, Jake reminded everyone that a church comes out of what a congregation is, not the other way around. "Take Emmett," he said. "Anyone can wear a plastic collar. You can give him a fancy title, an impressive office, and surround him with the most beautiful worship space imaginable, but, in the end, none of that is what makes him a minister."

Emmett looked away and twisted the ring on his finger.

"So too, beautiful worship and rich ministries don't make you a church. Only your relationship with God and one another can do that."

Many sitting at the table felt guilty for the way things had been at St. John's. Emmett, in particular, felt bad. He'd always liked being the rector of one of the most important Episcopal churches in New England. He enjoyed his office and the elaborate worship at St. John's. Deep down, though, he knew Jake was right.

Jake waited for the next dump truck to pass. "Before you come back next week, your homework is to write a personal definition of the church," he said.

"Impossible," one person said.

"I wouldn't know where to begin," said another.

"Oh, it gets worse," Jake said with a smile. "You must do it in one sentence!"

Jake assured them there were no wrong answers before he chose Trey to offer the closing prayer. The high school senior was startled but, to his credit, did as he was asked.

"Um, hi God," Trey began. "This is Trey, but I guess you knew that already. We're here because of your church. Ours burned, as you know, and we're trying to figure out what to do now. Help us feel that you're in this with us. Help us see the things we should be doing as we try to move forward. You're awesome and any help you could give us would be cool."

"Couldn't have said it any better," Jake said patting Trey on the back. Trey's prayer reminded Emmett of when he was young and God seemed like a friend. Somewhere along the way, things got formal.

Another dump truck drove away.

— 13 —

CHAPTER

Church

With his study door closed, Emmett pulled out some books from his shelves and tried to find quotations about the church from leading theologians. He felt, as rector, he needed to provide an impressive answer to Jake's question. His plentiful notes entangled him, but eventually, he wrote a complete, page-long description. Fitting a definition of the church into a paragraph would be difficult, but one sentence was impossible. Perhaps they'll allow me a little leeway at tomorrow's meeting, he muttered to himself.

CHAPTER 13

Jake and Emmett were finishing supper when Sam arrived unannounced. He apologized for interrupting but wanted them to know that it looked like the site would be cleared by Easter.

"Fantastic," Jake said.

"Well done, Sam," Emmett added.

"Would you like some pot roast?" Jake asked.

"Smells delicious, but I'm headed to an AA meeting."

"Good for you," Emmett said, but Jake took it a step further.

"Could we come?" Jake asked.

Sam looked to see if Jake was serious. "It's an open meeting. You can come if you want."

"Us?" asked Emmett.

"Yes, us," Jake replied, punching Emmett's arm lightly. "We might learn something. Let's go." Without waiting for Emmett to agree, Jake grabbed their plates and took them to the sink.

"You could follow me, or we could all ride in my truck," Sam offered.

"I vote for the truck," Jake answered as he marched out the door. Soon, the three men were riding side by side in a pickup truck. Emmett got the window seat.

"How long have you been sober?" Jake asked.

"Five years last Christmas," Sam said. "I'm sure you've heard about my public meltdown."

"I've heard worse. I liked the part about waking up in the manger."

"I'm still embarrassed about that."

"Sorry about your wife and the kids, though."

"Me, too," said Sam looking away.

"The way I see it, something inside you wanted to be closer to Jesus," Jake said.

Sam smiled at Jake. "Can't say I've ever seen it that way. I like that perspective."

"Where's the meeting?" asked Emmett.

"The basement of the Civic Center. We used to meet at the Congregational church, but they kicked us out after they did a major renovation. Some places don't like hosting AA meetings— too many cigarette butts outside and too much swearing inside."

"Were there meetings at St. John's?" Jake asked. Emmett looked out the window, searching for an answer. Recovery groups had approached the church at various times, but Emmett had always found an excuse to refuse.

"There weren't any groups at St. John's," Sam said.

"Well, I'm looking forward to this," Jake said as if they headed to get ice cream. "I've never been to an AA meeting."

"Me either," said Emmett.

Several cars were in the parking lot when they arrived. A group of smokers huddled beside the front door. "Getting their last puffs before the meeting," Sam explained as the trio climbed out of the truck.

Emmett and Jake took seats in the circle of folding chairs while Sam walked around and greeted friends. Emmett couldn't help but notice how comfortable Sam seemed. "Should we sit in the circle or off to the side?" Emmett asked when Sam arrived with three cups of coffee and a bunch of cookies.

"Everyone sits in the circle," Sam pointed out. He handed his guests their coffee and cookies: "This is our communion. It's not as fancy as what you give in church, but it serves the same purpose."

"Hear, hear," said Jake.

Everyone took a seat, armed with cookies and coffee, as the meeting began. Quite a collection of people, Emmett thought. There were men and women of all ages, some with piercings, others decorated with tattoos. Two looked as if they'd come straight from an office. Each time Emmett looked at someone, they turned away as if not wanting to make eye contact.

Sam whispered, "Most everyone here has been hurt by the church. Your clerical collar stirs all that up."

The meeting began with readings, then people introduced themselves by their first names and identified themselves as alcoholics. The crowd responded by calling their names.

"We do that as a way of keeping us mindful of our disease," Sam whispered. "We have what we like to call 'forgetters.' It's important to put it on the table at the start."

The meeting's topic was surrendering to a power greater than ourselves. Emmett was shocked by the level of candor. One person spoke about her need to surrender her family that she all but destroyed by drinking. Another spoke of surrendering his need for a job, and a third spoke about how she needed to surrender her need for approval. A newcomer shared he didn't like the whole idea of surrender. "It goes against how I was raised," he said. Holding out his two hands, he opened one and kept the second one closed to illustrate how he was willing to surrender some things, but not everything.

"I have a hole in my soul through which the wind blows," someone said at the end of the meeting. "I tried to fill that hole with booze, women, and even success at work, but nothing filled the hole. Finally, I had to admit complete defeat. That's when everything began changing for me."

The meeting made Emmett think about his own drinking. He wasn't an alcoholic, but Emmett understood what they were saying. He'd never heard such honesty in the church. People were hanging their laundry on the line and laughing at the polka-dotted underwear. They were not a glum lot. It made Emmett envious.

At the end of the meeting, they handed out plastic chips to welcome people to AA or to mark their progress. The last chip offered was for anyone who had returned to drinking but wanted to try sobriety again. A woman stood to receive what they called the start-over chip, and the applause was loud. Emmett thought it was like watching the father run out to meet the prodigal son. "For this son of mine was lost, and is found again," he said, quoting scripture under his breath. He'd never seen anything like it. Certainly not in the church.

On the ride home, Jake and Sam talked about the meeting. Sam explained that some groups are called "speaker meetings." "That's when someone tells their story."

"Seems to me most people would want to forget what happened," Emmett said.

"True," said Sam. "But there's power in remembering, in telling our stories. Sometimes what we say makes a newcomer feel like they aren't alone. Also, telling your story can help loosen its grip."

"Its grip?" Jake asked.

"Guilt and shame can squeeze a person right out of the room and back into the bar."

"I was surprised by the laughter," Emmett said. "You all shared your secrets and laughed."

"I was taught to think of it as if we're all survivors of a terrible shipwreck," Sam explained. "Many were lost, but the rest of us gather, wrapped in blankets, to talk about what happened and share our gratitude for being alive."

"I hope heaven's like that," Jake said. The other men nodded quietly. After a few minutes, Jake looked back over at Sam and asked, "Was your decision to get sober because of the Christmas tree lighting debacle, or was there more?"

After a long pause, Sam said, "There was more. There's always more. The sad part is that people forgive the drinking part. It's the other stuff they can't forgive."

"Doesn't seem fair," Emmett said. "You can't pick and choose grace."

"I hate to tell you, conditional grace is everywhere—even in the church," Sam replied.

Emmett stared out the window for the rest of the ride.

The next morning, Emmett didn't bother to bring his well-crafted paragraph to the meeting. He had finally found his sentence and looked forward to sharing it.

Stanley Fitzpatrick went first: "The church is a place of worship, period." Jake thanked him and agreed worship was a central part of the church.

"The church is a community of people gathered in God's grace," Sara offered. Emmett couldn't help thinking about the woman who had picked up her start-over chip the night before.

"The church is where the world is transformed, one meal at a time," Marty said.

Trey Prescott went next. "The church is where you go to hear about God."

"Just hear?" Jake asked.

"Well," Trey said, "that's part of it. There's a lot of talk about God in church. I guess I'd say it's also a place to wonder. There aren't a whole lot of answers, but it's nice to imagine God looking out for us."

A few smiled after hearing Trey's response. Emmett was next. With an impish smile, he put his hands together. His index fingers formed a steeple, thumbs the doors, and his other fingers were intertwined inside.

"Here's the church," he began, "and here's the steeple; open the doors, and see all the people."

He wiggled his fingers and almost giggled. As he looked down at his fingers, he thought about the men and women gathered in a circle the night before. He thought of the children he'd baptized and those he'd married and buried. He thought about those who were easy to love and those who were not. All of them were inside the church, he reminded himself. No exceptions.

"Now that's a sermon I get," Trey said, clapping his hands. Others laughed. Jake paused, hoping Emmett might explain.

"Too often, we make the church too complicated," he explained. "We say the church is this, then we add that, and before you know it, we've made it something cumbersome instead of letting it be the simple thing it was intended to be—a place to know and be known. The church is not the steeple, doors, or anything else. It's the people inside—warts and all. I confess I've often forgotten that. With God's help, I hope I don't again."

— 14 —

CHAPTER

Turning On the Water

"**T**ake a look at this," Emmett said as he slid the letter across the kitchen table.

"What is it?" Jake asked.

"You'll see. It's from 'His Holiness,'" Emmett said.

Jake unfolded the letter and saw the gold seal of the diocese at the top and the elaborate signature of the bishop at the bottom, complete with a cross before his name.

"Why does he put a cross before his name?"

"To remind everyone he's a bishop—as if there were any doubt with the seal and all."

"Dear St. John's Episcopal Church," Jake read out loud. "I write to inform you that after careful consideration and prayerful reflection, the diocese will not be taking legal action against your parish, nor anyone associated with it, due to your disregard of the requirement to ensure all diocesan property."

Jake folded the letter and returned it to Emmett. "Aren't you going to read the rest?" Emmett asked.

"Don't need to. What matters is you don't need to worry about what the bishop will do anymore. Now you know. You're free."

"Free? Feels like a reprimand to me. I'm thinking of writing back and..."

"Let it go, Emmett. Don't give the bishop such power."

"You don't understand how the Episcopal Church works."

"I think it's more than that," Jake gently admonished.

"Excuse me?" Emmett said, sitting up and facing Jake.

"Do the math. Your father was a bishop, and you wanted to be one, too. Now you're taking it out on a bishop who reminds you of that."

"So you're a therapist now as well as an architect?"

"I just think it's time to let it go. We've got enough to worry about." Jake stood to refill his coffee, watching Emmett to see how he would handle a direct confrontation. "Why'd you go into the church in the first place, Emmett?"

"To serve God and his people," Emmett replied without thinking.

"Answer like I'm not a seminary admissions committee."

Emmett stared out the window before responding. "I've always believed in God, even as a young boy, maybe especially as a young boy. It wasn't necessarily because of anything I learned in Sunday school or heard in church. I always felt God was near. I couldn't see him. He was just beyond my vision, but I felt God's presence somehow. When I watched the wind blow through leaves, listened to water flowing down a stream, or felt an ocean wave crash over me, I felt an overwhelming connection to God.

It made me grateful. It also ignited a sense of wonder. I started looking for God everywhere. When I got older, I wanted to be a part of that."

"A part of what?" Jake asked.

"The wonder. I wanted to spend my life noticing and pointing it out to others."

"Is that why you went into the priesthood?"

"Maybe it was too large a leap, but it made sense at the time." Emmett tapped the folded letter. "Little did I know the church was more about this than wonder." He took a sip of coffee and looked up at Abby's painting, "That's why I like the cabin so much. It's all about nature up there. Feeling close to God there is easy. It's feeling close to God here that's the trick."

"How does your father fit into all this?" Jake asked, looking at Emmett with a smile.

"I admired him, but I suppose you're right; I wanted to be like him, too," Emmett conceded. "The church seemed like the logical place to do that, but I'm not sure I've done a very good job."

"Yet," Jake whispered.

"Excuse me?"

"Your story isn't over yet. I'm no expert, but I doubt God called you so you could be like your father. I'll bet he hoped you'd be you, not somebody else—not Michael Phillips, not your father, or anybody else. It's not too late to be you."

Emmett smiled. "Where were you when I first came to St. John's? It feels like all I've done here is chase after something, achieve something, and be someone. I could have used that kind of reminder when I started."

"I wasn't born yet," Jake said, trying to lighten the mood. "But I'm here now, and you've got the chance to build a church, for Christ's sake. Not many people get to do that."

"We're a long way from building a church."

"It'll be sooner than you think. For now, think about the people," Jake said, imitating Emmett with his hands intertwined and the fingers being the people inside the church. "As you said, they're the ones who matter. Not the bishop and not your father."

Emmett left the kitchen table feeling a strange mix of agitation and relief. He decided to go over to the grist mill. The church offices were closed, but he needed some space from Jake and his probing questions.

The mill was silent other than the rushing from a spring thaw. The sanctuary was empty, and none of the artists were in their studios yet. Gladys and the altar guild had prepared the church for Holy Week. Lent was almost over. The Easter linen was removed from the altar. "He is risen" were words that needed to wait until Easter.

Sitting in his office, he looked at the Holy Week services. Looking over the services was the last thing he wanted to do after his conversation with Jake. He leaned back in his chair and listened to the river. He and his sister used to play in the stream behind their house growing up. A smile came to his face when he remembered standing in the stream with his pants rolled up and pretending to be John the Baptist. "Come to me," Emmett cried out to his sister with his arms extended wide, "and I will get you…" He struggled to remember the rest, then added, "Wet!"

He was playing church even back then, he thought. His sister complied with his charade and climbed down to be baptized. They laughed as Emmett reached down, scooped water in his hands, and lifted them above his sister's head.

"What, may I ask, are you doing?" his father asked with a voice so deep it made Emmett open his hands and cover his sister with water. "You should be ashamed of making fun of the church." The two walked back to the house like cowed dogs.

Emmett looked over at his father's crozier leaning against the wall. It was one of the few things salvaged from the fire. He stood, took the crozier, and walked slowly from his office to one of the windows overlooking the river. He watched the water cascade over the rocks to create the waterfall that used to give the grist mill life. A branch tumbled down the waterfall, bobbling up in the water below. Up and down, it looked like it was dancing its way downstream. Emmett was jealous. That's what free looks like, he thought, as he gripped his father's crozier tighter.

In a moment of spontaneity, Emmett walked out of the building and toward the river. The staff, once a sacred relic, worked perfectly as a walking stick as Emmett climbed down the steep bank to the water's edge. The rushing water made Emmett feel like a boy again. Mist from the falls coated his face as he drew near. He stood beside the river for a long time, letting the water carry his thoughts away. Breathing deeply, he thought the air was delicious. A breeze tugged at his pant legs.

He remembered the song he and his sister used to sing: "As I went down in the river to pray, studying about that good old way and who shall wear that starry crown, good Lord, show me the way." The song drew him closer to the water.

Then, another song came to mind. "Wade in the water," he began to hum, "wade in the water children, wade in the water, God's gonna trouble the water."

Why not? Emmett wondered, and he turned and sat on a nearby rock to remove his shoes. The ground was cold; the water frigid. Emmett gasped when it covered his feet. He remembered the time his father used him as an example during a foot-washing ceremony. Emmett couldn't stop giggling when his father took the towel and washed his feet. Even his father's angry stare couldn't control his laughter.

Unable to feel his feet, Emmett looked around to make sure no one was watching before he began wading into the river. His father's staff helped him navigate the slippery rocks. After almost falling, he knew better than to go any farther.

"Hey, Emmett!" Jake yelled from the parking lot.

Emmett turned suddenly and lost his balance. His father's staff couldn't bear his weight and snapped in two. Emmett fell backward, arms flailing, into the stream. Jake ran to help, but there was nothing he could do. The water was shallow, and Emmett was already crawling out of the river by the time Jake made it down the bank. Emmett shivered, so Jake took off his checkered jacket and wrapped it around Emmett.

"What on earth?" Jake exclaimed as he escorted Emmett back to the rock.

"Don't know what got into me," Emmett said.

"Glad you're all right," Jake said. He walked over and picked up one of the pieces of the crozier. "Sorry about this."

"The other half must've floated away," Emmett said. "Guess I took your advice about letting my father go." His attempt to make light of the situation did not hide his sadness.

"Breaking his crozier wasn't what I meant."

"It was my fault for bringing it here," Emmett said, looking at the piece in his hand. "I'm just glad no one was here to see that."

"I was! I saw the whole thing," Jake said with a laugh as he sat beside Emmett. "I only wish I had caught it on film."

"If you utter a word to anyone..." Emmett cautioned as he put on his shoes and socks.

"Don't worry, your secret is safe with me."

The two sat and looked out at the river. To their left, the grist mill's water wheel sat frozen in time. It loomed above the two as they sat at the river's edge, rust blended with chipped red paint.

"I bet that was something in its day," said Jake. "I hate that it's rusting away."

"I don't know. I bet it still has life in it." Emmett looked at Jake with his eyes opened wide. "I'm starting to sound like you!" Jake's laughter echoed off the side of the mill.

"Let's find out," Emmett said, handing Jake his jacket. "Follow me." Emmett turned and began climbing up the riverbank toward the entrance to the mill. Jake tried to keep up.

"You OK?" Jake asked as Emmett stood at the top of the river bank, bent over with his hands on his knees.

"A little too eager, I suppose," Emmett said between gasps. The two walked toward the mill and the two large grinding millstones in the corner of the sanctuary. "That's the lever the owner said opens the shoot for the water." Jake nodded as Emmett pulled a chair over.

"You're not seriously thinking of turning that," Jake said.

"It's the only way to see if the wheel still works," Emmett replied.

Emmett climbed onto the chair and reached for the lever. He almost fell, and Jake rushed over to support him. Once steadied, he tried pulling the lever. It was stuck. He tried again, but it only moved an inch.

"Probably best to let it be," Jake said from below.

"Let it be?" Emmett said in disgust as he tried again. "I thought you said to take risks and try new things."

"Yes, but not if it means breaking your neck."

"Let me worry about my neck," Emmett said as he tried one last time. The lever finally moved to the open position.

"Voilà!" Emmett declared as he climbed down and went to the window to watch. There was a deep groaning sound. They heard water going down the shoot, but the wheel didn't move.

CHAPTER 14

Water splashed over the sides and cascaded down the wheel, but it didn't move.

"I guess you were right," Emmett conceded. "Too old and rusted."

Jake put his arm around Emmett. "Let's get you home and into dry clothes."

They locked the door and drove back to the rectory. Once they were gone, the wheel creaked as it moved slightly. Chipped paint fell into the river as the wheel struggled to turn. As if waking from a slumber, the wheel seemed to lift its arms and yawn. Ever so slightly, with occasional pauses, the wheel inched forward. It finally made a full rotation, then another. Picking up speed, the wheel spun as smoothly as it ever had.

—15—
CHAPTER

Reorientation

"**L**ook at you," Jake said as he walked down the stairs and found Emmett preparing to leave. "All dressed and ready to go."

"I'm meeting Marty Starnes at the mill this morning to let her know Wednesday night dinners are a go."

"They are?" Jake said, turning to Emmett. "What made you change your mind?"

"My fingers, I guess," Emmett said as he put his hands together in the shape of a church and wiggled his fingers like children in the pews. "Or maybe it was my unexpected plunge yesterday. Either way, if it's truly all about the people, then Wednesday night dinners are the right thing to do, even if they're served in the sanctuary. I called around. The vestry members I spoke to were all for the idea. Guess it's always been me standing in the way."

"Marty's going to go nuts," Jake said. "Gladys and the altar guild might be a problem. You know how protective they are about the sanctuary."

"They'll get over it," Emmett said.

Just before Emmett left, Jake said, "While the effects of your swim remain, I want to ask if you're all right with me holding the next vision committee meeting over at the old church?"

"I don't see why not. What do you have in mind?"

"A field trip. It's time to get the committee out of their seats and doing something. I thought a trip to the old church would do some good."

"Whatever you think is best," Emmett said. "I trust you."

Jake smiled.

A crowd was gathered in the parking lot of the mill when Emmett arrived. Most of the artists from the second floor were there and some people Emmett didn't recognize. They were standing on the edge of the parking lot, pointing to the river side of the mill.

"Emmett!" Jewell cried. "Come here. You've got to see this."

"What is it?" he asked.

"The wheel. It's turning!"

He had forgotten about turning on the water yesterday. "I don't believe it," he said, looking like a child watching a magic trick. The large wheel spun as if a Ferris wheel at an amusement park. Water poured into each container within the wheel and fell back into the river as it turned. The crowd watched in awe; Emmett got chills. "When I turned the lever, nothing happened," he said.

"You did this?" Raj asked. "We always wanted to see if we could get it to work, but we never actually tried."

"It completely changes the place," said Jewell. Others nodded their complete agreement.

"The mill has come alive," Raj added.

Emmett stayed after the others went to their studios and watched the wheel until Marty arrived. Like the others, Marty was delighted to see the wheel spinning. "I thought that thing was rusted solid."

"Apparently not," Emmett said, as he escorted Marty into the church.

Emmett turned on the lights, "I want to commend you and your team for all you have done to get the food pantry up and running. It's been successful and is meeting a real need. I'm glad the space downstairs worked, but I wanted to meet with you not only to thank you but also to apologize."

"For what?"

"For refusing your request to use this space for the Wednesday night dinners." Emmett said, gesturing to the sanctuary. "I was so caught up in trying to make this place look like a church that I forgot to make it act like one. I was thinking only about Sunday mornings and not the other days of the week. Worship comes in many forms, as you so often point out. Your Wednesday night dinners are as sacred as any communion, and I'd like it very much if you would set your team loose and serve meals again on Wednesday nights. This time, in the church itself."

Marty looked at Emmett as if seeing him for the first time. She reached to hug him, catching them both off-guard. "What made you change your mind?" she asked.

"Several things. The church is supposed to be about the people. I forget that sometimes. Serving meals to those in need is the right thing to do. How soon can you get things started?"

Marty said she could be ready in a week or two. "But I need to rally the troops. Thanks, Emmett. You've surprised me," she said as she rushed toward her car.

"Is that a bad thing?"

"No," Marty called out over her shoulder, "it's wonderful."

"Why on earth do we need to meet at seven in the morning?" Emmett growsed. "I'd rather be in my pajamas enjoying my coffee."

It was only beginning to get light when the committee members arrived. They stood looking out at the cleared lot and the remaining portions of the foundation and walls. Once everyone was there, Jake climbed the steps and turned to face the committee.

"You're probably wondering why I've asked you here at this hour."

"You can say that again," Mac called out.

"It occurred to me that we've spent hours talking around a table. It's time we return here. We've had many conversations, some of them hard. We've agreed and disagreed, but we've also discovered some things about the church that maybe we'd forgotten. I thought it would be good to come here and see the church, literally, from a new perspective."

"At seven in the morning?" Mac grumbled.

"If that's what it takes. Sometimes it takes getting up early, or falling into a river, to see things in a new way." Jake said, smiling at Emmett. "The debris has been carried away, and the lot's been cleared. Now you can see what you have to work with."

"But why so early in the morning?" Stanley Fitzpatrick complained.

Jake smiled. "For centuries, churches have been built facing east. It is a theological statement: facing the rising sun was symbolic, as if looking at the new day of Easter every morning." Jake turned and pointed toward the remaining walls of the church. "St. John's was built in this direction, with the entrance here and the altar at the far end."

"That's right," Stanley said, "and the new church should be built exactly where the old one was." Many nodded when Trey interrupted.

"Wait a minute," he said, looking to his right. "The sun's rising over there. That's east."

People realized the old St. John's had been pointed in the wrong direction. "It was built that way to make the best use of the lot at the time," Jake explained, "but now that the church and Cutter Hall were gone, the lot is wide open. The church can be placed in a direction you want. A new orientation could lend itself to other ideas you come up with."

"There's a lot more room than I thought," Virginia said. The others agreed.

"It is a blank canvas," Jake said. "If you were to start from scratch, where would you put the church?"

"Right where it was," Stanley replied defiantly.

Others were willing to consider alternative ideas. "If we change the orientation," Virginia offered, "what would we do with the old church site? I'd hate to see it used for parking or something."

"It should be kept, somehow, as a reminder, or memorial of some kind," Simon offered.

"You have lots of time to decide what to do with this extra space. For now, I wanted to get your wheels turning." Mac nudged Emmett with a grin as he thought about the grist mill wheel. "You don't have to decide where the church will go this morning or what it will look like, but I thought you should come and wander around and think about how you might orient the new church building."

The committee members walked around the property in silence. A refreshing breeze blew through the leaves on the trees; spring always came later than people wanted in New England. Virginia wandered into the space where the church had been, thinking back to the baptism of her three daughters. Simon sat at the top of the granite steps and looked at the green grass covering the vacant space where the church had been. He closed his eyes and tried to imagine what the new church could look like. For the first time, he didn't see the old church when he closed his eyes. Sara walked along, sliding her hand along the one remaining wall, then paused to touch where her parents' window had been. She turned and leaned against the wall and watched the sunrise. Mac and Jake explored the farthest edges of the vacant space.

Everyone reconvened at the steps and shared their thoughts before Jake invited them to the rectory for coffee and breakfast casserole. The conversation was lively. Jake listened as the ideas poured out of committee members. Stanley didn't budge from his desire for the church to be built where it had been, but others spoke about how the parish hall could be situated beside the church so there would be increased parking. Someone suggested making a garden where the old church had been. Someone else mentioned a memorial. Sara tried to write down the ideas. After people left, Emmett kept coming up with ideas. Jake couldn't keep up.

News of the wheel turning at the grist mill brought the curious to church on Sunday as well as the regular attenders. Simon and the ushers scrambled to find enough chairs. Emmett departed from the scripture passages assigned for that Sunday and preached on the feeding of the five thousand in anticipation of his announcement about the Wednesday night dinners. He expressed his gratitude for Marty and her team—and asked for more volunteers.

On the first night of Wednesday dinners, Emmett arrived to help. The parking lot was full. There was also a crowd standing outside waiting for dinner, though the doors wouldn't open for an hour. Tables were scattered throughout the sanctuary, and tablecloths made it look more like a restaurant than a church. Gladys and the altar guild had surprised Emmett by throwing their full support behind the dinners. As Jake suggested, they made small flower arrangements in empty jars from the food pantry, using water from the river. When Emmett arrived, Jake and Sam were placing the arrangements on the tables. Simon and Sara set the last few places with napkins and utensils while Mac and others poured drinks. Virginia and Todd were working with Tom and Alice Smith to prepare the food.

When they opened the doors, the guests, as Marty insisted they be called, entered slowly. Looking at the space, they thanked the volunteers before finding a place to sit. Some were homeless, placing their possessions along the wall by the sanctuary's entrance. Others looked like families you would meet at the grocery store or on the street. Emmett recognized a few people and was surprised by their need. Marty welcomed each as if they were family members and encouraged them to sit wherever they were most comfortable.

"Look, Daddy," said one young boy pointing to the water wheel, turning outside the window. He must have been around seven years old with a haircut that looked like it had been given at home. His clothes were almost clean, torn in only a few places. "Can I go see?"

"I don't think that's a good idea," said the boy's father.

"Sure you can," Emmett interrupted, reaching out his hand. "I'll take you over and show it to you myself. We just got it to start moving."

While he explained how the wheel worked, the boy clung to Emmett's pant leg, looking up at the priest and taking in every word. Jake stopped and watched Emmett and the boy.

Once everyone was seated, Marty welcomed the diners and asked Emmett to say a blessing before the food was served. Walking up to the stage, Emmett realized the boy had come along and took his place beside the rector. "Let us pray," Emmett said. Everyone bowed their heads and held hands; the boy reached up and took Emmett's hand. There was a longer pause than usual as Emmett tried to compose himself.

"I don't believe this," Emmett said to Marty as his parishioners delivered the meals. "I've never seen such a turnout."

"People are hungry," Marty replied.

"No," said Emmett, "I was talking about all the parishioners."

"Like I said," Marty smiled. "People are hungry."

—16—

CHAPTER

Railings

Emmett was restless, irritable, and discontent. After many unsuccessful attempts at getting back to sleep, he got up and eased down the steps. He didn't want to awaken Jake. He wanted to be alone.

Walking across the common in the dark, he knew he should rejoice over everything that had happened since the fire, but something inside him was unsettled. The ups and downs of the past few months had taken their toll. He hoped a walk would calm him down.

The meeting about repositioning the church had been disturbing. Emmett was excited talking about rebuilding the church, but part of him agreed with Stanley Fitzpatrick. Why couldn't the new church be built where the old one had been? Why change everything?

The spring air was cool, and the granite steps were colder when Emmett took a seat in the empty space. He tried to focus on things like the flowers on the tables on Wednesday nights, the sound of volunteers laughing as they served guests, and the feel of the boy's hand in his as he said the blessing, but a gnawing worry intruded. The problem wasn't the money he needed to raise or the fact that they were worshipping in a grist mill. It was something deeper.

He reached over and held onto one of the mangled railings as he tried to figure out what was bothering him. A streetlamp glared its light onto the empty space before him. He gripped tighter.

Emmett felt trapped somewhere between the grist mill and vacant lot. Like the Israelites, he was in the wilderness, between Egypt and the promised land, and he prayed God would lead him forward. He prayed for the sadness to be taken away.

Trees swayed in the breeze, causing two branches to hit one another. It startled Emmett. He looked up but saw nothing. He listened and heard nothing. God no longer spoke to him. That, or he'd forgotten how to listen. He took a deep breath and was surprised by the wave of sadness that overtook him, or was it fear? Whatever it was wanted to come out.

Placing his head on his knees, he let the tears come. They were slow at first but soon flowed freely. He hadn't cried since Abby died three years ago. On the steps of the ruined church, Emmett cried for his dog that was hit by a car, for the penalty kick he missed that would have won the championship, and for his father, who was more often disappointed than proud. He cried because his name wasn't announced as bishop. He cried because everything he'd worked for was gone. All that remained were three steps and two twisted railings.

The morning light replaced the street lamps, and Emmett wiped his face and tried to compose himself. Tears are exhausting, he thought. He had led the church for 42 years, but it felt like sand slipping through his fingers. Parishioners were doing things without asking for permission, the sanctuary had become more of a town hall than a sacred space, and now they were talking about moving where the church once stood. "I'm losing my church," he said out loud.

"No, you're not," Jake said, standing on the path with his hands in his coat pockets.

"What on earth are you doing here?" Emmett asked, rubbing his sleeve across his face one last time.

"I heard you leave," Jake said, sitting beside Emmett. "Thought I'd check on you."

"I'm OK," said Emmett.

"That's what got you out of bed in the middle of the night."

"Couldn't sleep," Emmett admitted. "I feel like the church I've known, the church I've led, is slipping away.

"Slipping away or changing?" Jake asked.

"Is there a difference?"

"It won't last," Jake assured Emmett. "There's light at the end of the tunnel."

"It's killing me," Emmett said as he released the railing and brushed his pant legs.

"What's the church sign say?" Jake asked, pointing to the last remnant of the old church. "Darkness cannot overcome the light?"

"The light shines in the darkness, and the darkness has not overcome it. It's from John's Gospel."

"There you go," Jake said, trying to bring hope. "There's light even though there's darkness. We'll get through this. You, me, and the others. Trust me."

"I'm not all that good at trusting," Emmett said. "After running the show for so long, it's tough."

"How's running the show worked out so far?" Jake asked with a smile.

"Not good, as you can see," Emmett said, gesturing to the scene before them. "Not sure I have what's needed to get us through this."

"Then let others help. Let me help. Let Mac and the others help. Most of all, maybe let God help."

"God seems busy."

"Really? Maybe he's sitting right beside you, and you don't recognize him."

"Are you saying you're God?"

"You know what I mean."

"I do," said Emmett, looking away.

After a long silence, Jake changed the subject. "How 'bout we go get some breakfast?" Jake said as he reached down to help Emmett up. "Maria's must be open now. It's on me."

Emmett didn't reach the mill until mid-morning. Jewell was unloading something from her car as he arrived. He'd grown to like the artists, drawn by the optimistic way they approached life. He wandered upstairs more often, eager to see their most recent projects. "Can I help?" he asked.

"Sure," she replied, handing Emmett one of four rolled-up banners.

"What are these?" he asked

"Part of an art show that just finished. The theme was nature and art. I made banners representing earth, wind, water, and fire."

Emmett pulled down the corner of the one he was holding. "This one must be water," he said. Opening the banner further, the vibrant blues and whites captivated him. "What are you going to do with them now?"

"Put them in my studio closet with other finished projects, I guess," Jewell said as she handed Emmett a second one.

"Would you consider letting the church use them?" Emmett asked.

"Are you serious?" Jewell responded.

"It'd be a shame to put this in a closet. It needs to be seen."

"I agree. Just never thought you all would be interested."

The two went into the sanctuary and rolled the banners on the floor. Twelve feet long and four feet wide, the banners filled the space with color. Van Gogh would have approved of the dramatic color and unharnessed lines. Looking at her art reminded Emmett of when Abby would come to his office with her newest piece of art.

"They're magnificent," he said. "In fact, I don't want to borrow them; I'd like to purchase them on behalf of the church."

Jewell put her hands in her pink hair and looked to see if Emmett was serious. "Don't you think you should save your money for rebuilding the church?"

"This is part of the rebuilding," Emmett said. "I won't take no for an answer."

Emmett called Mac, and he arrived a short time later, towing the largest ladder he owned. Within an hour, Mac had all four banners hanging from the rafters, and Emmett and Jewell looked up in silence.

"Look at those!" Jake exclaimed as he entered. "They're as dramatic as any stained-glass window I've seen. Makes the place look like a church." He grinned at Emmett.

The other artists were surprised Jewell was able to convince the church to hang the banners in the sanctuary. "I didn't convince him. He convinced me!" she said.

On Sunday, Emmett used the banners as the focus of his sermon. He adapted Matthew's passage about letting one's "light so shine" and entitled his sermon, "Let your art so hang." The choir followed his sermon with an anthem from the hymnal.

> Earth and all stars, Loud rushing planets
> Sing to the Lord a new song!
> Hail, wind, and rain, Loud blowing snowstorm
> Sing to the Lord a new song!
> God has done marvelous things.
> I too sing praises with a new song!

Jewell was beaming, and the line of people wanting to speak to her after the service was long.

Gladys and Alma were not the only two trying to acclimate to the new normal at St. John's. The banners were all people could talk about during coffee hour. The youth seemed particularly drawn to them. They stared at them while munching on cookies and voting which was the best one. People were as startled by Emmett allowing such things in church as they were by the banners themselves.

Sara, Jake, and others were cleaning up from the coffee hour, and Emmett was hanging his vestments when Sam dropped in.

"Got a second?" he asked.

"Sure," said Emmett. "What can I do for you?"

"I was wondering," Sam began, sounding nervous, "if it would be all right for me to use the sanctuary from time to time to practice my guitar. I remember you have a thing against guitars in church, but I thought it might be all right if I played when no one was around."

Looking embarrassed, Emmett looked at Sam and said, "Of course, you can. I'm sorry I gave you that impression. I remember you playing the guitar when you were in high school. I'm glad you kept up with it."

"Much to my father's dismay," Sam joked. "At least I never joined a band and traveled to California, as he feared."

"Feel free to use the sanctuary any time you'd like," Emmett said and then offered his own attempt at humor, "but don't think I've changed my mind about guitars during church services!"

"I won't," Sam said, smiling. As he began to leave, he turned toward Emmett. "One other thing. Any chance you'd let that AA group you visited meet here? The Civic Center needs the space for another project. Some of the members of the group who came with me to church a couple of weeks ago asked if you'd consider such a thing. I said I'd ask."

Emmett paused and looked out toward the river. "Sure," he said, "Just make sure it doesn't conflict with Wednesday night dinners."

Emmett stood there as Sam walked away, then looked over at the three volunteers staring at him.

"Don't say a word," Emmett said, putting his hand up so he didn't have to look at the I-don't-believe-it grin on Jake's face.

"I won't," said Jake, "but sand slipping through one's hands makes the sweetest sound!"

"Funny," Emmett said. "Very funny."

— 17 —

CHAPTER

Opening the Cabin

"Can I come?" Jake asked when he heard Mac and Emmett were headed up to Emmett's cabin to open it for the season. It was a Memorial Day weekend tradition Abby and Emmett started when they first bought the place. Emmett continued it after she was gone, with Mac's help.

"I've been looking at this painting every morning," Jake said. "It's time I see it for myself." Mac and Emmett welcomed the extra help.

On the way, Emmett told the story of how a parishioner approached them soon after they arrived at St. John's and asked if they had any interest in a mountain place. "I told him we weren't interested, but Abby made me call him back that night after I told her about it. She felt a place of our own would be good for us. She was right. I can't tell you how often we came here to get away, just the two of us. She loved her role at St. John's, but at the cabin, we were just Emmett and Abby. I promised her I'd never sell it."

"Plus, it's frickin' gorgeous," Mac pointed out.

Emmett smiled. "It's rustic, but it does have an amazing view."

They opened the car windows to enjoy the cooler air as they headed to the mountains. Emmett stared ahead, lost in memories, as Jake filled the silence. He was curious how someone like Mac could find his way to an Episcopal church.

"There was an Episcopal church near where I was stationed in Japan," Mac explained. "A bunch of us went on Sundays, mostly to pass the time. When I was transferred a few years later, I missed it and found another Episcopal church near the new base. I liked that the services were almost identical. By the time we moved to Webster, I guess it was in my blood, so it made sense to join St. John's."

"But why church?" Jake asked. Mac turned and looked at Jake to see what he was after. "I mean, why go to church in the first place? If you'll excuse me for saying so, you don't exactly seem like the church-going type."

"Guess I'm hedging my bets."

"Hedging your bets?"

"You know," Mac said, pointing up, "I'd like a room when this is all over."

"Not exactly the most compelling declaration of faith," Emmett said, "but I think God'll let you in. You're a bit foul-mouthed, but I've never met a more caring soul."

"What the hell do you know?" Mac said, deflecting the compliment.

"What about you, Emmett?" Jake asked.

"What about me?" he asked.

"Why'd you go into the church? Did you feel a call to become a minister?"

"Suppose so," Emmett replied, shrugging his shoulders.

"That's not the most compelling declaration of faith," Mac offered from the back seat.

"Who really knows if they're called?" Emmett continued. "I always hoped to hear a voice or see a light, but it never happened. People in the Bible got them. Moses got a burning bush, for Pete's sake. Why not me?"

"You got a burning church," Jake joked.

"There you go!" Mac said, pushing against Emmett's seat. "That'll beat a bush any day!"

"Not sure that counts," Emmett said. "I'm embarrassed to say it, but I've never been completely certain about my call. I've always believed in God, but I've also always had doubts. I can't explain how doubt and hope can sit beside one another, but they do, at least for me. Doubts shout, but hope whispers. The whispers have kept me coming back, like God's going, "*pssst, pssst,*" to get my attention. Instead of an undeniable call, I seem to have been given a thousand whispers, hints disguised as coincidences."

"I like that," said Jake. "Can't that be enough?"

"At my age, it'll have to be," Emmett said.

He took the exit and pointed out the first view of Squam Lake. "This is where they filmed *On Golden Pond*," he said.

"Great movie," said Jake.

"Except when the main character carries the box of dishes and almost has a heart attack." Mac offered from the backseat.

"I loved his relationship with his grandson," said Jake, "and how they spent hours looking for that big fish."

"Walter," Emmett said.

"Excuse me?" Jake responded.

"Walter. That was the name of the fish. Named after his good-for-nothing brother-in-law, I think."

"I also loved how he became less of a crotchety old fart," Jake added.

"There's hope for you yet, Emmett," Mac joked.

"You're one to talk."

Emmett took a deep breath as he turned into the driveway for the cabin. "I lift my eyes unto the hills, from whence cometh my help," he said softly.

"I love it when you speak the king's English," Mac joked,

"What can I say? The place soothes my soul," said Emmett, "and lowers my blood pressure, which pleases my doctor."

The driveway was a dusty mixture of sand, dirt, and stones. It meandered through woods and climbed a hill until it reached an open field on top. To the right was a modest cabin and to the left was a breathtaking view overlooking the entire lake and surrounding mountains.

"My God," Jake sighed.

"Exactly," said Emmett. "You can really feel God's presence here. There's 25 acres, more or less. Developers have been after me to sell, but I can't."

"I'll bet it's worth a fortune," Jake said as they climbed out of the car.

"That's what they keep telling me, but it's the last piece I have of Abby. I'm not letting it go."

The three stood in the clearing, breathing in the mountain air. A gust of cool air made the three turn toward the cabin.

"The wind is a constant companion because it's so exposed." Emmett pointed to the shingles scattered on the ground. "They blow off all the time."

"Don't you have a fancy word for the wind?" Mac asked.

"*Ruach*," Emmett answered,

"That's it," Mac said.

"It's not my word. It belongs to the Hebrew people. Either way, the wind keeps it cool all summer."

"Makes me think of Jewell's banner," Jake said. "She'd love this place. In fact, all the artists would. You should let them come up here and have a retreat. If this place doesn't inspire a person, nothing will."

The screen door screeched its welcome as Emmett searched for the key. Jake jumped up and down on the porch to test its sturdiness.

"It's built like a tank," said Mac. "I replaced the deck several years back, and it's held up nicely."

"That's right," Emmett said, looking at his friend, "You rebuilt it when Abby got sick. She sat here all day wrapped in a blanket," he told Jake.

Mac looked away. He and Abby had been close. Despite Mac's colorful vocabulary, they spoke the same language, and she could reach Mac like no other. Building the porch had been his way of showing he cared.

Emmett opened the weathered lock and welcomed them into the musty cabin. Sheets draped the furniture, and dust coated the floor and tabletops. A two-story stone fireplace held court on the far wall with stairs leading up to a loft at the other end.

"All the stones came from the lake," Emmett told Jake, who rubbed his hands along the rocks. There's one bedroom down here and one upstairs. We always hoped the second bedroom would be for a child, but that never happened. Now it's an underused guestroom. Jake, would you bring some life to this place by starting a fire?"

Mac was in charge of replacing the lost or broken shingles. Emmett opened the windows and began sweeping each room.

"It's pretty hard, isn't it?" Jake asked as he knelt by the hearth, crumbling old newspaper.

"What? Sweeping?" Emmett responded.

"No, running a parish."

"It can be. You've seen how things work over the past few months. There are a lot of moving parts. It's hard to keep things running smoothly."

"You make it sound like a machine."

"That's how it feels, sometimes."

"Do you ever regret it?" Jake asked, looking back at Emmett.

"St. John's, or the ministry?" Emmett asked.

"Both."

"Sometimes. I hate saying that, but it's the truth. God once felt like a childhood friend. I always thought ministry would be like playing in a sandbox with God, making a fort or something, maybe something divine with others."

"It isn't?" Jake asked.

"Not very often," Emmett said. He paused and watched the dust blow out the window. "It's more like running a business—raising money and keeping perpetually disgruntled parishioners somewhat content—and don't even get me started on the bishop and the diocese. For all the talk about it being a holy institution, it can be pretty damn human, sometimes."

"Like us," Jake said. He continued to build the fire. After a few minutes, he offered a suggestion.

"Maybe building the new church can be your sandbox."

"Dream on," Emmett said as swept the floors.

"Remember," Mac called out from his ladder. "It's all about the people."

"Thank you for sharing," Emmett yelled back. "Mind your own business."

The fire chased out the remnants of winter. Jake decided to go outside and help Mac. Emmett started coughing and gasping for air just as he finished sweeping.

"You all right in there?" Mac called out.

"Yes, fine," Emmett responded between coughs. "Just the dust." As he put the broom away, he realized the last time he'd been to the cabin, St. John's was still standing. It was nice to think back to a time before the fire. It was nice to pretend, to picturing it sitting where it once did.

"Ready for lunch?" Jake asked as he and Mac came inside and found their rector on his knees, cleaning the refrigerator. "It's time to dig into that picnic Maria made us."

They ate on the front porch, and Mac did his best to name the surrounding peaks. Emmett stared out at the lake as if he was looking at someone.

"You all right?" Jake asked.

"Yes, I'm fine. Some of Abby's ashes are in that lake. Just saying 'hi.'"

"You're going to see her again," said Mac. "I don't know how this heaven stuff works, but I've got to believe you'll be together again one day."

"What do you think she'll say when that happens?" Jake asked.

Flustered by the question, Emmett looked at Jake and then back toward the lake. "She'll wonder what I ended up doing with the extra time I was given."

"And what'll you say?"

"Built a church?"

"Not bad. Not bad at all," said Mac. "She'd like that. She never liked it when you focused on what you hadn't done and who you hadn't become."

Emmett wanted to tell Mac to be quiet, but he knew he was right.

"Where are the rest of her ashes?" Jake asked.

"With me in Webster. I always hoped to put them at St. John's, but there's no graveyard." He took a deep breath. His arms and legs tingled. "This is my church," he sighed.

"How so?" asked Jake.

Emmett pointed out toward the view. "This never fails to inspire me. It's easy to believe in God when you look out and see this."

"It's inspirational," said Jake, "but what does it inspire you to do?"

"What do you mean?"

"It's not enough to be inspired. You need to do something with inspiration. Too often, people think the same way about church. They come hoping to be inspired by the music, the setting, or maybe the sermon. Then, they get on with their lives, forgetting whatever stirred their souls."

"Isn't the church meant to inspire people?"

"Yes, inspire them to be the extraordinary creatures they already are and do things no one else can."

"Speaking of which," Mac interrupted, "time to get back to work." He got up from his chair and reached down to help Emmett up. The three finished the rest of the work more quickly than expected, and Jake offered to drive back to Webster.

"It's always hard to leave," Emmett said as they walked toward the car. "Thinking about all that awaits us at home is overwhelming."

Jake reached out and patted Emmett on the back. "Think of it this way: if I said to go climb one of those peaks, what would you do?"

"I'd tell you it's against doctor's orders," Emmett said. Jake and Mac laughed. "Then I'd get in shape. I'd find my hiking boots, backpack, and walking stick. And I'd start hiking."

"That's what this year's been about," Jake said. "You've been getting in shape—you and the parish. You've found a temporary space, started some exciting ministries, and raised half a million dollars. You're getting ready to begin the hike."

"Feels like we've been hiking for months."

"The hike's only beginning." Jake pointed to the highest mountain, ignoring the disappointment on Emmett's face. "If you had to hike that mountain over there, how would you reach the top?"

"By putting one foot in front of the other."

"Exactly," said Jake. "Being nervous and overwhelmed is part of the deal. That's what being alive feels like. The trick is not letting them keep you from climbing. You're almost ready, Emmett. The whole parish is."

"I'm glad you think so," Emmett said as he climbed into the car. "Hope you'll let us know when you think we're ready."

"I will," said Jake. "I promise."

"I just wish the mountain we have to climb was as easy as those," Emmett said.

"You don't get to pick your mountain," Jake said.

"I know," Emmett said from the back seat, "but I sure wish we could."

─18─
CHAPTER

Stars

"All this momentum is fine and good," Emmett said to Mac during a small cocktail party at the rectory, "but none of it matters if I don't come up with the money. It always comes down to money."

"But it doesn't come down to you only," Mac pointed out.

"The clock's ticking, and we're not halfway toward the challenge."

"It'll come," Jake offered as he walked up to the pair.

"Yeah, yeah, yeah," Emmett grumbled. "Have faith."

"Yet you're still fussing."

"It's what I do."

Emmett excused himself and made his rounds to speak to the others. He was relieved when Sara and Simon pulled him over. "We were talking about the lock-in and what we would do this year," said Sara.

"Cancel it," said Emmett without hesitation. "We don't have a church to lock the youth in, and it's against our lease for anyone to spend the night in the mill."

"Yes, but..." Sara continued with a hurt look on her face. She had agreed to run the lock-in before the fire changed everything. Emmett often said it was an annual tradition to have the youth spend the night in the church to do God-knows-what. He'd never been to a lock-in, always delegating the responsibility. "Never really understood the purpose," he interrupted. "I suppose it was invented to engage the youth, but I've never understood what spending the night in a building, eating pizza, and playing tag have to do with the church."

"We could have it outside," Sara suggested, looking over at the common.

"Outside?" Emmett protested. "Like camping?" He pointed out that New England weather was notoriously unpredictable and chaperones were hard to find when it's inside, let alone outside. "It may seem like a good idea, but I don't think it'll work."

Emmett looked over at Jake, who was staring at Emmett and the other two, hands clasped and waving his fingers. Flustered, Emmett agreed to think about it. "Check with the youth, then see if any adults are willing to chaperone."

They were back at his office door a week later. "We've had a record sign-up," Simon reported.

"And we have more chaperones than we need," Sara sounded vindicated. "There's a catch, though."

Emmett looked up, expecting a request for funds.

"Trey is the head of the youth group this year, and he requested you attend."

"Me? Camp out? Absolutely not," Emmett said as he sat down and placed both hands on his desk. "I'm too old to sleep on the ground. But please thank them for their kind invitation."

"You don't have to spend the night. Just come for the first part," Sara replied. "The kids hardly know you."

"What do you mean? I baptized most of them and have been their rector for..."

"You've been their rector, but you've never spent time with them. They won't bite."

"You were young once," Alma hollered from the adjacent office, "or have you forgotten?"

"Hush," Emmett said in Alma's direction. Looking back at Sara and Simon, he added, "I'll stop by."

The weather was warm on the night of the campout, but clouds came up and a breeze stirred the trees. Mac and Jake had created a fire pit in the center of what used to be the church. A stack of wood that could burn all night and into the next week sat nearby. Simon convinced Raj, the woodworker from the mill, to make long sticks for s'mores. Sara and Virginia ordered more pizza and soda than the kids could ever eat.

Trey helped Sara unpack her car when three students arrived, armed with sleeping bags and ready to go. "Eager are we?" Trey said. "Pick a spot and unroll your sleeping bags. We'll wait for the others before getting started. Come to the fire pit once everyone's here."

"Don't you think it's kinda sick having a fire pit," one of the kids said, "given the church burned down and everything?"

"You can't camp out without a fire," Mac pointed out.

Emmett arrived as everyone gathered at the fire pit. His outfit of blue jeans and weathered hiking boots made kids look twice. It was the first time he had looked like a normal person, one boy whispered. Emmett offered an awkward smile, and Sara rushed over to escort him into the circle.

"First of all, I want to welcome everyone to the first St. John's campout," Sara began. "We almost canceled the lock-in because of the fire, but we felt it was an important tradition. Who knows, maybe it'll become a new tradition to hold it outside."

"The first thing we want you to do," Simon began, "is get up and find a seat beside someone you don't know well."

Emmett cringed as he remembered the group-building activities of his youth.

"Chaperones, too," Sara added, looking directly at Emmett.

Everyone hesitated before moving to new seats. Emmett found himself between Trey and Sam Tucker's son, Sam Jr. Each boy tried to hide their mortification over having to sit next to the rector.

"The point of tonight is to have fun, get to know one another, but it's also a chance to talk about some things," Sara said.

"What kind of things?" someone asked.

"You'll see," Sara said with a smile as she turned the conversation over to Simon.

"OK, everyone," Simon said as he stood and motioned to Jake for help. "Before the pizza gets here, and we lose any hope of your attention, Mr. Davidson and I..."

"It's Jake," the man in the red-and-black-checkered jacket said. "Mr. Davidson's my father. Why don't we agree to call everyone by their first name tonight, including your rector?"

There was a long silence as the youth looked at each other. Emmett realized they didn't know his first name. They chuckled when they heard Emmett's name. He'd always been Reverend Hodges. "This is so awkward," one girl said.

"So," Simon continued, "the first thing we need to do is build a fire. Does anyone know the best way to build a fire?"

A few raised their hands.

"Excellent," said Simon with more animation than Emmett had seen. It was like he was teaching one of his classes. He solicited help from two volunteers. "To build a fire, you grab the biggest pieces of wood and then find a match, right?"

"No," was the united chorus, but the kids knew from his class that this was his way of getting them to tell how to build a fire properly.

"You get some newspaper," the boy beside Sara told him.

"Then some bark and twigs," another added. "You know, small stuff."

Simon did as they suggested and threw it all in a pile in front of the kids.

"No!" a number exclaimed. "You need to put the paper down, then the smaller stuff on top of it. Then, you stack the logs." Simon complied with their instructions. "Be sure to leave room for air," someone called out as they watched Simon put the logs too close together.

"Now what?" Simon asked.

"You need a match," Trey called out.

Jake smiled as he got up and pretended to pick a match from behind Mac's ear like a magician. "Like this? Pay close attention," he said as he knelt and lit the paper. "See if you can't figure out a connection between the fire you just built and your spiritual lives." An audible groan went up when Jake mentioned their spiritual lives. "I knew this would turn all churchy," someone groaned.

"Don't worry," Simon said. "There's no test."

The fire spread from the newspaper to the twigs. A breeze blew the flames toward the smaller wood, where they gathered strength. Smoke rose, dancing in circles into the air. Pops and sparks announced the fire was catching, and Emmett smiled at Jake as they watched the captivated faces.

"What does that teach you?" Jake asked, pointing to the fire.

"That you shouldn't play with matches," Sam Jr. joked.

"That spiritual lives need to be built intentionally," Virginia offered, hoping to get the conversation moving in the right direction.

"You can't start with the big wood," the girl beside her added. "You need to start small and work your way up."

"How so?" asked Emmett.

"I don't know. We all drew pictures in Sunday school, but we moved on from there. We started reading the Bible, having discussions, and doing service projects."

"What else?" Simon asked.

"You need a match," one boy answered. "Something to get it started."

"Like what?" Jake asked.

"Maybe something happens in your life, or someone says something. Those can be matches, I guess."

"Not all matches are bad things, like someone dying or getting into an accident. It could be the birth of a baby sister or getting a spot on a team that you really wanted."

The group was quiet as they watched the fire.

"However it starts, it needs air if it's gonna grow," said one of the girls.

"Like that breeze that just came through," someone added.

"Otherwise, it'll go out," someone added.

"What gives your spiritual lives air?" asked Emmett.

"I don't know," said the boy next to Mac. "Hiking?"

"Hiking certainly breathes air into my soul," Emmett offered, then added, "at least it did when I was younger."

"Listening to my father play the guitar," said Sam Jr.

"Sitting with my friends," someone said.

"For me, I need to be alone," said another.

"Either way, you have to have the right wood," Trey offered.

"How so?" Jake asked.

"In Scouts, I learned there's soft and hard wood. Softwood burns but doesn't make much heat. It also causes a lot of smoke. Hardwood's best."

Mac stood and added wood to the fire. His smile made some think he'd given a clue. "A fire needs to be fed!" one of the girls shouted.

"You guys are good at this," Simon said. "The light in my spiritual life almost went out a few times, but St. John's helped that from happening. Do you all have something or someone who helps you keep the fire going?" Some mentioned their parents, another said a Sunday school teacher, and a third mentioned her coach.

Emmett hoped to hear his name but didn't.

The pizza arrived, taking away any chance of continuing the conversation.

"Before we eat," Sara said, "we need someone to say grace."

Emmett began to stand to offer a prayer when Jake turned to the girl beside him and asked if she would be willing to offer the prayer.

"Me?" she asked in horror.

"Why not?"

"I guess," she said. "Dear God, thank you for this pizza and this fire. You know we're hungry and a little cold, so thanks for giving us this time, this food, and this fire. Come join us. We'd love the company. Amen."

"Perfect!" Jake said as he clapped his hands. Virginia and Sara ushered the kids toward the pizza and drinks. When everyone reconvened around the fire, the conversations were between those sitting nearby.

"Is it hard being a rector?" Trey asked Emmett.

"That's a heck of a question," Emmett said as he tried to think of an answer. "Yes and no, I suppose."

"What part's yes, what's no?"

"Trying to meet everyone's expectations is the hardest part, and always having to have answers is a close second. Everyone's got an idea of what a rector should be, and it's hard to be everything to everyone."

"What's the good part?"

"When things happen that you don't expect, and you know God's at work behind the scenes. That's when it feels like a church and God's right there. It becomes a spiritual adventure, more than work."

Trey nodded as he returned his focus to the pizza slice.

"Is it hard to be Trey Prescott?" Emmett asked, catching his dinner companion by surprise.

"Yes and no," Trey replied, trying to swallow and talk simultaneously. "I mean, I'm lucky. My family's got all we need. So, in that way, it's easy, but it's not as easy as some people think. There are a lot of expectations. I'm always told to represent the family well, and I don't even really know what that means. Friends also make assumptions, which I don't like. They think we're loaded. They think we've got it easy and don't have the same kind of problems they have. It makes you wonder who your real friends are."

"I get that," said Emmett. "Not the rich part, but the rest." Jake started collecting everyone's trash.

"Sometimes I feel like a cartoon character or something." Trey continued in a deep voice. "That's Robert Prescott's boy; He's a chip off the old block." Emmett stared at the fire and thought about his childhood. "It makes it hard to be human," Trey added.

"What do you mean?"

"I got caught drinking beers with some friends at the Webster quarry last summer. Someone saw our parked cars and called to complain. My father was pissed. He said I embarrassed the family. I made a mistake, and so did everybody else, but somehow it was worse because of my last name."

Emmett let out a brief chuckle, which caused Trey to look over in surprise. "I got suspended from school when I was your age," Emmett said, looking at the fire. "I punched a kid. I don't remember why. I think it was because the guy picked on someone. I think part of me wanted to be someone other than 'the bishop's kid,' which is what they always called me."

"Wow," said Trey. "Our minister's a badass."

"Hardly. It was probably the last time I did anything bold. My father was pissed too. From then on, I pretty much did what people expected."

After a long pause, Trey asked, "Do you ever wonder what caused the fire?"

"Sometimes," Emmett said. "Do you?"

"Sometimes. The kids talk about it, but I figure what's done is done."

"We've got more marshmallows, chocolate, and Graham crackers than we can possibly eat," Virginia called out, lifting an assortment of boxes. Hearing that as a challenge, the kids scrambled to be first in line for dessert. While standing around the fire roasting their marshmallows, Jake started talking.

"I'm new around here. What was your church like before the fire?"

"Your basic church," one boy replied.

"It had an amazing organ with some pipes in the back which were used for special hymns."

"I loved those," someone said.

"They scared me," shared another.

"It was dark and formal."

"Smelled like a museum to me."

"I thought it was too quiet, like a library," one person said. The others laughed but knew what she meant.

"It smelled good at Easter," someone said.

"Christmas, too," someone else agreed. Everyone nodded.

"I liked the windows," one boy said. "When the sermon was boring, I'd look at the windows."

A few looked over at Emmett to see if he was offended by the remark. "Don't worry, some of the windows were better than any sermon I gave," he said, looking over at Sara.

"I was baptized there," said a boy reaching for a third marshmallow. "I don't remember it, but I remember my grandmother's funeral. I like that we had a place to go for important stuff like that."

"I remember the first time I had communion. I didn't know you were allowed to chew the bread, so I tried to swallow it whole. Almost choked to death." Some laughed because they had almost choked on the bread too.

"I nearly spit the wine out the first time I tasted it," said Sam Jr. "Now, I just dip my bread in the wine like chips and salsa."

"Intinction," said Emmett, which caused everyone to look over, perplexed. "It's called intinction, but go on. I love this."

"My favorite memory was when you invited us to bring our pets to church. It was in honor of some saint."

"St. Francis," Emmett said.

"All I remember is that I was allowed to bring my dog to church. He was the most important thing I had, and I've never forgotten that the church let me bring him to a service."

"Remember when Margaret Collins brought her horse?" Mac asked.

Everyone laughed as they remembered the arrival of the big brown horse and how it ran onto the common when Emmett tried to bless it.

"I remember when we went over to the rectory around Christmas. Your wife always made it feel like it was our house."

Emmett smiled.

"When I had my tonsils out, you and your wife brought a quart of ice cream over," said Trey, looking at Emmett.

"I remember the time you wrote me a note when my cat died," said the girl standing beside Sam Jr. "I still have it."

"You wrote me when I finally scored a touchdown," said one of the boys. The memories surprised Emmett.

"How about when you knocked over the chalice and spilled the wine down the front of the altar?"

"Oh, don't remind me," Emmett said with a smile.

"I thought Mrs. Fitzpatrick was going to kill you."

"She almost did," Emmett joked.

"What about when it was boiling, and you decided not to wear pants under your robes? You almost got away with it until the Jones kid lifted your robes and shouted, 'hairy legs!'"

"OK, OK!" Emmett said, trying to cut off the litany of embarrassing moments.

Everyone sat back and watched the fire, moaning that they had eaten too much. They watched as the sparks twirled into the night sky. Thunder could be heard in the distance.

"Look at the stars," someone sighed. "I love stars."

"Me too," said Mac. His participation caught everyone off guard. "They saved my life once when I was in the Navy."

Everyone looked over at Mac. He was a fixture at St. John's, but the kids never dared to speak to him. Some called him "The Bear" because of his size and how he growled when he worked on the furnace.

Mac started to talk, telling the kids about his experience in the war, when his boat sank in the Pacific, and he spent two weeks in a lifeboat.

"We used the stars as a map," he said, causing the kids to look up into the sky at the stars with renewed appreciation.

"To think," someone else offered, "the stars have always been there, but we never looked up."

"We couldn't," someone pointed out, "the church was in the way!" The kids laughed.

"Now there's a sermon!" Mac whispered to Jake.

"On that note, I bid you all good night," Emmett said as he struggled to stand. "Thank you for allowing your old and very stiff rector to join you tonight. Enjoy your sleeping bags. I'm headed home to my cozy bed."

A clap of thunder in the distance let everyone know a storm was approaching. Sara and Virginia looked at each other and wondered if they should begin calling the children's parents, but Simon assured them the storm would pass. It didn't. The rain started just as everyone was getting into their sleeping bags. Soon, it was a downpour. Trey told the other kids to grab their things and follow him as he ran across the common toward the rectory.

"Not sure Emmett's going to like this," said Sara.

"It'll be fine," said Jake.

"Might do him some good," Mac added.

Emmett answered the door in his bathrobe and pajamas and tried to hide his surprise.

The chaperones called the parents and assured them everyone was safe in the rectory and they could come to get them in the morning. It took a while for the children to settle. The living room was covered with sleeping bags and whispering children as Emmett climbed the stairs.

Abby would have loved this, he thought.

— 19 —

CHAPTER

A Minister

"I'm quite aware of how we used to do things," Emmett said to Alma as he handed back the service program proof. "Would you please just do as I asked?"

Jake stood off to the side until Emmett returned to his office. "What's up with him?"

"It happens every year before the bishop's visitation. I can set my watch to it," Alma explained.

"The bishop's visitation?"

"The bishop's required to visit every parish in the diocese once a year. He visits St. John's on the first Sunday of September."

"Why does it make Emmett so surly?"

Alma stopped what she was doing and looked up at Jake as she decided how to explain. "Well, you know that he and the bishop don't exactly get along. They were seminary classmates. Then, they ran against each other for bishop. Things get a little tense until the visitation is over."

Jake decided now was not the time to discuss his recent ideas for the vision committee. "It can wait," he said to Alma as he excused himself and headed upstairs to see the artists.

On the Sunday of the bishop's visitation, Emmett was up and out of the house before Jake came downstairs. Although he wasn't preaching, Emmett nervously paced around the mill. Despite his anxiety, the congregation looked forward to the bishop's visit, and the volunteers were well-versed in their duties. Still, Emmett worried something would go wrong. That this was the first visitation at the mill only made him pace more quickly.

"You're going to wear out those floorboards," Mac said with a grin when he arrived.

"You don't understand..." Emmett tried to explain.

"Yes, I do," Mac shot back, "more than you know."

The bishop's Mercedes turned into the parking lot, and Simon moved the orange cone and waved him into the reserved spot. Even though there were plenty of open spaces, Emmett knew the bishop liked a reserved parking space.

"Good morning," Emmett said as he greeted the bishop. "Can I help carry anything in?"

The bishop offered a warm greeting before handing Emmett his vestment bag. He knew better than to ask Emmett to carry his crozier.

"This is," the bishop paused as he entered the mill, "different."

"It's nothing I could have ever imagined, but we've made it work." They entered the building.

"What are those?" the bishop asked, pointing to the hangings in the sanctuary.

"Banners. Made by one of the artists upstairs. They represent the four elements. I thought they'd bring some color to the place."

"A bit trendy," the bishop said, "They do lighten the place up, though."

Gladys was ready to take the bishop off Emmett's hands and show him where he could vest for the service. Emmett returned to his office as if he had something pressing to do, but he just wanted to get away from the bishop. He knew the two would meet after the service to discuss the parish and how things were going. He was required to show the bishop the membership rolls and a list of all baptisms, weddings, and funerals since the last visit.

"Sounds like a physical," Jake said when Emmett described what happens during an episcopal visitation. "Aren't there more important things to ask about, like how you have served the poor and made a difference in the community?"

"It's easier to stick with the numbers and be done with it," Emmett pointed out.

"Does he ever ask how you are doing?" Jake wondered.

"Not that I can remember."

"A good crowd," the bishop whispered to Emmett as they stood waiting for the processional. Emmett was pleased almost every seat was filled. When he saw Jewell's pink hair and guests from Wednesday night dinners in blue jeans and tee shirts, he worried about what the bishop would think.

Bishop Phillips preached on the cost of discipleship and urged people to follow the disciples' example by picking up their crosses and following Christ. Emmett tried not to roll his eyes. "Even if it means dying for another," the bishop said. Emmett tried to listen, but the way the bishop waved his hands in the grist mill like it was a revival tent stood in his way. Emmett waited for the bishop to finish with his adoring crowd so they could meet and discuss the health of the parish.

"So, tell me, Emmett, how are things? You and your parish have been through a lot."

"We have. I know I should tell you it's all been awful, but it hasn't," Emmett said. "In fact, in some ways, it's been good, maybe even wonderful. Losing the church was a tragedy, don't get me wrong, but walking through this dark valley has brought us together as a parish in ways I couldn't have imagined."

"Glad to hear it. I was also delighted to hear about your receiving a million dollars."

"A million-dollar challenge. We only get the money if we raise the same amount."

"Still, it's quite a lot of money."

"It will be if we can meet the challenge. We're just over half, but I'm not sure we will be able to find the rest in time."

"I hope that means you'll be able to support the diocese again now that you're back on your feet," said the bishop as he looked around the small office.

"Back on our feet?" Emmett laughed. "You must be joking. We're worshipping in a grist mill, breaking bread on an altar made of sawhorses and planks of lumber. We're far from on our feet."

"But you'll get there. I have faith."

"That's nice to hear. All I remember from our last conversation was that we were on our own."

"You need to do something about that anger of yours," the bishop said. "It's unbecoming of a minister, let alone one of the senior priests of the diocese. We need to set an example for our people. They expect us to be like Christ, even when we don't feel like it."

"I might say the same to you," Emmett muttered.

"Excuse me? What do you mean by that?"

"Just that you, as bishop, are supposed to be a minister to the ministers, or have you forgotten? Being a bishop isn't about purple shirts, fancy cufflinks, and people bowing whenever you enter the room. It's about being with people when they're hurting, forgiving them when they make mistakes."

"And this is something you know about firsthand?" the bishop asked, not expecting an answer. "I know you're still bitter about losing the election to me. I know you're disappointed that your ministry hasn't amounted to more, but that's not my fault. It's yours, and the sooner you learn to accept things as they are, the better for you, your parish, and even the diocese."

The rest of the conversation blurred for Emmett. Eventually, he found himself standing at his desk, left with the smell of the bishop's expensive cologne filling his tiny office. He looked forward to returning to the rectory and, for the first time, wished he had the place to himself. As if reading his mind, Jake announced he was going to Mac's cabin for dinner. Emmett tried to disguise his delight.

He spent the evening on the patio thinking about the bishop, not just the recent visit but their entire history. Emmett gripped his wineglass tighter as he thought about Michael's arrogance and self-centeredness. Then he remembered what Sam once said, that pointing a finger at someone only means three fingers are pointing back at you. Emmett put down his glass and pointed his finger. Looking at the three fingers curled up and pointing back at him, he began thinking about his role in their toxic relationship. He tried to blame Michael for their problems but knew he had a role in things. He left the wine on the table and went up to bed.

The morning after the bishop's visit felt more like a day to mop up than get back to work. He brought Alma a cup of coffee, just the way she liked it. He thanked the altar guild and choir for their fine work and met with Virginia to review what he and the bishop discussed.

He was making a list of parishioners who might increase their contribution to the challenge when there was a knock on his office door. He tried to hide his frustration as he welcomed whoever it was. His father often said ministry happens in the margins, but it didn't make interruptions any less inconvenient. No matter how adamantly he argued, Abby always said interruptions were the ministry.

Emmett was surprised to see Trey at his door. "Sorry to bother you. I was wondering if I could have a minute?" he asked.

"Certainly," Emmett said. "Have a seat."

"I came over before school, hoping you'd be here. I need to ask you something."

"Shoot," said Emmett

"Did I cause the fire?"

Emmett froze, and he gripped the edge of his desk. "Why on earth would you ask that?"

"It's been on my mind for a while. After the fire, there was a lot of talk about what caused it. Some of my friends joked it was probably my candle that caused it. I know they were only kidding, but the idea keeps bugging me. I need to make sure it wasn't my candle."

"I'm glad you came by," Emmett said, trying to buy time to think. "As I told the congregation, there was no conclusive evidence on how the fire began. It was likely a candle, but there's no telling which candle."

"I've thought about it," Trey said. "I tried to put myself back in the service, but I can't remember blowing mine out that night."

"I'm sure you did," Emmett offered.

"Are you?" Trey asked. Emmett looked away for a second, and that was all Trey needed. "You're holding something back. It was my candle. I'm the one responsible for burning the church down." He did not wait for Emmett to respond. Trey thanked Emmett for his time before scurrying out of his office. After Sunday's service, Trey returned to see Emmett.

"I need a favor," he said as Emmett took off his vestments. "I found the fire marshal's report in a drawer in my father's desk. I didn't understand all of it, but it said they thought the fire came from a candle near the altar, probably on the right side. That's where I sat, and my candle was in the stand beside my seat. That makes it clear my candle caused the fire." Emmett tried to argue, but Trey wasn't listening. "So, there's something I need to do. I'd like to own it."

"Own it?" Emmett asked.

"You know, apologize," Trey explained. "I need to tell the congregation it was most likely my candle that caused the fire and how sorry I am."

"I can't let you do that. We don't know for certain..."

"For certain? I know. But it most likely was my candle. That's enough for me. I've hidden behind my family's shadow all my life. For all I know, my father offered the million-dollar challenge. I'm sick of it. I need to stand up and admit my mistake. It won't change the fact that we lost the church, but at least it'll stop the masquerade that's been going on my whole life."

"Won't bringing it up make things worse?" Emmett asked.

"Maybe, in the short term, but at least the secret will be out and the wondering will be over."

"We should discuss this with your parents," Emmett said.

"No," Trey demanded. "They'll only try to talk me out of it, like you."

Emmett had no intention of Trey making such an announcement, but he said Trey could say something at next week's service. Emmett planned to figure out a way to keep Trey from making such a public pronouncement. He knew there was much to be lost by such an announcement, and little to gain.

Over dinner, Emmett told Jake about Trey's visit and his desire to apologize to the congregation.

"You're not going to let him, are you?" Jake asked.

"Of course not," said Emmett.

"I'm impressed by the boy's desire to own it, but it would do more damage than good."

"I've got to figure out a way to fix this," Emmett said.

"Sounds like a job for God, not you," Jake said.

Emmett looked out the window and smiled. "But I'm all we've got."

Emmett grew increasingly agitated as Sunday drew closer. Trey didn't need to live with the guilt and blame for the rest of his life, Emmett kept reminding himself.

That Sunday, Emmett meandered down to the river as people began arriving. He was still searching for what to do when he took his seat after the sermon. The sermon had been about the adulterous woman brought to Jesus by a crowd with stones in their hands. Jesus wrote something in the sand before addressing the crowd. Emmett wondered what he had written. Whatever he said, whatever it was, caused the crowd to drop their stones and walk away.

The choir sang a variation on the hymn, "Lift High the Cross," before the announcements, and Emmett welcomed the visitors and encouraged everyone to stay for coffee hour. Instead of going right into the offering, Emmett looked out and saw Trey sitting beside his parents. Putting his prayer book under his arm, Emmett spoke candidly to the congregation.

"We've been through a lot. We lost our parish almost a year ago and have struggled to find our way through the darkness of the tragedy. Much good has happened, but ever since the fire, there's been this gnawing concern: what caused the fire, or, more specifically, who was responsible? I've heard the grumbling, the theories, and the finger-pointing, and it's time to address this issue head-on. This morning I'd like to tell you what happened and who's to blame."

Trey took a deep breath and began to rise.

"It was me," Emmett said. An audible murmur arose from the pews, and Trey sat down. "The fire was caused by a candle I left burning." Trey looked at Emmett. This wasn't what they had agreed to. Emmett continued. "I sent the ushers and acolytes home after the service. I said I'd close up. I guess I was distracted. The fact is, I missed the lit candle, and the rest is history. I'll regret what happened for the rest of my life." After a pause, he added, "You should know, I offered my resignation to the vestry soon after the fire, but they refused to accept it. Now you know the truth. Someone did cause the fire. You're looking at him."

The congregation sat in silence before the service resumed. When it was over, some parishioners seemed angry; others offered their support to Emmett. Trey stood off to the side waiting for his turn.

"What was that?" he asked after most of the crowd had left. "We had an agreement."

"I couldn't let you take the blame," Emmett said.

"But I was ready to…"

"Yes, I know."

"So, you lied to me."

"We don't know for certain that it was your candle, and I was responsible for closing it up. So, technically, it was my fault."

"Was that stuff about resigning true?"

"Yes," Emmett said, "but the vestry forgave me and told me to move on. Now, it's your turn to do the same."

"It's not what we agreed to," Trey said as he stormed from the church. A few people noticed his dramatic exit, including Trey's parents, who were standing nearby. Robert looked at Emmett with a kindness he'd never seen before.

Emmett took a seat in the empty sanctuary after everyone left. He looked at the altar and the twisted cross he'd found in the ashes. Raj and Mac had done their best to restore it.

"I didn't see that coming," Mac said as he joined Jake and Emmett for lasagna at the rectory that night.

"What?" asked Emmett.

"You taking the hit for Trey."

"Not how I'd put it, but it was the right thing to do."

"How'd it feel?" asked Jake.

Emmett looked away before responding. "Like I was a minister."

"Trey will never forget it."

"Neither will I," Emmett said as Jake filled Emmett's wine glass.

—20—
CHAPTER

Home By Another Way

"**Y**ou're ready," Jake said to Emmett while they were on a morning walk.

"Excuse me?" Emmett replied.

"You asked me to tell you when I thought you were ready. I think you're ready."

"We haven't raised all the money we need."

"I wasn't talking about the money; I was talking about you and the people of St. John's."

"It won't do much good if we're ready but don't have the money."

"That may be true," Jake said, placing his hand on Emmett's shoulder, "but it's nice to know you've done the work and are ready if or when the money comes."

As the days grew shorter, Emmett worked harder. They were still $232,000 short with less than three months to go. He closed the door to his office and listed every gift made. He compared that to the parish register and searched for people who had not yet participated. He also returned to the donor list and circled the names of those he felt might be willing to give more. When he finished, he saw the stark reality. "We're not going to make it," he sighed.

"I don't know where we're going to find the rest," he shared with Jake, "and don't say it'll be all right. Don't tell me to have faith."

"Okay, but it will, and you should," Jake said with a smile. "Keep in mind all the other things that have happened since the fire: the church now has a standing-room only Wednesday night meal program, four different twelve-step groups are using the space during the week, and the youth have suddenly become a part of the parish."

All Emmett could see was the list of names on the sheet before him and the amount left to raise.

"Don't you think Robert would give you an extension, particularly after what you did for Trey?" Jake said.

"I didn't do that to get an extension," Emmett replied.

"I know you didn't."

Emmett remembered how Robert looked at him after taking the blame for the fire. Maybe he would be open to an extension, Emmett thought, but he quickly dismissed the idea.

An early snowfall greeted parishioners as they arrived for the Thanksgiving service. It was the first time all the churches and the one synagogue of Webster had worshipped together. Emmett came up with the idea while having lunch with Rabbi Kaplan at Maria's. "We've worshipped apart for too long," he said before sharing his idea. "What better day to worship together than Thanksgiving?"

The service was held in the mill, and the sanctuary was packed. People who had never attended a service of any kind were there, and the artists from upstairs filled several rows with artists from throughout the state. There was an article about the service in the *Webster Times*, and Emmett was surprised to receive several gifts from people who had nothing to do with St. John's. They'd heard about the fire and wanted to support such a church.

The snow continued for a week, and on the first Sunday of Advent, there were piles of snow pushed to the corners of the parking lot. Advent was Emmett's favorite season of the church year, but his mind was more focused on meeting Robert's challenge than preparing for Christmas. He hardly noticed the new altar hangings Jewell made. The altar guild began decorating the sanctuary as they had the old church, a little each week until it was fully decorated by the Christmas Eve service.

There was an echo in the season's festivities that year, a palpable sadness intertwined with the traditional joy. Each wreath and holly branch reminded parishioners of what happened a year ago. Advent became a reminder of all that had been lost. Gladys was particularly bossy, and Alma treated Emmett as if it was his first year leading the parish.

"People are still grieving," Sam said as Emmett shared his observations at a men's breakfast at Maria's. "They show it in all sorts of ways."

"It's only been a year," Mac pointed out.

"Feels longer than that," said Emmett, "but then sometimes it feels like weeks ago."

"Maybe you should preach about that," Jake offered.

"The season's too depressing already," Mac said under his breath.

"You're quite a pair," Jake said, waving down their waitress for more coffee. "You give the bleak midwinter a whole new meaning."

"Calling it as I see it," Mac said.

"Then start seeing it differently. Didn't the rabbi tell us to look out at the abundant harvest surrounding us in his Thanksgiving sermon?"

"That was last week," Mac said. It made the others laugh.

"In AA, we're told to practice an attitude of gratitude," Sam said. "You can't host a banquet and a pity party at the same time."

"I like that," Jake said.

"Christ is coming, one way or another," Emmett said, taking a sip of coffee.

"I hope he has our new address," Mac quipped.

"Are you all coming to the tree lighting ceremony on Friday?" Emmett asked.

Everyone nodded, but Sam said he wasn't sure he was ready. "I'm still pretty raw about what happened."

"That's too bad," Emmett said, reaching his hand across to Sam's sleeve. "The committee was hoping you'd be the one to flip the switch this year." The look on Sam's face caused the others to stare in silence.

"You're kidding," Sam said. "I don't know what to say."

"'Yes' would be good," Mac said, trying to lighten the mood.

"OK," Sam stuttered. "Yes."

"I didn't know the committee wanted Sam to light the tree," Jake said to Emmett as they walked back to the rectory.

"They didn't," Emmett said with a grin.

"Be careful, Emmett," Jake said. "You're becoming unpredictable."

When Jake and Emmett reached the rectory, Sara stood by the kitchen door. "It's about time!" She hopped from foot to foot, unable to keep her excitement at bay.

"Sorry," said Emmett as he reached for his keys. "Did we have a meeting?"

"No. This is a spontaneous visit." She waved a piece of paper above her head.

"What's that?" asked Emmett.

Before he had time to remove his jacket, Sara thrust the paper in front of Emmett. "You remember when I told you I was looking into foundations that might help us raise the money to rebuild."

"Yes," said Emmett, "but I remember you saying foundations don't give to religious institutions or building projects."

"That's true," Sara said, "but I found one that I thought might at least consider it. It's called The Cram Foundation, named after some architect."

"Ralph Adams Cram," Jake said. "He was one of the leading Gothic Revival architects in American history."

"Right," Sara nodded. "It turns out they support the restoration and preservation of Gothic buildings." Emmett pointed out that St. John's had nothing to preserve or restore. "I know but thought it was worth a try, so I approached them and asked if they would ever consider supporting the building of a new church if it was built in Gothic style. They said they would consider it, so I sent an official application." Emmett was surprised to hear this for the first time. "I wanted to keep it a secret so you wouldn't get your hopes up. Virginia signed the application, and Jake helped me with the architectural lingo."

"You did?" Emmett said, looking over at his house guest, who looked away sheepishly.

"We sent the application in September, and I got this letter this morning. It says they're awarding St. John's a $250,000 grant toward building a new church in the Gothic Revival style."

"But we haven't designed the church, let alone picked a style," Emmett protested.

"I know, but this might help us decide," she said.

Emmett was familiar with Cram's work and welcomed the possibility of building the new St. John's in such a style, but he knew it was not his decision to make. He'd have to get the vestry's approval and parish buy-in. He might also need to run it by the bishop. The thought of doing that nearly made Emmett want to refuse the grant.

"We have a week to accept or decline the grant," Sara pointed out, startling Emmett.

"That's impossible."

"It's not," Jake pointed out. "Everything's possible, and if my math's correct, it means you've just met the challenge."

It took a moment for Jake's words to sink in. Emmett looked over at him and offered a weak smile before walking away.

The next day, Emmett called for a vestry meeting, and they agreed to the conditions of the grant. They also decided to keep the news secret so Emmett could announce it at the Christmas Eve service. Mac sensed something when he saw the look on Emmett's face later that week, but Emmett did not let on to the good news. "Either you've taken up with a woman, or you've been hanging out with the artists upstairs smoking whatever it is they smoke."

"Neither," Emmett said as he arrived at the mill. "I think both might kill me. I'm just happy. It's going to be a merry Christmas, old friend, a very merry Christmas."

Sam was off in the corner playing a song Emmett had never heard, one about the wise men going home by another way. "Who wrote that?"

"James Taylor. I used to sing it to my kids every Christmas Eve."

"Why don't you sing it to them this Christmas Eve?" Emmett asked.

"Can't. They live with Jenny."

"I know, but sing it to them anyway, at the Christmas Eve service." Sam stopped playing and looked at Emmett with a bewildered look. He could tell Emmett was serious.

"Sing in the Christmas service?" he asked. "Who are you, and where did you put the rector who swore there would never be guitars in church?"

Emmett chuckled. "I don't know where he's gone, but I'd love you to sing that song after the sermon. I think it's time your children see their father for who he is, not who he was."

Emmett was gone before Sam could refuse. He thanked the altar guild for all their hard work. Jewell had made a remarkable altar cover of green, red, and gold. Gladys wasn't sure she could use it since it was not the correct liturgical color, but Emmett assured her it was fine.

"It's more than fine. Let's see if we can find flowers to complement her work."

When Emmett met with the participants to go over the service, he was upbeat like in the old days before Abby's death. "You should hire a brass quartet," Emmett told David Livingston.

"You said we couldn't afford one."

"I was wrong. Abby always said, 'It's not Christmas without brass,' and she was right." Emmett sounded like a boy talking about his favorite type of ice cream.

When selecting readers, Emmett wanted to ask some new people. Marty almost fell off her ladder when Emmett came down to the food pantry to ask her to read. Sara tried to refuse, citing her fear of speaking in public, but Emmett would have none of it. "Simon can work with you," he said. "He has a knack for preparing readers."

"We still need one more acolyte," Gladys informed Emmett. After thinking for a moment, Emmett said he knew just the person. It was a long shot, but he had to ask.

Emmett waited in the school parking lot, standing beside Trey's car. As other students walked by, they looked at him as if he were from another planet. Emmett waved, which only made them look down and rush to their cars.

"Trey?" Emmett called out as he saw his young parishioner approach.

"What are you doing here?"

"I was wondering if I might have a word."

"I'm not sure we've got much to talk about."

"I know you don't like that I told the congregation I left the candle lit, but I did what I thought was best."

"Clearly. We agreed I'd take the blame."

"I only agreed so I could figure out another way. In the end, I did, and it was for the best. Anyway, I didn't come here to rehash our disagreement."

"Your betrayal."

"Our disagreement. I came to ask if you'd be willing to serve as an acolyte at the Christmas Eve service."

"You've got to be kidding," Trey said as he put his backpack on the hood of his car. "Are you rubbing it in my face? Aren't you afraid I'll burn down the church again?"

"I'm not rubbing anything in your face, and there's no one I'd trust more. You're the head of the youth group, and this is your senior year. You're a perfect choice."

Trey shook his head. "You've got the wrong guy. Ask someone else."

Simon and the other ushers used every folding chair, including those belonging to the three recovery groups that met weekly in the sanctuary. People began arriving while the musicians unpacked their instruments. Emmett mingled with the choir and the last-minute stragglers searching for seats, while Gladys arrived with the crucifer and one of the acolytes.

"Where's the other acolyte?" Emmett asked.

"He's coming. Always a bit late," Gladys said with a coy smile. Then Emmett looked up and saw Trey walking quickly down the aisle while still trying to put on his robe.

"Don't think this means I've forgiven you," he said to Emmett, who smiled gently.

As the service began, Emmett bellowed from the back of the sanctuary, "For behold, I bring you good tidings of great joy, which shall be to all people, for unto you is born this night in the city of David, a savior which is Christ the Lord."

"Oh boy," said Adam, the young boy from Wednesday night dinners who had become a front-row participant at all services. Many chuckled as they stood to sing, "O Come, All Ye Faithful."

Emmett watched as each reader who came to the lectern brought the Christmas story alive. From his seat, he could see Marty's legs shaking, but when she read the passage from Isaiah, the congregation was enthralled.

"The people who walked in darkness have seen a great light; those who lived in the land of darkness, on them light has shined. For a child has been born for us, a son given to us."

Emmett read the final lesson, as always, then waited to deliver his sermon.

"I want to begin by saying I hardly recognize you. I see faces of people who were not with us a year ago. Artists from upstairs, volunteers from our food ministry, and guests for our Wednesday night dinners. What a gift it is to have everyone with us tonight. The St. John's family has grown, and that's a good and joyful thing, as the prayer book says."

"But what brings us to a grist mill this Christmas Eve was not good or joyful. One year ago, we lost our church. I still see the flames, smell the smoke, and hear the cries of those standing beside me as the church burned. It horrifies me and fills my soul with sadness. But I also see all that has happened since that fateful night. When we met in homes because we had no church, I thought St. John's was a thing of the past. When we sifted our hands through the ashes, I thought we were as much like dust as the church, and when Jake began asking us to look at what it means to be a church, I wasn't sure we'd come up with an answer."

"But we did."

"We found a grist mill in which to gather. We found ways to be a church without a building. We found things inside us that we didn't know existed. We learned to sing to the Lord a new song, even if we did so wearing colorful robes." Emmett turned and looked at the choir. "It leaves me grateful beyond words."

Emmett's sermon was about how encountering Christ changes a person. "You cannot go to Bethlehem and see this child and not be transformed. It was true 2,000 years ago, and it's true today. It's true not only for individuals like you and me but also for churches like ours."

"We just heard about how the wise men traveled home by another way. Perhaps, because of what has happened over the last year, we know what that means. You and I are traveling home by another way. We may be stumbling, but at least we are stumbling in the right direction. We are no longer walking single file but side by side. In fact, we aren't walking so much as we are dancing, if you will, and that must be because we have encountered Christ in some way. I can't explain it, but I believe it's true."

"I know we've got a long way to go, but there was a time I didn't believe we'd get this far! While I can't see it, I believe we'll make it to next year, and the year after that. Who knows, we may even build a building along the way. The good news is we're becoming a church, with or without the building, and that, I believe, is the greatest news I can offer tonight."

The congregation sat in silence as Emmett returned to his seat, and Sam stood and adjusted the microphone. "Um, hi," he began. "I'm as surprised by my being up here as you are. I guess this is me dancing my way home, as Emmett said. I've picked a song I used to sing to my children before bed every Christmas Eve. I don't have that chance anymore, so I guess this'll have to be our home," Sam said, gesturing to the mill. Then, looking at his son and daughter, he added, "Either way, this is for you."

The congregation sat in stunned silence once Sam finished. He put down his guitar and walked back to his seat. Adam began applauding, and the congregation followed his lead. St. John's had never been a church where people clapped, but that night they were.

"I've completely lost control of the place," Emmett said with a big smile and an exaggerated tone to one of the choir members on his way up to make his announcements. After the usual announcements, Emmett took a deep breath and said he had one more. "As you know, we received an exceedingly generous challenge from an anonymous donor. If we could raise a million dollars by the end of the year, this donor would match it dollar for dollar. More than a few times, I didn't think we'd make it, and a few weeks ago, I was ready to admit defeat, but tonight I am happy to announce that, together, we have made it! As of last week, we've raised just over a million dollars!" Emmett lifted his hands so high, he looked like a referee indicating a touchdown. The congregation stood and cheered.

Back at the rectory later that night, Emmett was beside himself. "I just can't believe it's happened," he said to Jake. "Now that we have the money, we can build the church."

Jake lifted his glass toward Emmett's as if to toast. He didn't have the heart to tell him they didn't have anywhere near the money they'd need to rebuild the church.

NEW LIFE

—— 21 ——

CHAPTER

New Thinking

It was a silent Christmas morning, but Emmett could still hear the congregation's cheers the night before. Jake left for Maine after the service to surprise his dad, so Emmett had the rectory to himself. He'd grown used to having Jake around but welcomed a morning alone. With coffee in hand, he wandered toward his study, took his seat beside his Bible and prayer book, and settled himself into a morning of reading and prayer. Then, the doorbell rang.

He was startled, then annoyed. No one was there when he opened the door, only a small package with a card. "Merry Christmas, from a member of the church." The card was unsigned. He looked out to see if he could find the giver, but the street was empty. He returned to his study, only to have the doorbell ring again moments later. Like before, there was no one, just a package with an identical message in someone else's handwriting. By the third time, Emmett knew something was up.

"It was a Christmas version of ding-dong-ditch," Sara shared when she saw Emmett the next day. "The kids came up with the idea. They didn't like the idea of you being alone on Christmas, so they came up with the idea of dropping off small presents all day."

"And they did!" said Emmett. "I hardly had time to sit."

"I hope you didn't mind. I shared one of my favorite Christmas stories with them about a bunny who leaves gifts for others in the forest, and they came up with the idea of leaving you anonymous gifts."

Remembering the 23 small packages lined up on the mantel, Emmett didn't mind. He was touched.

Between gifts arriving, Emmett took a yellow legal pad and wrote down every idea he had about a new church. Building a church was something he had dreamed about, and he didn't want to forget a thing. Looking down at his long list, he didn't know where they should begin.

When Jake returned from spending Christmas with his father, Emmett presented a litany of questions. After he shared the list, he put the pad on the table and looked at Jake. "We can't do this alone. We need an architect. I know you only agreed to get us ready, but now that we're ready, we need your help in designing the church."

"I'm flattered," Jake said, "but you need an architect who does this sort of thing on a regular basis. I can suggest some names."

"I don't want names. I want you."

"I've never built a church from scratch."

"Neither have we. Can't we figure it out together?"

"That's a risky proposition," Jake said.

"Aren't you the one who's always telling me to take risks, to have faith?"

Jake laughed and said he'd think about it. Ultimately, he agreed to be considered, provided the vestry committed to considering other architects and picking the best one.

Robert Prescott was keen on working with a famous architect from New York. "He's the best there is," he assured everyone. "He's won countless awards, and whatever he designs will be impressive and worthy of our parish."

"I don't want it to be impressive," Sara offered. "I want it to be inspirational."

"Aren't those the same things?" Robert asked.

Marty suggested an architect in Boston known for creating multi-purpose buildings. The church should be a place of worship and service, she insisted. The architect she recommended could create a one-of-a-kind church and service center, as she called it. "It will be a useful church. Plus, constructing one building instead of two will save a lot of money."

There were other architects to consider, but Emmett asked that Jake be the third candidate. The following month was full of interviews and visiting examples of their work. The vestry met late into the evening to decide which architect to select, but, in the end, they chose Jake.

"You already know us and understand what we want and need," Emmett told Jake when he and Virginia came to ask him to design the church. Jake couldn't hide his surprise.

"My methods might not be conventional," he reminded them.

"Nothing about you has been conventional," Emmett said with a grin. "Why should this be any different?"

"Then, I accept," Jake said with a smile. Emmett offered to help form a design committee, but Jake had other thoughts. "I don't want a committee," he said. "I'd like to open this up to the entire parish and people in town. It might mean we get too many thoughts and opinions, but it's worth the risk. People will feel a part of the project, and that will outweigh the inevitable chaos. Let's invite people and see who shows up."

Emmett was uncomfortable with Jake's approach but knew he had to let Jake lead the process as he saw fit. That Sunday, Emmett announced the first meeting of "The Designers," as Jake called them. Emmett invited anyone who wanted to participate in designing the church to attend the meeting, then offered his traditional offertory sentences before turning toward the altar to prepare communion.

"Not so fast, Reverend," said a familiar voice from the back. Emmett turned and saw Mac and Raj, the woodworker from upstairs, walking down the aisle, carrying something long. Taking a place beside Emmett, Mac continued. "As you know, we're about to embark on a special journey. As wonderful as we all are," Mac added sarcastically, "and as good as our ideas will be, we're going to need a shepherd to guide us. I, for one, know of no better shepherd than this fellow beside me. So, we thought it would be fitting to give you what every shepherd needs: a staff!"

Mac handed Emmett the long, wrapped object. "The journey will be long, and the path full of twists and turns. We thought you could use something to keep you from losing your footing, and you can also use it to poke and prod us if we start wandering."

Emmett smiled as he pulled a long walking stick from the wrapping.

"The wood comes from one of the beams of the old church. Raj gave it shape, and then a bunch of us gave him ideas for the carvings, which he can explain."

"Each carving tells the history of St. John's, beginning at the bottom with the first sanctuary. They work their way up to the top with various chapters in the parish's life carved throughout, including this one," Raj said, pointing to the day he and Abby arrived. Emmett noticed the top was uncarved. "The top is blank because the story is still being written."

"And you are going to help us write it," Mac said as the congregation rose to their feet and applauded. Emmett tried to hide his discomfort in being presented with a gift. "Yes, it's just like a bishop's crozier," Mac whispered to Emmett while the congregation applauded, "only, this one's yours."

Emmett brought his new walking stick and a long list of ideas to the first design meeting. He was eager to see who would show up. Jake was already at the mill, setting up tables in the sanctuary with some of the artists from upstairs. Others began arriving soon after. "Don't you want to push the tables together?" Emmett asked as he saw three distinct areas being set up.

"No, this is going to be a different kind of meeting. I've asked our friends from upstairs to help." Jake saw the look on Emmett's face. "Don't worry; it's going to be fine."

"Sit wherever you like," Jake announced as people entered, "but don't get comfortable. You'll be moving around."

Simon and Sara sat together, which Emmett noticed they were doing more often these days. Virginia sat with other vestry members, and Jake was delighted to see that Rabbi Kaplan and another member of his synagogue had accepted his invitation. They sat next to Sam, who brought friends from the Tuesday night AA meeting. There were also faces Emmett did not recognize. Maria explained they were people who had seen the notice on the diner wall and wanted to help. Robert and Trey arrived just as the meeting began.

Jake introduced himself and welcomed everyone. He then asked Emmett to say a few words and offer an opening prayer.

"Come, Holy Spirit, come," Emmett prayed. "Fill this space and fill our hearts with your life-giving presence. Inspire us to see thee more clearly, follow thee more nearly, and love thee more dearly as we gather to build your church, day by day. Amen."

"Today's meeting will be a little different," Jake explained. "I see some of you brought lists of ideas. I'm happy you've already begun thinking, but today is a day to think in new ways. Our job is to design a church, and that will involve thinking about the church, but I want us to think about church in ways we haven't before. This is our chance to reimagine the church, to see it as if for the first time."

Jake continued. "You're sitting in one of three separate areas. Think of them as separate classes. When I ring the bell, you'll move from one table to another. By the end of the day, you'll have visited each table. The artists from upstairs have come up with ways to help our minds think and our hearts feel in new ways."

"Jason Abrams, the potter from upstairs, will teach us using clay, and Jessica, who's a painter, will teach us through drawing. Tom, who specializes in sculpting, and Jewell, who makes collages and works with fabric, will teach us using broken plates." Many were intrigued by the plan, but Jake could see others were skeptical.

"I thought we were here to design a church," Stanley Fitzpatrick grumbled.

"We are," Jake responded. "Your job is to find the connection between each activity and designing a church." Then, with a pause, Jake smiled and said, "On your mark, get set, go!"

Jake wandered from table to table as the artists began leading their groups. Jason gave each person at his table a piece of clay and encouraged them to play with it in their hands as they talked. Some held the clay reluctantly as if they were concerned about getting their hands dirty. When Jason compared it to playing with Play Doh, people began squeezing it and rolling it more freely as Jason described his work as a potter.

"It's messy work. You take clay and mold it in your hands or on a wheel. Eventually, it takes shape. It always begins as a lump of clay. That is, until it gets into the potter's hands. Then it becomes a bowl, cup, or plate."

"Sounds biblical," Virginia said.

"How so?" Jason asked.

"The Bible says we're created out of clay. I guess that makes God a potter," Virginia responded.

"Reminds me of Ash Wednesday," someone else offered. "Ashes to ashes, dust to dust."

"Clay is dust with water mixed in," Trey pointed out.

"I like molding it," chimed in one of the participants from the diner.

"Yeah, but it's hard on the clay," Trey said.

"Anyone here ever been molded?" Jason asked the group. Those at the table sat in silence as they looked down at the clay in their hands. Eventually, they began to talk about challenging situations they had experienced. Jake listened to people share about times when they felt God molded them. One person spoke about her divorce, another when he lost his job.

"Molding may be necessary, but it sure can hurt," someone shared, and others nodded.

"What does this have to do with rebuilding our church?" Stanley asked.

"Fair question," Jason said to his hostile participant. "What do you all think this process says about the church?"

The group was quiet for a few minutes as they continued to work the clay. Then someone offered, "Maybe churches get molded, too, just like people."

"Has St. John's been molded?" Jason asked.

"In the last year, it sure has," Virginia said, then added, "and I'm not sure it's over."

"Does the clay have a role in the molding?" Jason asked.

"I suppose," said Virginia. As she grabbed a sponge and squeezed it over her clay, she added, "it needs to stay moist. Otherwise, it dries up and becomes brittle." She resisted the urge to look at Stanley. "Churches, like clay, need to be able to bend and move."

The conversation moved into how churches can stay flexible and bend. Jake smiled as he moved to the next group.

Jessica was giving her table an art demonstration. Using a still life arrangement on a table, she presented a new way of drawing. "Instead of drawing the objects themselves, I'm drawing the space between the objects. It's called the negative space," she said. The people at her table looked confused, but slowly they saw the random shapes between the objects begin to reveal the objects themselves.

"Wow," one person said as she recognized the objects from the still life.

"When I took up painting," Jessica explained, "I needed to challenge my way of seeing. You've heard the expression: looks can be deceiving. We look at things as we think they are, not as they really are. Drawing the negative spaces keeps our minds from filling in the blanks with what it thinks it sees—or wants to see."

"In churchy terms, this process is called *via negativa*, or the negative way," Emmett pointed out. "It means we describe everything using negatives. The thought is, by describing what something isn't, you eventually describe what it is."

"Didn't Michelangelo do something similar to that when he carved the statue of David?" Simon asked. "I remember reading about how he didn't carve David so much as take away all the rock that wasn't David."

"Exactly," said Jessica. She stepped back from the canvas so everyone could see the finished drawing—a beautiful interpretation of the still life.

"So, what you're telling us..." Simon began.

"I'm not telling you anything," she corrected. "I'm just showing you a way to draw." Jessica looked over and smiled at Jake standing behind the others.

"What I'm getting from this," Simon ventured, "is that we should be careful not to assume we see things as they are. We sometimes see them as *we* are."

"Maybe when we look at God, or the church, we need to consider all the things God isn't," Emmett said, then added, "But it's hard when you've been looking a certain way for a long time."

"It's tough even when you're young," one of the teen members added.

"What do you think it would look like if we took away everything that isn't the church?" someone asked. "What would we find in the end?"

The third table was the loudest. Everyone wore smocks, gloves, and protective eyewear. Tom placed colorful ceramic plates in front of each person and told them to smash the plates with one of the mallets. It took a few practice swings before they let themselves swing freely, shattering the plates into pieces. Jewell pushed all the plate shards into the center of the table and told everyone to reach in and grab a handful.

"You're probably wondering what on earth we're doing," she said, as some participants offered exaggerated nods. "All those wonderful plates are now broken. They were once useful plates, and now, they're..." She paused in hopes someone would complete the sentence.

"Useless," Sam said with little hesitation.

"Are they?" Jewell asked as she took a handful of shards and placed them beside one another. "In my work, I take pieces of fabric, glass, or whatever I find, usually something others have thrown away, and turn them into a piece of art."

"You make them into new creations," Tom suggested. Jewell smiled as she continued to place the shards beside each other.

"It's your turn," Jewell told the group. "Grab a pile of shards and see what you can make out of them."

"Like making a mosaic," someone offered.

"Exactly," said Jewell. "I grew up Greek Orthodox before I became a Buddhist. We had mosaics all over the church. I remember staring at them as a child, trying to see the picture, until my father walked me up to one day and showed me that it was one picture made up of thousands of tiny pieces. I was hooked from then on. I've been putting broken, discarded pieces together to make art ever since."

The table fell silent as the participants began arranging the broken pieces—some arranged the pieces by color, others by shape. As with the other tables, they wondered what the exercise had to do with the vision committee's work.

"I guess this is what the church is supposed to be," Sam offered. Tom encouraged him to say more. "It takes broken souls and makes them into art, at least it's supposed to."

"I love that idea," Jewell said.

"But sometimes there's a limit to how broken someone can be," Sam offered.

"Really?" Jewell asked. "I don't recall any of you deciding which pieces were too broken. You just grabbed a pile and got to work."

"Plate pieces are different from people," Sam pointed out.

"Some of my best pieces come from some of the most broken pieces," Jewell said.

"I remember an album cover that was really cool," Tom shared as he placed his pieces together. "On one side was a prism with light shining through it. On the other side, it showed all these different colors."

"Wasn't that Pink Floyd's 'Dark Side of the Moon?'" Sam asked.

"Yup, exactly," Tom said.

"But what does that have to do with this?" someone asked.

"The imperfections break the light into colors," Tom explained. "I think our imperfections break us into color."

"Take a minute and tell us what you see when you look at the broken pieces you are arranging," Jewell instructed. One person talked about her family growing up, how it was never the same after her parents divorced. Another person talked about close friends he had lost over differing political views.

"I see my soul," one of Sam's friends said, without looking up. "I'm starting to think I was born with a perfect soul, but it was eventually shattered or splintered because of things I did or the approval I sought. I'm not sure I can put it back together."

Those around the table were unsure how to respond. Jewell let the people at their table work silently before resuming the reflections. "Sam, you sang on Christmas Eve, and I couldn't help but notice your guitar was kinda beat up."

Sam smiled and nodded. "Yes, it's been through a lot. It's definitely got character, you could say."

"I'll bet all that character changes the sound of the guitar," Virginia said.

"It does. Makes it better. It's sort of like musical patina," Sam said.

"But what does that have to do with building a church?" someone asked.

"Maybe it's that no matter how wonderful or perfect we think we are as a parish, the fact is we're a bunch of broken people doing the best we can," Sam said. "I think we need to accept the brokenness and begin to make art."

"I think God is with those who are crushed, the ones who don't just believe in God but need him," someone added. "God renews souls by making them into art. He changes the sound of their song, if you will."

"Amen to that," Jewell and Tom said in unison.

The conversation took similar paths as the groups circulated from table to table. The members of the congregation started to see some connections between the art they were creating and the vision work to which Jake was calling them.

After almost everyone left, a core group stayed behind to clean up.

"What are we supposed to do with these?" Virginia asked, holding up a list of ideas.

"Throw them out," Mac joked. "Not sure our old ideas are going to work. Sounds like we're headed into uncharted waters."

"Don't throw them out," Jake interrupted. "They'll come in handy later."

——22——
CHAPTER

Textbook

"**I**t's time for a field trip," Jake said to the group as they gathered for their second meeting, "but before I tell you where we're going, we need to discuss something first."

Unlike the first meeting, this time, everyone sat at one large table. Jake asked people to sit beside someone they didn't know well. Textbooks were stacked in the middle.

"What are those?" Trey asked, fearing the meeting was going to be like school.

"Grab one and see," Jake said. "In fact, pair up and take one. They're old textbooks Simon brought from the high school. Don't worry about the subject. Focus on the textbooks themselves." Jake allowed time for each pair to find a book and begin looking through its pages. "Look at the table of contents. How is it

CHAPTER 22

organized? Then, look at individual chapters. What do the specific pages look like? Is there anything that catches your eye?"

Jake heard some reminisce about books they once had; others talked about subjects they had loved—or hated—in school.

"Not sure I know what this has to do with building a church," Stanley muttered.

"Oh hush," said Gladys from across the table.

"You'll see, Stanley," said Jake with a grin. After giving the group time to examine the textbooks, he continued. "I wanted you to look at textbooks because, in many ways, that's what we'll be designing."

"A textbook?" asked Trey. "I thought we were building a church."

"We are, and, although we don't often think of churches like this, in a way, they're just fancy textbooks," Jake paused as people made bewildered faces. "Instead of covers, the church has walls. Instead of pages, it has windows and furnishings. But before we get to all that, tell me what you notice about the textbooks."

"Ours is organized systematically," Simon observed. "Each chapter built on the one before and leads to the next one."

"Ours has quotations in colorful boxes spread out throughout the chapter. I'm sure they have something to do with the text on that page," said Rabbi Kaplan.

"Ours doesn't have quotations, but it has lots of pictures," someone offered.

"Ours is a math textbook," said Gladys. "Some pages have shaded boxes with specific equations; others have questions. It's nothing like the books I had as a child."

"No, I'm sure they're very different," said Jake. "Through the years, textbooks have progressed and developed more effective ways to present the material."

"The more pictures, the better," Trey announced. "This one's got lots."

"Why do you like pictures?" Jake asked.

"Because it means there's less to read," Trey said to the amusement of everyone but his father. "Pictures are sometimes easier to understand."

"But what if you showed that book to someone who couldn't read? Do you think they could understand something just by looking at the pictures?" Jake asked the group.

"Sure," said Simon. "The pictures are also easier to understand."

"A picture is worth a thousand words," someone offered.

"I know I sound like a broken record, but what does this have to do with designing a church?" Stanley said, closing his textbook with a thud.

"A long, long time ago," Jake began.

"In a galaxy far, far away," Trey added.

Jake smiled at Trey's *Star Wars* reference. "Early Christians built dedicated spaces for worship. They were simple, nothing like the churches of today, but, over time, they progressed. People learned how to build spaces that were bigger and more open. They also learned how to construct walls in a way that allowed larger windows than the small ones in the early churches. At one point, all church services were in Latin. Fewer people spoke Latin. Eventually, only the clergy and well-educated did, but the service remained the same. People came to church and had no idea what was being said."

"I know what that's like," Trey joked.

"Then this exercise is for you, Trey," Jake said. "Eventually, people decided to let the building teach the Christian story. In other words, they turned the buildings into textbooks, sermons of their own."

"Is that why stained-glass windows show biblical scenes?" Trey asked.

"Exactly, but not just the windows. Every part of the building became a part of the storytelling."

"Visual sermons," Emmett offered.

Jake nodded with delight as he walked over to Emmett's new walking stick. "Here's a perfect example. In my hand is a piece of wood. Raj shaped it in such a way as to serve a specific purpose, to be a staff or a walking stick. Then, with input from Mac and others, he carved things into the staff—people and moments from St. John's life. Without anyone saying a word about St. John's, I think you can learn a lot about a church just by looking at this staff. It's the same with churches, or at least it should be." Jake passed the staff around the table for people to examine. "So, the question is, what do you want your church to say?"

After many suggestions, Jake told everyone to keep a running list of ideas. "We'll need them later," he said as he returned the walking stick. "All buildings say something, or, to use a churchy word, all spaces have their own theology. That leads me to the field trips I mentioned earlier."

Jake nodded to Simon, who brought an offering plate full of folded pieces of paper and stood beside Jake. Simon explained, "We're going to pass this around the table. Each pair should take one piece of paper. Don't look at yours until I tell you to."

He waited until everyone had theirs, then nodded to Simon to continue. "On that piece of paper is the name of a place here in town. Your assignment is to visit that space as a team and look for its theology. Every space says something; your job is to figure that out."

The group looked around the table like a pop quiz had been given. "There are no wrong answers," Jake assured them. Reluctantly, each pair unfolded their paper as if opening a fortune cookie.

"First Baptist Church," Virginia read out loud.

"St. Francis's Catholic Church," announced another pair.

"The Webster Library," Robert said with a scrunched face. "I thought we were looking at churches."

"Libraries can say as much as any church," Jake said.

The Quaker meeting house and the Congregational church were assigned.

"Mt. Sinai Synagogue," Sam and Sara read in unison. Rabbi Kaplan perked up, sitting taller in his seat.

"Maria's," read Mac, sounding like he'd grabbed the golden ring on a merry-go-round. "Can I do this work while I have breakfast?"

"Sure," Jake said. "Just make sure you look around while you're eating."

"You shouldn't have any problem doing that given how much time you spend there," Emmett added.

Mac looked at Emmett. "Look who's trying to make a joke, everybody."

"I've never been to Maria's," Gladys said. Mac, her partner for the excursion, gave her a smile.

"Then you're in for a real treat," Emmett replied.

Once each team had announced their assignment, Jake gave final instructions. "You have two weeks to complete your assignment. We'll reconvene the first Saturday in February, at the rectory, at 9 o'clock sharp. Bring boots and jackets because we'll go over to the church site after breakfast."

Emmett was surprised he'd be hosting the next meeting. Jake's spontaneity took some getting used to.

When the group assembled two weeks later, everyone was buzzing with excitement to share about their excursions, but Jake asked them to wait until after they ate breakfast. Jake asked the group to gather in the living room when they finished.

"This reminds me of when Abby was alive," Virginia said, touching Emmett's sleeve tenderly. "Remember how often this house was full?"

"I told you spaces have theologies," Jake began. "Let's go around the room and hear from each pair about what you observed."

"Stanley and I went to St. Francis's Catholic church," Simon began. "We were surprised at how similar it was to our old church."

"The altar was up front, where it belongs," said Stanley, "and the lectern was on the left and pulpit on the right same as old St. John's."

"The service was also similar," Simon continued. "Many prayers were identical to ours, which was interesting. The eucharist was clearly the most important part."

"How'd you know?" Jake asked.

"The altar was center stage," Stanley added. "Bells rung at certain moments during communion."

"Sanctus bells," Emmett offered. "I always thought they sounded like a phone ringing."

"We noticed two other things. A bowl of water sat at the front of the church, and people dipped their hands and put water on their foreheads as they entered."

"Like they were baptizing themselves," Stanley said.

"Or recalling their baptism," Emmett offered.

"The other thing was the cross."

"How was it different? Don't all churches have crosses?" Jake asked.

"Jesus was still on their cross. He's not on ours," said Stanley. "I was told in Sunday school that he wasn't on the cross to remind us of what happened on Easter."

"Why do you think their crosses have Jesus on them?" asked Jake.

"To scare people," one person offered.

"To remind them of Christ's sacrifice," said another.

"Sounds like heavy-duty theology," said Jake.

"Trey and I went to the Baptist church," said Virginia. "It was nothing like what you described. The altar was not in the middle. In front were chairs and a pulpit used for both reading the scriptures and preaching."

"But behind the pulpit was this big glassed-in pool area," Trey shared with unusual excitement. "It had palm trees and hills painted on the wall behind the water; I even saw a camel or two. Someone got baptized on the Sunday we were there. He was a grown man, not like the babies in our church, and the minister dunked the guy."

"Dunked him?" someone asked.

"Grabbed him by the shoulders and put him all the way under. It was like a baptismal dunking booth."

"I guess it's pretty clear why they call themselves Baptists," Virginia pointed out.

"But why all the way under, clothed and everything?" Trey asked.

"I don't know. Maybe it has something to do with giving up one life and starting another," Jake said.

"We went to the synagogue," Sara said. "The first thing we noticed was that it was round. It took getting used to, but Sam and I thought the design brought an intimacy to the place."

"Their Bible was a scroll," Sam shared. "They unrolled it on a table that looked a lot like an altar."

"The service was in Hebrew," Sara added. "It was hard to understand what was going on, but I loved listening to the language while looking around the space. There were stained-glass windows with Hebrew words written on them. One had lanterns, and another showed an elaborate chest that looked like the ark of the covenant."

"As in *Indiana Jones*?" Trey interrupted.

"I believe the movie got it from the Bible," Sara smiled. "Above the place they read were carvings of two scrolls set side by side. We thought they might be the Ten Commandments, but someone explained that one scroll represented the law, the other the prophets."

"On the way home, we talked about Jesus being Jewish. We wondered if the service we heard was like the one he went to. We also remembered the story of when Jesus went to the temple. Seeing people read from a scroll made it easy to imagine."

Each group found something interesting in the spaces they visited. Those who went to the state capitol mentioned the statues and famous speeches engraved on the walls. The library emphasized learning and Webster history.

When it was Mac and Gladys's turn, people were eager to hear what theology they found in a diner.

"You were right," Mac looked at Jake, "Maria's *definitely* has a theology. I treated this lovely lady to breakfast at Maria's, and I'm happy to report she lived to tell the tale. Hanging on the walls are pictures of each president who has visited Maria's while running for office. Instead of putting them all on one wall, in chronological order, the pictures are divided, Democrats on the left, Republicans on the right."

"There are also framed sayings scattered on the walls, which I liked," Gladys said. "One of them said, 'today is the first day of the rest of your life; don't screw it up.'" Gladys tried not to blush. "Another said, 'If you don't like New England weather, wait a minute.' Then there was this one that Mac really liked, 'Don't say a word until I've had my coffee, and then only if you must.'"

The group laughed at the sayings and talked about how close the dining tables are at Maria's and how that leads to common conversations in the diner, whether people like it or not. "It's a place of hospitality," Jake said, smiling at Maria. "It also honors our being the first primary state."

After a short break, Jake told them to grab their coats and hats. "Follow me," he said. "It's time to focus on what you want your church to say. Time to begin our work."

"Finally!" Stanley said.

Jake had asked Mac and Simon to shovel the walkway up to the church steps for this part of the meeting. Mac had added a stake in the snow due east. Those who'd been at the reorientation gathering knew why that was important.

"Pretend you're the church. Go to the stake Mac put in the snow and form the shape of the church." People trudged through the snow and formed a large rectangle.

"Needs to be bigger than that," Simon offered. "Attendance has grown almost 30 percent since the fire."

"Who would have thought your church would be growing?" Jake said, smiling at Emmett.

"What about that space?" Marty asked, looking over where the old church had been and the extra land surrounding it.

"There's lots of space for all sorts of things," Jake said. "That's for the parish center and parking." Marty smiled for the first time since the meetings began. "I see you've formed the church in the shape of a rectangle."

"That's right," Stanley grumbled. "Just like the old church."

"That might be best, but you might want to consider building it in the shape of a circle. Sam and Sara said the circle created a sense of intimacy when they visited the synagogue. When you think about what you want the church to say, what's the most important thing?"

"Love," Sara said.

"Forgiveness," Sam added.

"How can you say all that from the very beginning?"

"Build it in the shape of a heart," someone suggested timidly.

"Interesting thought," Jake said, "but what's a more Christian way to express love?"

"The cross," said Emmett. "We should build the church in the shape of the cross."

"Cruciform is the word you're looking for. Emmett's right. Start your textbook at the foundation. A church built in the shape of a cross for all that follows. People will get a sense of what the church is about when they first enter."

Mac and Simon ushered people into a new shape, and people saw the cross.

"Do you think people will notice the shape?" Virginia asked.

"Some will, some won't, but the building will tell the story from its foundation, whether people notice it or not."

Jake encouraged everyone to shuffle their feet in the snow, then return to the shoveled pathway. Once back, he asked them to look at the space they had created.

"Take in this moment," Jake said. "You're looking at something few will ever see, or at least see in this way. Behold, the beginning of your new church."

"I love it," Virginia said, and others agreed.

"It's only the beginning. Now you'll have to build on the foundation by writing the book."

They stood in silence for a few minutes before the cold in their feet prompted them to head back to the rectory. Marty remained, and Jake went over to see what was on her mind. "The parish center," she said. "There's all this talk about the church. I don't want the parish center to be forgotten."

"It won't," Jake assured her. "That's why you're here."

—23—

CHAPTER

Pages

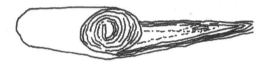

"I don't want to mess this up," Emmett said from his seat at the kitchen table.

"We will," Jake replied. "It's only a question of how."

"Always the bearer of good news."

"It's what I do," Jake said as he patted Emmett on the back and took his seat. "When I first became an architect, I felt like you do now. I wanted my work to be perfect, to stand out from others. I was excited about the possibilities. I was determined not to make any mistakes. Turns out that's the worst way to be an architect."

"And person," Emmett added.

"I tried to be clever. My early work was good, but it wasn't great. It was functional, but it wasn't inspirational."

"What was missing?"

"Soul. Buildings are like people that way," Jake answered. "Some people live functional lives, and other people live inspirational ones. The difference is where the life springs from. Inspirational lives spring from within. They have soul."

"How do we make our church have soul?" Emmett asked.

"I have some ideas," Jake said, "but it's up to you and the others to determine how this church gets built. You can build a church that functions or one that inspires, and if we get lucky, it might do both."

Emmett stayed behind as Jake went upstairs to get dressed. They had been talking about the building, but Emmett couldn't help but think about his ministry. Like Jake, he had wanted his ministry to be perfect, to stand out. Looking back, he wondered how much he had used his head instead of his heart in his ministry. He wondered what it might have looked like had he lived it from his heart.

"It's time to fill the pages," Jake said as he rubbed his hands together like a child about to blow out candles on a birthday cake. The group sat at a table in the grist mill, clearly anxious for the next step. "There's a lot of work to do, but, in the end, you'll have built a church."

"And parish center," Marty added.

"And parish center. Thank you for that, Marty. The two buildings are equally important, like two sides of the same coin."

"Two sides of a parish—worship and service," Emmett added.

"I'm glad to hear you say that," said Marty, "because parishes usually care more about worship than service."

"Not us," Emmett said. "At least, not anymore."

"Can I quote you on that?" Marty asked. Emmett nodded.

Robert spoke of this as a defining moment in St. John's history and how generations to come would look back on the work they were about to begin. Simon followed Robert by reminding everyone about the parish's significant role in the diocese. When someone suggested they design the most impressive church in the state, Emmett stood and invited everyone to join him by the windows.

"I've always loved streams," he began. "And I've grown fond of this one now that we've spent a year on its shore. I've listened and watched it flow. Heck, I even fell in it not too long ago." Emmett opened one of the windows and continued. "There was a time when I wanted to be like this river. I wanted to draw people's attention, showing them what a wonderful river I was. But I've realized I had it all wrong. I was never supposed to be the river. I'm supposed to be the stream bed. My job is to make a place where the water can flow."

"Why are you telling us this?" Robert asked.

"It's the same with the church we're designing. The building is not the river. It's the stream bed. As tempting as it might be to build something impressive, something that makes a lot of noise and draws everyone's attention, the important thing is what flows through it."

"So, we should build something average?" Robert asked.

"Not at all. But the point is not the buildings themselves. It's what goes on inside them. It's what flows through. Whether we're talking about the the church or the parish center, our job is to create the best spaces possible for God's grace to flow, just like the water below."

Once everyone returned to their seats, Jake continued. "It's time to look inside the buildings and figure out what will flow through them. We'll begin with the church, then move to the parish center."

"Where do we start?" Simon asked.

"With the windows," Jake said. "They're like the pictures in the textbook."

The group had a lengthy discussion about what to put on the windows. Some wanted only scenes from the Bible; others wanted to include moments from church history. One person thought the windows should depict scenes from American history. In the end, the group decided to stick with stories from the Bible.

"Instead of sitting here and deciding which stories should be depicted on the windows, I'd like to ask each of you to go home and look through your Bibles," Jake said. "Pick one story that speaks to you on a personal level. Over the next few months, we'll present our selections to each other and see what happens."

"You're not serious," Robert said.

"I don't even know if I have a Bible at home," said Stanley. "I'm sure I got one when I was confirmed..."

"I know where it is," Gladys said, glaring at her husband.

"Sounds touchy-feely," Robert muttered under his breath.

"You'll have to excuse our hesitancy," Emmett said to Jake. "We pride ourselves on our ability to create rich liturgy, perform inspirational music, and offer sound theology. But we're not known for speaking about our faith."

"Maybe it's time you try," Jake said.

People squirmed in their seats as Jake let the sound of the river fill the sanctuary.

"Lent's coming up," Emmett said. "Maybe this could be our Lenten devotion. We could use the forty days to present the stories that matter most to us."

"Of course, you'd tie it into the liturgical year," Mac said, shaking his head.

Sam raised his hand. "I'll go first. I know what story speaks to me."

"You're on!" Jake said, pointing to his first volunteer. The rest of the group passed a sheet of paper around the table, signing up for their turn.

Sam was standing at the end of the table when everyone arrived. "I volunteered to go first because there's one parable Jesus told that's always been my favorite." Lifting his Bible, he cleared his throat and took a deep breath. "There was a man who had two sons. The younger of them said to his father, 'Father, give me the share of the property that will belong to me.' So he divided his property between them. A few days later, the younger son gathered all he had and traveled to a distant country, and there he squandered his property in reckless living...'"

Those around the table listened as if they had never heard the parable of the prodigal son. Having it read by Sam Tucker, who they watched embarrass himself at the Christmas tree lighting ceremony years ago, changed how it sounded. When he finished, Sam closed his Bible and placed it on the table before looking at the group.

"I've always related to the younger son. I squandered a lot of my life in reckless living. I lost everything. It sucks."

Trey laughed at Sam's word choice, giving the others permission to do the same.

"My father didn't run out to greet me. There was no fatted calf for a celebration. All I got was two months of rehab. But in the end, it allowed me to begin the long journey home. I'd like to tell you I've made it, but I feel like I'm still on my way. I think the only reason I've come back to St. John's is because of this parable. That, and the fact that Emmett encouraged me."

Sam took his seat, and Jake looked at Emmett with a grin.

"I love that parable," Simon said. "The way the father comes out to the son and welcomes him home touches my heart."

Others shared their appreciation for the parable and Sam's willingness to speak honestly, but Robert asked for Sam's Bible. "I've never cared for this parable," he said as he opened it to where Sam had left off. "Meanwhile, the older son was in the field. When he came near the house, he heard music and dancing… The older brother became angry and refused to go in. So his father went out and pleaded with him. But he answered his father, 'Look! All these years I've been slaving for you and never disobeyed your orders. Yet you never gave me even a young goat so I could celebrate with my friends. But when this son of yours who has squandered your property with prostitutes comes home, you kill the fattened calf for him!'"

When he finished, Robert explained, "I guess I have a hard time with this parable because I've always identified with the other brother. Where was his feast? Where was the celebration for his doing the right thing?"

"I appreciate your honesty, Robert," Emmett said. "I used to identify with the older brother, too, but then I realized the father went to both sons, as if Jesus was saying both were lost."

"But isn't the father the point?" Trey asked, causing everyone to look at the group's youngest member. "I get the whole messing up and the staying home stuff, but it seems to me Jesus wants us to think about God being like the father."

Emmett stared at Trey. "Out of the mouths of babes," he sighed, "come some of the most authentic sermons."

"You OK?" Jake asked when he entered the kitchen and saw Emmett steadying himself on the counter's edge.

"I'm fine. Just tired. Building a church can take a lot out of a person," he said.

"You don't need to do this by yourself, you know. In case you haven't noticed, a lot of people want to help."

"I have noticed, and it's very gratifying," Emmett said. "The parishioners have rolled up their sleeves like never before."

Jake stood by the window and took a deep breath. "I can't wait to hear what the others come up with."

Over the next several weeks, the design team members followed Sam's example. Virginia read the passage where Jesus met the woman at the well. "She never expected to encounter Christ at such a place, at such a time," Virginia explained. "I have to admit that's what it was like for me. I met Christ when I least expected to. My kids were struggling, and my marriage was headed in the wrong direction. I got tangled up in all my problems, but Jesus showed up anyway."

Robert read the story Jesus told about the successful man who built silo after silo, only to be told his time was up. "I've spent most of my life building silos," he confessed. "This is a story that's always haunted me."

"I hope you'll forgive me," Rabbi Kaplan began when it was his turn, "but I chose a story from the Hebrew Scriptures. You are building a Christian church, but I needed to go to the Bible I know."

"It's ours too," Emmett said, hoping to encourage Rabbi Kaplan.

"That's right," Simon added. "It was Jesus's Bible."

Rabbi Kaplan smiled and read the story of Moses at the burning bush. "I have always loved God coming to Moses in such an unexpected and dramatic way, but what moves me most is that he chose Moses. Moses had killed a man and was not the best speaker. He was an unlikely person to lead the Hebrew people, yet he was God's choice. That gives me comfort when I think I'm not qualified to do the work of leading my synagogue."

"That's a great story," Emmett said. "I've always loved God choosing Moses in such a dramatic way. I've always been a bit jealous of Moses, but I must admit I've found it unfair that Moses leads the people out of Egypt and into the wilderness but never gets to enter the Promised Land."

Rabbi Kaplan laughed and agreed. "You'd think after all that work in the wilderness..."

"I picked something from the Old Testament too," Trey said when it was his turn. "I've always liked the story of creation." Trey read the creation story from Genesis and then explained that he liked the story because it kept God big. "I like to think of God as the God of the universe rather than some dude walking around Jerusalem years ago."

"It doesn't have to be either-or," Emmett pointed out. "God is the creator—and the dude."

"I guess so," Trey continued, "but God made the whole world, the atoms and the Big Bang, the sea and the mountains.

Sometimes people shy away from putting science and religion together. I don't think science disproves God. Quite the opposite. I think it points to how amazing God is. If you ask me, people make God too small."

The group nodded thoughtfully.

"I've always loved Ecclesiastes, but I picked a passage from Micah, the prophet," Sara said as she picked up her Bible. "'He has shown you, O mortal, what is good. And what does the Lord require of you? To act justly and to love mercy and to walk humbly with your God.' Sometimes I think we make things too complicated. Micah always reminds me what really matters."

Marty went next. Like Sara, she went to sentiment more than story. "I'm not that religious, if by religious, you mean someone who goes to church and knows the Bible by heart. My grandparents came to this country with two suitcases and a bunch of hope. Inscribed on the Statue of Liberty were the words, 'Give me your tired, your poor, Your huddled masses yearning to be free... Send these, the homeless, tempest-tossed, to me; I lift my torch beside the golden door.' More than any others, these are the words that have guided me. I think God cares about the poor and tired, the huddled masses. I think God cares more about how we treat each other than he does about buildings and fancy services. God is in each of us, I believe. That's why I do what I do around here. When we serve each other, we're serving God."

"There's a passage from the Bible about that," Emmett said. "It's from the Gospel of Matthew. It says, 'For I was hungry, and you gave me something to eat; I was thirsty, and you gave me something to drink; I was a stranger, and you invited me in; I needed clothes, and you clothed me, I was sick, and you looked after me, and I was in prison, and you came to visit me.'"

"Exactly," Marty said with a smile. "Couldn't have said it better myself."

Maria read about the feeding of the 5,000 and spoke of her passion for feeding people. "I think feeding people is a ministry of sorts. It welcomes people, comforts them. We've fed many more than 5,000 at the diner, and we're going to keep feeding people as long as we're open."

Gladys read the story of how Jesus turned water into wine at the wedding at Cana and spoke about how she met Stanley after her marriage of 30 years fell apart. "It was like being given new wine, the best wine, late in life," she said.

Stanley went next and read from Matthew about building one's house on rock. "The foundation is what matters," Stanley said. "The foundation is crucial, whether it's the church we're building or the lives we're living. I know you think I'm an old curmudgeon because I don't go in for all the trendy ideas we've talked about, but all I care about is our foundation. I care about the church that was here long before I arrived, and I care about building a new one on the same, strong foundation."

"Sounds like a hymn," Emmett said, smiling at Stanley.

At dinner that night, Mac shared his intention to read the story of Jesus and the thief on the cross. "I've always taken comfort over Jesus forgiving the bum that late in the game. If he can forgive him, I figure there's hope for this bum."

"What are you going to choose?" Jake asked Emmett. Emmett put down his napkin and let out a long sigh. "I've given it a lot of thought. Part of me wanted to read about when Jesus taught in the temple as a boy."

"Because he was going about his father's business?" Mac asked. "Teaching in the temple like you do every Sunday."

"No, because he was left behind by his parents," Emmett said, looking away. "But I decided to go with something a little less depressing. The nativity story's my favorite. It's what first captured my imagination as a child, and it's what has given me the most hope over the years. The idea that God has come into the world to let us know we're not alone still speaks to me after all these years."

"Hear, hear," said Jake, lifting his wine glass as if to make a toast. "Here's to the little boy who was left behind and the man who was eventually found."

When it was Jewell's turn to share, she asked the other artists to join her. "Remember, we're artists, not theologians. But we came across a fascinating story when we were looking in the Bible for something to share," she said. "The disciples were gathered upstairs, much like we are in our studios, and a mighty wind descended, then there was fire, and people spoke in tongues."

"That was the day of Pentecost," Emmett explained. "It's the day the Holy Spirit filled the disciples, which empowered them to become the church."

"We feel like we're the people of wind and fire. Through our art, we speak in many languages."

"God is the great artist," Jessica added, "and each time we paint, mold clay, or arrange broken pieces into mosaics, we feel like we're working beside God."

"Co-creators," Emmett said. "I love that. But I could do without the fire part. We've had enough fire."

Jewell waited for the laughter to settle down. "I know fire took your church away, but if you look around, you've also been on fire recently. This place was like a ghost town when you moved

in. Now, look at it. You have something going on every night of
the week."

"Maybe we should rename St. John's 'The Church on Fire,'"
Trey said, which caused his father to scowl.

Jake laughed loudest and said, "There are worse things to call
a church."

By the time everyone had presented the scripture passages
that were most meaningful to them, Emmett felt as if he'd met his
parishioners for the first time. He wondered what Jake planned to
do with all the stories.

"Don't worry about that right now," Jake said when someone
asked him about it. "We need to turn our attention to the parish
center now."

"Finally," Marty said.

"We've spent a lot of time on the church, but the parish
center is equally important," said Jake. "The two buildings will
sit beside each other, connected by a covered walkway. They're
like a train ticket I once had, the kind with a perforated line and
words that read, 'Not good if detached.' Our job is to keep the two
attached. We need to put just as much effort into the parish center
as we have been putting into the church."

The conversation began with the entrance itself. "Every sign
I've ever seen says, 'The Episcopal Church welcomes you,'" Sam
pointed out. "I think we should design an entrance that's truly
welcoming."

"Why not print the words that Reverend Hodges read on
the wall facing people as they enter? You know, the one about
feeding the hungry and visiting the sick," Trey suggested.
"They would be perfect to represent all that ministry you keep
reminding us about."

Emmett tried to hide his smile. Trey was right, even if he had a funny way of saying it.

The kitchen and parish hall were next. Marty was put in charge of figuring out what kind of kitchen the church needed, and others focused on the parish hall. At first, they wanted to design a multi-purpose space that could host wedding receptions and 12-step recovery meetings, but Sam convinced the group to dedicate a separate room for 12-step ministries, as he called them. Sara suggested a parish library that she and Simon agreed to design. Virginia mentioned a quiet center for prayer and meditation.

"There needs to be a youth room," Trey pointed out.

"A youth room?" Jake asked.

"We always get pushed into some faraway place," Jake said. "Before, in Cutter Hall, we met in this cramped room. I wondered if we could have a dedicated space in the new church, a place where we could meet and hang out."

"What kind of room?" Jake asked.

"You know, with couches and comfortable chairs, maybe a TV and a fridge."

"Sounds like a clubhouse," Jake said.

"It would encourage kids to come around more often."

"I'd like that," Emmett said as he placed his hand on Trey's shoulders.

At the end of May, Emmett hosted a dinner to thank everyone for their hard work, and Jake waited until after dessert to invite everyone into the dining room. In his hands were two long rolls of paper. Everyone knew what they were.

"Keep in mind," he said, "these are preliminary drawings. A friend from graduate school who has a firm outside Boston let me use their equipment to make these. There's still much to discuss, but at least they'll move us along."

Everyone stepped closer like children crowded around a new puppy. Jake and Emmett unrolled the drawings slowly to build suspense. The first drawing showed an aerial view, with the church in the shape of the cross and a walkway connecting it to the parish center. The next drawing showed the inside of the church with the altar, pulpit, and lectern in place, along with a diagram of each window.

"There are twelve large windows, one on each end and four more along each side," Jake explained. "There will be smaller windows below each bigger one, expanding upon the biblical story that each one tells."

The next drawing showed the parish center with a large lobby, industrial kitchen, and ample parish hall. The offices were clustered at one end of the hall with meeting rooms at the other. "And look," Jake said to Trey, "there's a youth room on the second floor."

"Looks like you have one more office than we need," Emmett pointed out.

"That's because you need to think about the future. The way things are going, you will need additional staff. You can't do it all. It won't be long until you'll need to hire an assistant priest." It had been a long time since the parish had needed (or been able to afford) additional staff, but thinking about another minister brought a smile to Emmett's face.

"What's over there?" Stanley asked, pointing to where the old church used to be.

"That's a very special feature, Stanley. It comes from something you and Emmett said. You spoke of this place being a memorial, something to remind future generations of those who came before, and Emmett said he always wanted a place to put Abby's ashes. The place you are asking about does both. It's a memorial garden."

"You mean a columbarium?" Emmett asked.

"A what?" Virginia asked.

"A columbarium is a kind of memorial garden. People's ashes are placed there with plaques with names and dates on them." Stanley was silent, but the look on his face told Jake and others he liked the idea.

"But what's the circle in the middle of the garden?" Trey asked.

"That," Jake said with delight, "is a fire pit!"

"Really?" Trey sounded like he'd found another gift under the Christmas tree.

After telling the group about the night the youth gathered around a bonfire, Jake explained his hope that the space could be used for the living as well as the dead.

The discussion took off, everyone excitedly talking and brainstorming until Robert brought the evening to a crashing halt with one question. "So how much will this cost?"

──24──
CHAPTER

Let the Building Help

"**Y**ou're joking," Emmett said, spitting out the words. "I knew it would cost more than we have, but $8 million?"

"You're building two buildings," Jake pointed out.

Staggering toward the coffee, Emmett's disbelief turned to anger. "Why did you let us dream like that? The stained-glass windows, memorial garden, and state-of-the-art parish center are beyond what we can afford. I wish you hadn't deceived us."

"Deceived you?"

"Yes, you convinced us all things were possible. Now we know that's not true. Only some things are possible. We'll have to start over."

"You won't," Jake said, unfazed by Emmett's anger. "It's a big number, I'll grant you, but you've already raised $2 million. You're a quarter of the way there. This is just another challenge."

"A big one," Emmett sighed as he returned to the table.

"Keep in mind that $8 million is a rough estimate. I doubt it's far off, but it could be less. Plus, we can adjust things to lower the costs."

"By $6 million?" Emmett asked, shaking his head.

"No, but we can lower the costs. Let's see what we can do, then decide if we need to start over."

Emmett mustered a halfhearted nod before Jake went upstairs to dress. He felt like a fool. Looking out the window across the common, he dreaded sharing the news with the others.

"Well, that's no surprise," Robert said with an I-told-you-so tone as he threw the estimate on the table. "We'll have to start from scratch."

"Or maybe we should just focus on one building," Stanley suggested.

"Don't tell me," Marty said with disgust, "we should just build the church."

"That's what St. John's is, after all," Stanley replied.

"One building or two, it doesn't matter," said Simon. "We don't have enough money either way."

Jake tried to calm the growing frustration by pointing out how natural it was to run into financial issues, but Marty was eager to continue to debate.

"At some point, we need to step back and ask whether we should build the church in the first place," Marty said.

"Oh please," Stanley muttered.

"I'm serious," Marty said, ignoring the comments. "Spending that kind of money on a church and parish center is nuts. Do you have any idea what we could do with that kind of money? We could build affordable housing, feed every family in our community who needs our help—plus, we could make sure every student in this county had a good, warm lunch."

Emmett listened, knowing how important it was to let people vent their frustrations. He thought about the picture behind the bishop's desk, a black-and-white drawing of a bishop holding a cathedral in his hands and a beggar on his knees before him. The image had always stirred Emmett as a profound criticism of the church. As he listened to the others, he thought about how the drawing had become hauntingly real.

"Without the church, there's no congregation," Robert pointed out, "and without a congregation, there's no money. Without money, there's no helping the poor."

"I know," Marty conceded, "but just because we can build a church doesn't mean we should."

"You raise an important point, Marty," said Emmett, surprising many at the table, "but I believe the answer lies somewhere between throwing out all of our ideas and building something we cannot afford."

"There's always sticker shock at this point in a building project," Sam pointed out.

"But $8 million?" Mac responded. "That's more like sticker electrocution!"

"Every project needs revision after the first numbers come in," Sam continued. "I suggest we look for ways to cut and see where that leads us."

Many agreed, but others looked like children learning there was no Santa Claus. Anticipating this, Jake presented a list of changes that could save money without changing the buildings too much. "The balcony could go, and we could reduce the size a bit. We could also build the church out of wood instead of stone." With each suggestion, the pain increased, but everyone knew they had no choice but to make significant cuts. It took several meetings before Jake was able to provide revised numbers. The changes saved more than $1 million. The initial delight over the savings soon gave way to the fact that they were still a long way from being able to afford to build anything.

"You'll just need to raise more money," Jake said to Emmett as the deflated group walked to their cars.

"You say it like there's a spigot to turn, and money will pour out. I did everything I could to raise the money we have. I could go back to donors and ask for more, but people were pressed to give what they did. I'm out of ideas, Jake. I don't see how I can pull this off."

"It's not up to you alone. If you've learned anything, you should know you're not in this by yourself. This is a group project. The parish is full of clever people who can think of solutions we can't. Plus, I believe this building wants to be built. I know that might sound New Age to you, but I believe it. Perhaps you need to let the building help."

"The building help?" asked Emmett.

"Yes. What you've designed is special, but no one other than the design group knows about it. It's time to introduce your dream to others. People may be drawn to your vision. They might want to help make it happen financially. An ordinary church might not inspire them, but this one might."

"How do you propose we 'let the building help,' as you say?" Emmett asked.

"Let 'em in on the secret."

"How do I do that?"

"You don't. We do! Ask the group what they think and see what they come up with."

It took a while for The Designers to imagine how to introduce the church and parish center to others. Robert didn't believe it would work the way they needed it to, but the artists helped the group see the possibilities.

"Whenever one of us has an idea, we meet for coffee and listen to the person," Jewell explained. "We don't say a word; we just listen. Then, we wait and see what stirs within us and share that with whoever presented the idea."

"Sounds like the Quakers," Emmett said. "They seek the Way and listen for it in a still small voice within."

"We're going to need something a lot louder than a still small voice," Robert said cynically. "We're going to need a megaphone."

"When I make lesson plans," Simon explained, "I map out what I want to say on a whiteboard, then I think about the best way to present it."

"I use storyboards whenever we present an ad campaign," a local advertising executive shared. The artists looked at one another and nodded.

"What?" asked Jake.

"We were thinking," Jewell began. "You told us we're creating a textbook. Why not make boards for the story we're trying to tell? In the art world, we call them cartoons— something to help us envision what we're going to paint or write. We could do that for each of the windows and display them here in the sanctuary."

CHAPTER 24

"Don't do it here," said Trey. "Do it at the church. Put the cartoons on easels where the windows will be."

"That's a great idea," said Virginia, "but let's not stop with the windows. Let's try to create a sense of the whole place."

"How do you propose we do that?" asked Stanley.

"We could outline the footprint of the building with white chalk for a start," Sara suggested. "Then people could see the space in the same way we did when we shuffled our feet through the snow."

"I could get the folks who line the football field at the high school to help," said Simon.

"Have them outline the parish center while they're at it," said Emmett, much to Marty's delight. "If we're going to show them our dream, let's show them the whole dream."

"Simon, Sam, and I will come up with something to show where the altar and other furnishings will go," Mac offered.

Marty suggested serving refreshments where the parish hall would go, and Alma agreed to set up mock offices.

"I'll get a coffee pot and some folding chairs to show people the 12-step room," Sam said. That idea inspired Sara to offer to set up a church library.

Jewell agreed to draw the stained-glass window boards, and Jessica said she would color them.

"Only color part of the cartoon," Jake said. "That will give them a partial taste of what could be. Leaving them unfinished will allow people to consider helping us finish the drawing, so to speak."

Trey said he and his friends would set up chairs to look like a church and make a fire in the pit. The choir volunteered to provide music for the event.

Mac chimed in, "I'll get my buddies in the fire department to bring an extension ladder to show people how tall the church steeple will be."

"Get them to 'lift high the cross,'" Emmett joked, but Mac decided to do just that: attach a cross to the top of the ladder.

It took more than a month to pull things together, but the enthusiasm was contagious. Parishioners who had done nothing more than show up for an occasional service became regular visitors to the mill. People in the diner who heard about the event volunteered to help, as did members from several local churches.

"I told you God wants this building built," Jake said as he stood with Emmett and watched everyone working.

"I wish God would write a check," Emmett whispered.

"He has," Jake pointed out. "He's written lots of them, through others, and I'm sure more are coming. Now that we've done all we could to lower the costs, it's God's turn to take it from here."

"When do you think God might show up?" Emmett asked.

Jake shook his head in disbelief. "Don't you see? God's been here the whole time. He's here now. Just look." Jake said. All Emmett could see were volunteers scattered throughout the sanctuary.

A crowd assembled at the church an hour before the event started. "These are just the volunteers," Jake pointed out as he and Emmett crossed the common. After greeting all they could, the two climbed the steps and offered some final instructions.

"Remember, we're the only ones who have seen the design," Jake began. "It's time to let others in on the secret."

"Let them experience what the new church and parish center will be like," added Emmett. "Paint a picture in their minds. Tell the stories of the windows. Make the church come alive."

Virginia and Sara had assigned specific duties to the volunteers. Ushers would lead visitors through the entrance and to the volunteers at different stations. The volunteers would explain the biblical story that their window represented. Other volunteers would speak about the altar and furnishings. When the visitors completed the tour of the church, they would be taken into the makeshift parish center. Marty, Alma, and their team would serve refreshments while describing the ministry that would happen there. Stanley and Gladys stood by the old church walls and explained the memorial garden. Trey and his friends stoked the fire in the fire pit and prepared to talk about the youth program.

"All we need are some visitors," Emmett said, looking toward the street. "It's early," he added.

Jake had placed an ad in the *Webster Times*, and Emmett reluctantly called the bishop to ask if he would let the diocese know about the event.

"Someone out there might want to come and help us build the church," Jake said as they waited.

The unpredictable New England spring weather cooperated, and the first visitors arrived on time. By the time the first group began their tour, the second group was almost full. Cars lined the four streets around the common, and only half were parishioners.

When they were ready to begin, Emmett and Virginia stood on the small riser Mac had built beside the future entrance. In a moment of inspiration, Mac had taken the Revere Bell out of storage and placed it on a temporary stand beside the stage. "I'll ring it when you're ready," he said. "It'll make them think they're going to church."

Emmett addressed the crowd. "On behalf of the people of St. John's and the folks who have worked for months to dream and plan a new church, we welcome you to what we're calling 'Our Unveiling.' With the help of your imagination, we invite you into our new church to show you what could be, and then invite you into our parish center for refreshments."

Virginia continued. "You'll enter through the doors on your left. The church will face east. The new orientation allows plenty of room for our parish center to serve others. It's a vital part of who we are. The old church site will become a memorial garden."

"The new church will be in the Gothic style, built in the shape of the cross and filled with stained-glass windows. From creation to resurrection, you'll see drawings of the windows and hear the stories they tell. Volunteers will answer any questions you may have."

"As senior warden, I welcome you and invite you to consider joining us to make this dream a reality. These buildings are expensive, but we believe our vision is worth it."

She turned to Emmett, who launched the event with arms opened wide: "Come, enter his gates with thanksgiving and his courts with praise. Give thanks to him and praise his name." Mac rang the bell.

Simon and Sara stood at the entrance and welcomed people into the new St. John's. "The cross at the top of the fire ladder shows the height of the church. It creates a sense of awe when you see or enter it," Sara explained.

"It's also intended to right-size a person, as one of our younger members likes to say," Simon added. "It reminds us that God is bigger...and we are smaller...than we often think."

A dramatic swirl of blue and white dominated the creation window, with stars and planets and seven panels depicting the seven days of creation. "We wanted to capture the dynamic nature of creation and tie it in with the biblical account," Terrance explained. "Creation happened when the spirit of God moved across the surface of the earth long ago. But that spirit still moves over the earth and all around us."

The next window showed Adam and Eve in the Garden of Eden. With lush plants surrounding them, the window speaks to the garden-like relationship human beings once had with God. "That relationship was lost because of our desire to be God," Sam explained.

Rabbi Kaplan stood barefoot beside the Moses window and invited those who were willing to remove their shoes as well. "We cried to the Lord, the Lord heard us, remembered the covenant he made with his people, and acted," he said. "This window captures that moment with Moses holding his sandals in his hand because the ground on which he is standing is holy ground." The rabbi had brought many from his synagogue to the unveiling. He was proud the group was committed to telling the entire biblical story, not just the part found in the New Testament.

The fourth large window showed Israel becoming a nation. "You'll see King David dancing before the ark, with the Tent of Meeting close behind," the volunteer explained. "The biblical story says he danced naked before the ark, but we decided to offer the G-rated version for the church." Each group found the decision funny. "The tent and the ark were the two spiritual traditions of the northern and southern halves of the kingdom, the law and community. David brought them together in Jerusalem. This window reminds us of the need for both in our church today."

"But Israel was never supposed to be like other nations," the next volunteer said. "They experienced great success and failure. Eventually, it took prophets to remind them who they were called to be. The people listened at first, but then they turned back to their foolish ways. They lost the promised land, the land that represented their covenant with God, the land that made them feel like God's chosen people."

"But God didn't forget his people," Virginia and Sara explained as they showed the drawing of Isaiah promising a messiah. "God would come and be with us, and this window leads to the windows on the south side, which tell the Christian story."

The nativity window was first. Sam's children took turns pointing out the shepherds and the wise men. "He came for all people," Sam Jr. explained, "shepherds and kings alike."

"That's why we included both Matthew and Luke's accounts of Jesus's birth," Sophie added. "People often only think about the story from Luke, but the Bible has two stories, each with its own take on the event. We wanted to remember that Jesus came to us all."

The next three windows showed Jesus's public ministry of teaching and healing before the transfiguration when the disciples saw Jesus for who he truly was. "The windows in the south transept depict Holy Week, and the ones behind the altar are the Easter windows, one for each of the four accounts found in the gospels," a volunteer said. "In the middle, between the Easter windows, will be a large window showing Jesus after the resurrection, his arms open wide, welcoming all."

Emmett greeted each group at the altar. He explained why the lectern was on one side and the pulpit on the other. "The church has a theology. On one side, the word is spoken; on the other, it's proclaimed, and in the middle is the altar, where God is made known in the breaking of the bread."

"What's going in that window?" someone asked, looking back toward the entrance.

"You'll have to ask him," Emmett said, pointing to Jake. "That's where the rose window will go, the only round window in the church. He's keeping that window a secret."

As the visitors finished the tour of the church, Emmett heard some of their comments.

"It's like the Bible in glass," one visitor said.

"It's like a sermon in color," said another.

"The bigger windows are the themes," the volunteer said, "and the smaller windows are illustrations of the themes."

More people arrived as others went through what would be a covered walkway leading to the parish center. Like the church, chalk outlined the footprint of the parish center. Greeters stood in what would be the lobby—or welcome center, as they planned to call it. "At one end of the hallway will be the rector's office and other administrative spaces, and at the other are designated rooms for specific ministries. The volunteers standing down there will describe those in greater detail."

"There will be a library and a quiet center," another volunteer said. "We want the two rooms next to each other to remind everyone the spiritual life involves study and contemplation."

"What's in there?" asked a visitor, pointing to a room with a coffee pot and metal chairs in a circle.

"That's our recovery center," Sam said with pride. "We feel strongly that the church needs to be a safe and encouraging place for 12-step ministries, not just alcohol but all types of addiction. Although we are not a sponsor of any group, this room is a dedicated space for recovery meetings of all kinds. Unlike other places in town, they won't have to share the space. They'll be able to leave the seats up and coffee mugs ready."

"St. John's doesn't just allow recovery groups," Sam pointed out, "we welcome and celebrate them."

In the parish hall, Marty and her many volunteers waited with refreshments. "Here at St. John's, we take service seriously. This parish hall will host weekly dinners for those in need. The kitchen will be specifically designed to accommodate our work."

"What are those?" a child asked.

"Backpacks," Marty replied. "We want to start a backpack ministry for students who don't have food for lunch. We're hoping to start by giving 50 students backpacks, which we'll fill each school day. But the need is greater than that."

Emmett had hesitated when Marty asked if she could mention the backpacks and ask for help. It was supposed to be a fundraiser for the church, but Jake assured him it was the right thing to do. "It's important the people get a sense of everything we do and the building we hope to build," he said.

The volunteers were exhausted and elated when the day was over. No one wanted to leave. Jake and Emmett had dinner waiting for everyone in the rectory. During dinner, Emmett shared that three people had approached him, expressing interest in donating money to fund some of the windows. Simon shared that someone had asked about giving money for the pulpit, and Mac announced a group had formed, calling themselves The Steeple People. "They're determined to fund the bell tower and get the Revere Bell back to its rightful place."

"Remarkable," Emmett said to Virginia while they refreshed their glasses in the kitchen.

"I've never been more excited," she said. "The fire was the worst thing that ever happened, but I must admit, this might be the best. I feel guilty saying it, but I felt so lost when we lost the church building. Today, I've never felt so found."

Before The Designers went home, they agreed more unveilings should be scheduled since some parishioners could not make it and others wanted to return with friends. Once Emmett and Jake had the rectory to themselves, they sat in silence in the living room. Emmett struggled to climb out of the chair on his way to bed.

"You look tired," Jake said.

"It's been a long day."

The enthusiasm continued for several weeks. People asked Emmett for private tours, and within a month, people had donated enough money to pay for seven of the windows.

"You're not going to believe this," Sam said without saying hello as he entered the rectory one morning. "A friend of mine, a confirmed atheist, or at least that's how he describes himself, wants to donate the recovery room in the parish center."

"Seriously?" Emmett asked.

"Folks from the synagogue stopped by when you were out the other day and said they were interested in donating the Moses window in Rabbi Kaplan's honor," Jake said.

"I don't believe it," said Emmett.

Donations were not the only excitement that summer. Attendance on Sundays grew to an all-time high. Marty and Sam convinced Emmett to hold a service before the Wednesday night dinners. Sam agreed to form a band to play music, and parishioners said they'd take turns delivering the message. Emmett was surprised not to be asked to participate, but Jake reminded him to focus on his parishioners' initiative. "I guess this is what the ministry of all believers looks like," Emmett said.

"Most churches focus on the clergy and treat the rest of us like chorus members standing in the back," Jake said.

By the end of the summer, they had raised half the amount needed. Sam and his father agreed to donate granite from their quarry for the church, and a roofing company offered to provide the materials at cost and labor for free. After a long night of poker at his cabin, Mac convinced the owner of the local HVAC company to donate all the equipment the church needed.

At the next vestry meeting, Jake broke the bad news. "You've raised a great deal of money. Be proud of yourselves. A year ago, you never dreamed you could raise such a sum, but you only have enough to build one building, not both."

"We're not done yet," Marty said. "There's still time. It's only August. There's still money out there."

Knowing Jake was right, the vestry still agreed to go forward with the plan to construct both buildings. They decided to wait until the last minute before deciding to build one or two buildings.

They stood at the same crossroads a month later, despite finding several new donors. "Could we break ground and begin construction, knowing that we might only be able to build one of the two buildings?" Sara asked.

"Begin as if we're building both buildings and then decide at a certain point?" Jake asked. Sara nodded. "I suppose so. The important thing is to pour the foundations before the ground freezes. There's time before you must decide."

"Let's say we have to decide which building to build." Marty interrupted. "Which one would be built?"

"The church," Stanley declared as he hit the table with his fist like a judge with a gavel.

"Hold on, Stanley," Emmett said. "Marty raises a good question. We need to take our time considering the advantages of each. Hopefully, we will be able to build both, but we should have a plan."

The vestry decided to break ground at the end of September. By the groundbreaking ceremony, they would also have a drop-dead decision date for whether they would build one or two buildings. Certain vestry members were convinced they could raise the money in time, but Emmett knew it was impossible. He also knew which building would be first—and who would have to break the news to Marty.

—— 25 ——

CHAPTER

Broken Ground

"**L**ook who's getting all creative," Jake said as he heard Emmett's plan for the groundbreaking. "I've never heard of a groundbreaking where everyone brings a shovel. Usually, it's just the important people."

"Why not?" Emmett said. "Everyone's been important. Plus, the church belongs to us all. It might even be fun."

Jake smiled as he sat across from Emmett in his office.

"What?" Emmett asked.

"Nothing. I just don't think I've heard the word fun come from your mouth, especially about the church."

The groundbreaking ceremony took place on a crisp fall morning. Gathering people to break ground was something

Emmett knew was important. The bulldozers would arrive in the morning, but the dirt belonged to the congregation for now. They had worked hard to reach this moment.

Everyone was asked to bring a shovel. Some brought shovels from home; a few younger children brought plastic spades with matching buckets. Parents tried their best to keep their children from digging in the loosened dirt before the ceremony. Sam had his workers move the granite steps to where the new entrance would be, and Emmett stood at the top to welcome the large crowd.

"In church, we break bread, but this morning we're going to break ground. Like with communion, when we break this ground, the ordinary will become sacred, and Christ will be made present," Emmett paused for a moment. "For a long time, I thought this church belonged to me. I thought it was up to me to make this the church God intended. How silly. How arrogant." Emmett looked out and saw Michael Phillips standing beside Jake. He watched as Jake handed the bishop a shovel. "This is God's church, and all we can do is show up and stick our shovels in the dirt. God will take it from there."

After offering a prayer, Virginia read a lesson from the apostle Paul to the people of Corinth: "For we are God's fellow workers; you are God's field, God's building. According to the grace of God given to me, like a skilled master builder I laid a foundation, and another man is building upon it. Let each man take care how he builds upon it. For no other foundation can anyone lay than that which is laid, which is Jesus Christ. Now if anyone builds on the foundation with gold, silver, precious stones, wood, hay, straw—each man's work will become manifest; for the Day will disclose it, because it will be revealed with fire, and the fire will test what sort of work each one has done. If the work which any man has built on the foundation survives, he will receive a reward. If any man's work is burned up, he will suffer loss, though he himself will be saved, but only as through fire."

Before inviting everyone to grab their shovels and join him at the base of the steps, Emmett offered a response to the reading. "Working together, we've done what many of us never thought possible. This morning, we stand at the threshold of a new church. Yes, we're building two buildings," he said, glancing over at Marty. "God's buildings, but they're not the point. They'll allow us to gather as children of God to worship and serve other children of God. That is what the church has always been about, or at least what it should have been about." Looking out at Jake, he continued. "We've received countless blessings over the last 20 months. We've dug deep and discovered the true foundation of this thing we call the church buried deep beneath our old church. It is on that foundation that we will build our new church."

"It has taken much gold and silver, as Paul put it, but, like the buildings themselves, the gold and silver have been a means to an end. As much as we needed financial support, such generosity only brought us here, to this place, right now. Paul says the builder will be saved only through fire. I would put a different twist on it. We, the people of St. John's, have been saved through fire. Through fire, we have been given new life. As we lift our shovels and dig the dirt, may we celebrate that new life and give thanks to the one who gave it to us in the first place."

Emmett climbed down the steps and invited everyone to come forward. He motioned to Virginia, Jake, and the bishop to stand beside him as everyone took their position along the chalk lines of the church and the parish center. On Sara's cue, the youth began the countdown. People gripped their shovels and did their best to dig deep when the moment came. New England dirt, like its residents, is tough and hard to penetrate, but people did their best. The congregation stood side by side, like a family, digging into the dirt as if it was a garden waiting for seed.

The choir sang the hymn, "The Church's One Foundation," as people stuck their shovels in the dirt. When they finished with the first official dig, everyone cast their shovels aside, clasped hands, and sang:

> The church's one Foundation
> is Jesus Christ her Lord;
> she is His new creation,
> by water and the Word;
> from heav'n He came and sought her
> to be His holy bride;
> with His own blood He bought her,
> and for her life He died.

The sound of trucks awakened Emmett the following day. When he pulled his curtain, he saw a convoy positioning themselves and the workers unloading equipment.

He rushed to awaken Jake. He didn't want him to miss the moment.

"We've got to get going," Sam explained when the two men made it to the common. "The foundation's got to be dug and poured before the ground freezes."

Emmett offered a silent prayer as the engines fired up. It's really happening, he thought. The first layer of dirt folded like an accordion under the bulldozer's blade, revealing many rocks below. Laying a foundation in such soil would be difficult. Emmett watched for as long as he could, but he knew the clock was ticking. He had until the foundations were poured to find the rest of the money.

When Emmett arrived, Marty and the food pantry volunteers were downstairs filling backpacks and artists were upstairs working. The vestry had hired Raj to build the pulpit and lectern, and Jewell and Jessica were working together to design and make the stained-glass windows. With Jewell's mosaic talents and Jessica's painting abilities, they brought the drawings to life. Jake was delighted to learn Jason, the sculptor, had studied stained-glass making in graduate school and was eager to help once they were ready.

Emmett took the list of phone messages and the draft for this week's service leaflet from Alma and was about to get to work when Marty arrived. "Got a minute?" she asked. "I think I've come up with a way to raise money while also making sure the church expands its ministries."

"I'm all ears."

"Last night, I had this idea I think will help us. I want to rent space in the parish hall to nonprofits. In fact, I'd like to rent out the entire second floor to people and organizations who are doing important work. It would generate revenue and add to the activities of the church."

"I love the idea, but we need a building before we can think about renting."

"I know, but rent will help with the costs once we build."

Emmett gave a halfhearted smile.

"You're not having second thoughts, are you? We're still building the church and the parish hall, aren't we?"

"I promise. That's the plan. But we need to find the money before we can guarantee anything."

"While you're finding the money, I'm going to find renters. I spoke to a friend who works for the New England Environmental Society, and she said they'd love to have their office near other nonprofits. Sam said the 12-step central office is looking for space, and I am sure there are others. I'll keep looking while you find the money." Marty started to head back to the pantry before turning back around. "And Emmett, thanks for proving me wrong. I thought when push came to shove, you would side with the folks who are set on only building the church."

Emmett wanted to explain that he wasn't on a side, but Marty was already gone.

The construction was the main topic of conversation around town that fall. When trucks carrying the steel beams drove past the diner, the excitement grew. Donations increased. "People want to be a part of something this exciting," Jake pointed out.

The Steeple People were the first to reach their goal. They hosted a fun run on a Saturday with T-shirts featuring a drawing of the church's steeple. They raised the money needed to give the Revere Bell its new home. The recovery groups took up a special collection at each meeting, and Sam and the choir organized a concert to help raise money for a new pipe organ. Gladys and others organized a garage sale. Although it was not likely to raise the kind of money needed, Emmett appreciated the effort. "Maybe I should sell my collection of presidential signatures," Stanley offered. "I'm sure they're worth a lot."

Emmett was full of gratitude as he sat at the kitchen table, sipping his coffee the next morning. People were giving their all to help the church raise money, and he felt he should too. It wasn't until his grandfather clock struck eight that he knew what he had to offer.

"You're kidding," Mac said when he heard Emmett's plan to sell the clock. "That's your prize possession. Didn't you and Abby buy that on your honeymoon or something?"

"Tenth anniversary."

"You can't part with that," Mac said.

"I can. It's what she would have wanted."

After the foundation was poured and set, the steel beams were lifted into place, and truckloads of granite arrived. The foundation of the parish center was covered to protect it from the winter weather. They hoped to have the roof of the church completed by November 1, All Saints' Day, so they could keep working when it was cold.

"How much time do we have before we have to decide about the parish center?" Emmett asked.

"Spring. Easter, at the latest," Sam said.

During a particularly frigid week, Marty met with Emmett at Maria's to see if she could use the enclosed church as a shelter for the homeless. There was no heat yet, but at least folks would be out of the wind and weather.

"I'd love to, but the city would close us down if they found out."

"They won't. I promise," said Marty.

"Can't risk it," Emmett stated.

"But it's below zero. What harm could it do? I really wish the church would start living the gospel and not just talking about it. The church could be a shelter for people desperate for a place to get in from the cold."

"My hands are tied," Emmett said before excusing himself. Marty remained at the table, taking the last sips of coffee and trying to calm down. It was then she noticed the set of keys Emmett left on the table. They were the keys to the church. At first, she thought Emmett had left them by mistake. Then, she realized he had done it on purpose. Unbelievable, she thought, smiling to herself.

Throughout the winter, Marty and her team focused their efforts on raising money for the parish center. They convinced Maria to start a fundraising campaign for the kitchen. Each donor got a free cup of coffee at the diner if they made a gift. On the wall was a drawing of a large coffee mug, like the thermometers used in other fundraising efforts, and the coffee mug slowly filled as they moved toward a $50,000 goal.

Work at the church seemed to slow once the walls were up, but Jake assured Emmett that progress was still being made. People were eager to go inside, but they had to wait until spring to gather on the lawn to watch the Revere Bell being lifted to its new home. It felt as if the entire town had come to watch. After a long wait, the familiar sound rang over the town of Webster once again. People cheered and embraced one another.

Despite all the efforts, Emmett could tell they would not have enough money by Easter. Although they had far exceeded every fundraising effort in St. John's history, it was clear they wouldn't be able to build the parish center.

"There must be something we can do," Virginia said before the vestry voted.

"We could take a loan," Terrance suggested, although he knew St. John's had a strict rule against borrowing money. Simon suggested keeping the space in the mill to make it a ministry center, but nothing would lessen the disappointment of not building the parish center.

"Who's going to break the news to Marty?" Virginia asked.

"I will," said Emmett after the vote. "I'm the one who promised, and I need to be the one to break that promise."

Emmett went to find Marty the next morning. She was unpacking a recent delivery to the food pantry when he knocked on the door. Without saying a word, she knew what he was there to say.

"I knew it," she said, shaking her head.

"I wish I had better news. It wasn't from a lack of effort."

"No, but you promised."

"I promised we'd build both if we raised enough money. We've raised over $5 million. We don't have what we need to build the parish center. We're $1.7 million short. We'll have to wait."

"You chose the church over the ministry," Marty said with a growl as she turned away. Emmett knew better than to respond. "I can't say I'm surprised," she added, "just disappointed because I thought you had changed."

—26—

CHAPTER

Death

Jake had breakfast ready, but Emmett was apparently sleeping in. The night before, he had looked weary. The conversation with Marty had worn him out, he said, and Emmett asked Jake if he would do the dinner dishes so he could retire early.

Jake ate his breakfast and put Emmett's in the oven to stay warm, but after an hour, he became worried. They had two meetings later that morning, so Jake went upstairs to check on Emmett.

Standing outside Emmett's door, Jake leaned close to see if he could hear him stirring. He knocked softly but still no response. Turning the handle slowly, he entered the dark room.

The light from around the curtains helped him navigate toward the bed. The room seemed unusually still. Something was wrong.

"Emmett?" he said as he approached. He heard no breathing. Even in the dark, Jake could see Emmett's mouth draped open, and his hand rested on his chest. Surprised by the chill of his hand, Jake realized Emmett was gone.

"No, no, no!" he said, shaking his friend as if it would revive him. He sat on the edge of the bed. He knew he should get up and call someone, but Jake didn't move. He sat in the dark with his friend.

Eventually, he went down the stairs and sat at the kitchen table. Workers hammered on the roof of the church, and a truck arrived with another load of stone. Don't they know the rector's dead, Jake said to himself. He knew he should call Mac and Virginia, but he wanted the world to stay the same for a minute longer. Abby's painting reminded Jake of the porch of their cabin and its incredible view. He hoped Emmett was there now, with Abby, holding hands and looking at an endless view.

Jake wept.

"Yes?" Mac answered.

"Mac, it's Jake. I don't know how to say this," he paused. "Emmett's dead."

"What?"

"He died last night in his sleep."

Jake continued to supply details, but Mac had long hung up. He pulled into the driveway minutes later.

"I don't believe this," Mac said as he stormed into the kitchen. "What the hell happened?"

"No idea," Jake said as he offered Mac some coffee.

"No, thanks," Mac excused himself to go upstairs. Jake remained in the kitchen and waited. Once Mac finally returned, the two sat at the table and waited for Virginia.

"I figured he'd always be around," Mac sighed. "That he'd outlive me. In fact, I used to joke about what he'd say at my funeral." Jake smiled pensively and looked out at the church.

"We talked about that," Jake shared. "Emmett said he never wanted to do it. Hoped you'd outlive him. Guess he got his wish."

Mac looked away. "What now?"

"What Emmett would want...finish the church," Jake said with certainty, then added, "Won't be the same, though."

News of Emmett's death traveled quickly. Virginia burst into tears when she walked into the kitchen, and the three of them took turns calling vestry members. Sam had the flag on top of the crane at the church lowered to half-mast. There was a hush in the usually boisterous diner, and Maria excused herself more than a few times throughout the day to be alone. Jake noticed Sara standing by herself in front of the church, as if holding vigil, later that afternoon.

"No," Marty cried when Jake told her. "He couldn't have. He was just here, meeting with me." Marty looked away as she recalled their heated conversation. "I'm afraid I said some pretty ugly things."

"He understood," Jake said, trying to comfort her. "He knew the parish center was important to you. Because of you, it had become important to him. He hated that you doubted that. Making the decision to put it on hold was harder than you know. He told me just last night that he'd find a way to make good on his promise."

Virginia called the bishop, and they planned a meeting to discuss funeral arrangements. "It's customary for the bishop to preside over the funeral of any member of the clergy," he told her.

"Hell no," Mac said when she told him.

"It's customary," she said.

"I don't care. Emmett couldn't stand the man. It's not what he would have wanted," Mac said. Jake distracted Mac by focusing his attention on what was needed to keep the building on track while Virginia and others planned the funeral. Later that week, Virginia asked Jake and Mac to meet her for breakfast at Maria's. Mac hoped to convince her to keep the bishop out of it, but he failed. Virginia told Mac the funeral would involve the bishop. "But he won't be preaching," she said with a coy smile as she sipped her coffee.

"That's a relief," said Mac. "Who will?"

"You."

"Me? Are you nuts?"

"No one knew him better. It's either you or the bishop. You choose."

Mac scowled at Virginia. She had cornered him, and Jake sat back, enjoying the show. "I need some air," he growled after agreeing to speak. No one saw him at the diner until the funeral, although Jake spotted him early one morning wandering the construction site.

"It would have been nice if we could have had the service in the new church," Sara said as she stood with Simon, waiting to hand out programs. They'd both gone to the cabin the day before and picked wildflowers for the altar, something Emmett had done for Abby's funeral. The artists helped the altar guild, and the choir planned to sing one of Emmett's favorite anthems. Virginia had asked as many people as possible to participate.

Someone placed flowers on the stairs of the new church site. Although no one said a word, everyone wondered how they'd carry on without Emmett.

The sanctuary filled early. When Mac arrived in a suit, Sara and Simon took a second look. Gladys showed him where he would sit during the service, and Virginia was assigned to assist the bishop.

"I am Resurrection, and I am Life," the bishop read as he processed into the silent sanctuary at the grist mill. "Whoever has faith in me shall have life, even though he die."

Jake, processing beside the bishop, continued. "And everyone who has life, and has committed himself to me in faith, shall not die for ever."

"As for me," read Sam, "I know that my Redeemer lives and that at the last he will stand upon the earth. After my awaking, he will raise me up; and in my body I shall see God."

Sara was next. "I myself shall see, and my eyes behold him who is my friend and not a stranger. For none of us has life in himself, and none becomes his own master when he dies."

The bishop climbed the steps onto the stage as he completed the readings. "For if we have life, we are alive in the Lord, and if we die, we die in the Lord. So, then, whether we live or die, we are the Lord's possession. Happy from now on are those who die in the Lord! So it is, says the Spirit, for they rest from their labors."

The congregation sang, "O God, Our Help in Ages Past," one of Emmett's favorite hymns, then Virginia read the first lesson from the Bible Emmett had found in the ashes of the church. It still smelled of smoke. "Do not let your hearts be troubled," she read, her voice trembling. "Believe in God, believe also in me. In my Father's house there are many dwelling places. If it were not so, would I have told you that I go to prepare a place for you."

Marty read the Beatitudes, words Emmett suggested be written above the kitchen in the parish hall. Trey read about the two sons who were asked to work in their father's vineyard, one of which eventually obeyed. Mac cleared his throat and fidgeted in his seat as his moment approached.

"You all know I'm not much of a public speaker," he began. "I'm not much of a public anything, but Emmett had a knack for getting me to do stuff I didn't want to do." The congregation laughed. "I see, by your reaction, I'm not alone. Maybe that's what his job was—to get us to do stuff."

"I know I am supposed to stand up here and tell you all the things Emmett did during his life, but none of that seems important to me this morning. With him gone, I'm more interested in who he was than what he did."

Mac paused and got a grin across his face. "As I thought about Emmett these past few days, I kept returning to the moment we were standing on the street looking at the church burn. Like the rest of us, he had grabbed his coat and ran to the church. But Emmett didn't change into his clothes first, so he came with his pajamas sticking out from under his jacket. They were Disney pajamas, *The Lion King*, to be exact, which still makes me laugh. I remember the look on Jake's face when he saw them. Who knew the rector of St. John's wore such things? Every time after that, when I saw Emmett dressed in robes for services and heard him speak with that pontifical tone he had when conducting services, I thought of the man in the Disney pajamas. I know they were gifts from his niece and nephew, sitting over there, now adults, but something makes me wonder if Emmett didn't fancy himself the mystic of the pride lands."

"I know Emmett was our priest, the senior minister of the diocese, but it was the minister in pajamas, the boy within that priest, I loved the most. With a father like his and expectations like those placed upon him, I'm sure it was hard to keep that boy alive. Although Emmett loved the ministry, I think he sometimes missed the boy within. What we do can sometimes get in the way of who we truly are." Mac stopped for a moment, cleared his throat, and then continued.

"Something happened the night our church burned, though. I can't put my finger on what it was exactly, but it was as if the boy within the man started to return. I saw it when Emmett lifted his hands and explained what he thought the church was all about," Mac said as he lifted his hands and formed the church with the people inside. "I saw it in the way he interacted with the artists upstairs. It was like he was looking over a fence longingly. I think his love of you wackos, as you call yourselves, was evident when he bought your banners, Jewell, and had them hung for all to see here in the mill."

"But the moment things really changed was a scene I didn't get to see. I wish I had. I would never have let him live it down. One morning, Emmett decided to go down to the river. But he ended up falling in. That same day, he reached over and pulled the lever, which caused the water to turn the wheel." Mac looked over toward the wheel and paused. "That was not the Emmett I had known before. It was like he had rediscovered his adventurous child. His eyes opened wide that day, his heart wider still. From then on, it was as if I was watching my friend become someone new, someone marvelous."

"I know I should be more impressed with his achievements, his role in the church and the diocese, but it's this change I celebrate most this morning. It was as if he became a new creation, and we were all invited to watch—or come along. Maybe we still can." Mac looked as if he was going to say something else but decided against it. He returned to his seat instead.

The bishop invited the congregation to rise and sing "My Song is Love Unknown."

> My song is love unknown,
> My Savior's love to me;
> Love to the loveless shown,
> That they might lovely be.
> O who am I,
> That for my sake
> My Lord should take
> Frail flesh, and die?

Before communion, the bishop stood for announcements, then added words of his own. "Many of you probably know that Emmett and I were classmates in seminary. We met on the first day. I'm not sure when it began, but somewhere along the way, he and I became competitors. You name it, we saw it as an opportunity to outdo the other. Maybe the rivalry pushed us to achieve, but it also got in the way of what could have been a meaningful friendship. A few years ago, we both ran for bishop. The rivalry took on new proportions, and I'm sorry to say, the result was a permanent wedge between us." The bishop looked over toward the windows before continuing.

"I have a confession to make this morning. When Emmett came to me after the church burned, looking for money to help St. John's rebuild, I refused. There were reasons, but the one never mentioned was that I was jealous. Part of me, the part

I'm embarrassed to talk about, didn't want him to succeed in rebuilding the church."

"It's scandalous, I know, but it's time I admit it and set things right. As I understand it, you've raised enough money for the church but not the parish center. As bishop, I'd like to offer you an interest-free loan for the remaining money to complete the two buildings. I should have done this while Emmett was alive, but I am doing it now. I do so not for your gratitude but your forgiveness."

The bishop's offer was all people could talk about at the reception. Some were ecstatic over the possibility of completing the whole project, but others felt it was too late for such a gesture.

"Feels like a deal with the devil," Mac grumbled as a pudgy man in a tattered sport coat interrupted.

"Excuse me, but I was wondering if you could direct me to whoever is in charge."

Mac refrained from pointing to the urn full of ashes sitting on the altar. "The tall woman beside the bishop is the senior warden. She's who you're looking for."

"Who do you think that is?" Mac asked as the stranger made his way toward Virginia.

"Beats me," Jake replied. The two watched as the man handed Virginia a business card.

Resurrection

J ake and Mac attended the construction site meeting with Sam and the foreman to revise the schedule since they could only afford to build the church building. Despite the bishop's offer, the vestry had decided to wait until the parish could raise the necessary funds. While they talked, they could hear someone trying to open the large front doors. When Mac went to help, Virginia came rushing in.

"Wait!" she called out, her voice echoing off the unfinished walls. She rushed down what would be the center aisle of the church. "Wait," she said with both hands lifted like a traffic cop. The group turned in her direction. "Change in plans," she announced with a smile.

The group waited as she caught her breath. "Last week, after Emmett's funeral, a man introduced himself to me. Seems he is Emmett's lawyer. Lives up near the cabin. He's been a friend of Emmett and Abby's since they bought the place."

"He said he needed to meet with me to discuss Emmett's will. So, I went and met with him this morning. Turns out Emmett revised his will in last few weeks and didn't tell anybody," Virginia stopped, the dramatic pause pulling in the group. "He left his place in the mountains to St. John's."

Mac stepped closer to Virginia. "You're kidding."

"I'm not. He left some of his other assets to his niece and nephew, but he didn't have children, and the church was his family. He figured we could decide what to do with it." The group looked at one another as they thought about the cabin. Virginia continued. "Apparently, there's already been an offer to purchase it, and the lawyer wants us to make a decision as soon as possible."

Mac took a few steps away from the group as he thought about the cabin and what it meant to Emmett. "As long as I'm living," he could hear Emmett say, "I'll never sell the place."

"Do you think the church should sell it?" Jake asked.

"How much?" asked Mac.

"Two million!" Virginia replied.

"Really?" asked Sam. "That's enough to..."

"Finish the church and the parish hall," Virginia said. "I know."

"What did you tell him?" Mac asked.

"I said I needed to take the offer to the vestry, but I don't see how we could refuse."

Mac looked around at the unfinished church and thought about the parish center. "I hate to think of selling the cabin, but there's something wonderful about the cabin making it possible to finish all this," he said, looking around the church. "His final gift to this place."

"Almost," Virginia said with a grin as she walked over to Mac. "There's one more gift. Emmett left this for you." Virginia reached out and placed Emmett's signet ring in Mac's hand.

"I don't believe it," Mac said, closing his hand around his friend's cherished ring.

Jake turned to Sam: "I'd say you need to rework the schedule. Looks like we're back to our original plan."

The vestry agreed to sell the cabin, and everyone cheered when Virginia made the announcement on Sunday. Sam brought in additional workers to work on the parish center so they could catch up construction there with the church. "We won't be able to finish them at the same time," Sam pointed out, "but we'll do what we can to move things along quickly."

No one cared about when the parish center would be completed. They were just happy that it was going to be built, especially Marty. She began crying when she heard the news and spent the rest of the day wandering around what would be the new parish center. "You kept your promise, Emmett," she said, wiping away tears. "I'm sorry I ever doubted you."

The diocese was eager to send an interim minister to St. John's after the funeral, but Virginia did her best to stall them. They hoped to make do until the church was completed. Parishioners took turns leading worship, and it reminded everyone of the home churches they started after the fire. Virginia invited parishioners to tell their faith journeys as the sermons. The congregation continued to grow, and the Wednesday night dinners had become so crowded that they had to expand to two seatings.

The first window, the creation window, was installed later that month. Jessica had combined the biblical account of creation with science by arranging seven circles in the window, one for each day in the biblical narrative, surrounded by a dramatic swirl of blue and white depicting the Holy Spirit moving over creation. There were stars and planets, mountains and valleys, streams and oceans, and people of all ages and races.

"I hope it's not too dramatic," Jessica said to the group.

"Not a chance," Trey responded. "I think it's cool."

"Capturing God creating the universe was bound to be dramatic," Sara added.

They held a brief service of dedication before the window was lifted into place. A similar service was held for each window as it arrived. Mac sent a champagne cork flying through the church after each dedication—carefully aiming away from the glass!

The slate floor was installed a month before the chairs arrived, and Raj brought the lectern he'd built soon after. Instead of the traditional eagle, the lectern featured a dove with extended wings holding the Bible. Four columns made up the base, representing each of the gospels, and the 66 shields around the edge represented all of the books of the Bible. On either side of the lectern were small shelves that could be pulled out to hold a candle. "I thought they would come in handy for your Lessons and Carols service on Christmas Eve," he explained.

The organ installation began in early September and was being tuned when Raj delivered the pulpit. It was placed on the right, across from the lectern. On each panel of the pulpit were carved images from scripture: loaves and fishes, Jacob's ladder, animals climbing onto the ark, and Jesus calming the storm. "It's like looking at the Bible," Trey commented. Raj smiled proudly.

After Thanksgiving, Raj brought the final piece he was asked to build: the altar. Unlike the old church, the altar was put in the center of the crossing instead of facing the far wall as it had in the old church. Mac wasn't sure Emmett would have approved: "He was a stickler about the traditional altar facing away from the congregation."

"This was his idea," Raj said. "He specifically asked that I design it to be placed here. It's made from wood we got from his property at the cabin." Mac drew close and rubbed his hand along its smooth surface.

"The grain makes it look like a work of art," Simon pointed out. Jake remembered the kitchen table and Abby's coffee rings that Emmett circled with his finger.

"I suppose this is as good a time as any," said Jason, who lifted a large chalice and patten in the air. "Emmett wanted something out of the dirt for the new church, something to complement the fancy silver. So we used the dirt and clay to mold the vessels for communion."

Tom followed his fellow artist and presented the candlesticks he'd sculpted out of metal from the old railings from the church entrance. The group stood back and admired the altar, pulpit, lectern, chalice, patten, and candlesticks.

"We should have communion," Virginia said in passing.

"I was hoping you might feel that way," said Jake. "That's why I asked Gladys to bring these." Lifting a loaf of bread and bottle of wine, Jake invited the others to draw near.

"But there's no priest," Gladys said.

"I know," said Jake, "but I think Jesus would be okay with us having communion anyway. I think he'd love that we're celebrating communion together like this."

Mac tore away the last of the packing paper around the altar while Gladys and others prepared the table. "We don't have any altar linens," Gladys pointed out, which caused Jake to remove his red-and-black checkered jacket and place it on the altar.

"There you go," he said to Gladys, who looked unnerved.

"Who's going to lead us?" Simon asked, and everyone looked toward Virginia.

"Not me," she said as she nodded at Jake.

"Let's do it together," he said. "I'll start, but don't blame me if I mess up the words. I know how you Episcopalians are about your words." He added with a smile.

Standing at the altar with everyone gathered in a circle around him, Jake began. "Long ago, Jesus sat with his disciples, knowing his time was coming to an end. He reached for bread and lifted it up for everyone to see. He gave thanks to God before breaking it and handing it to his disciples. 'This is my body,' he said. 'Take and eat it and know that I am with you, and in you, through this bread.'" Jake lifted the loaf of bread and broke it in half and handed each half to the people standing on either side of him, saying, "Christ is present, now and always."

Sara took the chalice with both hands and lifted it as she remembered Emmett doing every week. "Like the bread, Jesus took the wine and lifted it up for the disciples to see. 'This is my blood,' he said, 'shed for you and everyone. Drink it, knowing you're forgiven. No matter what others say, no matter what rules or conditions people try to put between you and this wine. You are forgiven, now and always.'"

Sara offered the chalice to Jake, who drank from it and passed it to Trey. "You are forgiven, now and always," each person said as they passed the wine around the circle. Trey passed the chalice to his father.

When everyone had received the bread and wine, they said the Lord's Prayer and sang "Day by Day," a simple hymn everyone knew. Because it was short, they sang it twice:

> Day by Day
> Dear Lord, three things we pray
> To see thee more clearly
> To love thee more dearly,
> And follow thee more nearly
> Day by day.

When they finished, they greeted one another as if meeting for the first time. As they left the church, they looked over at the frame of the parish center. "I wish Emmett was here," Virginia sighed. "He would have loved this."

"I'm sure he's watching every bit of it," Mac said. "It's because of him that we are able to complete the building."

The final window installed was the rose window. It had taken the longest to design and construct, and this was the window Jake had kept secret, much to the frustration of others in the congregation. The installation took over a week, and only the workers were permitted in the church while it was being put in place. A curtain was hoisted over the window before its dedication, and the group was invited to be there at 5:30 sharp, just before the autumn sunset.

Jake stood on the scaffolding beneath the rose window. Sara stood beside him. "This moment is not as we planned or hoped." He began. "Emmett was supposed to be standing where I am. But I know he is here in spirit." Jake turned to the side and lifted his arm, pointing to the window behind him. "The rose window is unlike the other windows, and Emmett was intrigued with this one in particular, so it was difficult to keep what you are about to see a surprise."

"As you remember, when we began this process, we met in the ashes. We searched for pieces of the church, and this woman beside me began looking for pieces of the windows. I tried to convince her it was a futile exercise, that the pieces would be hard to find and impossible to use, but she was determined. Slowly, her pile grew. It took hundreds of hours of combing through ash, but in the end, we had enough for a window. Together we decided the pieces should be used for the rose window, and here it is." Jake took one string, Sara took the other, and, with a nod, they pulled them at the same time. The sheet fell, revealing what they called "The Resurrection Window." Made up of thousands of shards of glass from the old windows, the rose window was a collage of color. Unlike the other windows, there was no scene or picture, only pieces of glass cut like diamonds to capture the light. The afternoon sun made the window electric.

"The colors move from dark to light as you journey toward the center," Jewell explained.

"Looks like a mosaic," one person said.

"I reminds me of a visual labyrinth," said Jewell. "It represents the spiritual journey, one in which we travel out of darkness into light."

"It's like your church sign used to say, 'Light shines in the darkness, but the darkness has not overcome it,'" said Jake.

"It's also a reminder of what we've been through," someone added.

"And who we are," said Jewell. "Like the glass, we're all broken but capable of coming together into a glorious piece of art."

"I love it," Virginia said. "And Emmett would have, too."

Jake gathered The Designers together two days before the church dedication on Christmas Eve. He wanted those who had played a significant role in the design and building of the church to share a moment alone to celebrate their years of work. Glasses of champagne waited, and once everyone assembled, he proposed a toast. "Emmett would not have wanted us to miss this moment," he said. "He would have wanted us to stand here and take in this marvelous church. I can't help but see each of you in this building. Like those shards of glass in the rose window, there are tiny pieces of you in this place. Tonight I want to pause and say, 'You did it!' Here's to you."

"And here's to God," Sara added. "We never could have pulled this off without divine help."

"Hear, hear!" the others said as they lifted their glasses.

"Wait a minute," Stanley interrupted. "I don't know why I never noticed it before, but something is missing." The group looked around to see what was missing before Stanley shouted, "A cross! We forgot the cross."

"No, we didn't," Jake said with a sheepish grin. With a nod, Mac walked toward a transept door. "Give me a hand," he said to Simon, and the two returned carrying an enormous, dark cross. Unlike traditional crosses, this had four arms, one pointing in each direction of the church.

"I made it with Raj's help," Mac said as Sam attached the cross to waiting cables. "Jake designed it so that you'll see the cross wherever you sit.

"Smells like smoke," Trey pointed out.

"It should," Mac replied with delight. "It's made from the charred beams of the old church."

Sara began sobbing as Sam hoisted the cross above the altar. The rest stood in silence as they looked up at the cross. Thoughts of all they had been through filled the sacred space. After a few moments, Jake invited everyone to join him outside before leaving. There was one more thing he wanted to show them. A gentle snow had begun to fall, and people held on to one another as they walked outside.

"What about the sign?" Stanley asked Jake. "Will it be there in time for the dedication?"

"Yes, Stanley, it will," said Jake. "It's being installed tomorrow morning."

"Good. Like the old one?" he asked.

"Just like it."

"With the quotation?"

"It'll include a quotation from John's Gospel. Don't worry."

When they were halfway down the path, Jake told them to turn around. Jake intentionally left the lights on so they could see the church illuminated in the night.

"Oh my," Virginia sighed.

"The windows look like jewels," Sara added.

"If Emmett was here," said Trey, "he'd say, 'There's a sermon in that.'"

"Indeed," said Jake.

CHAPTER

Life

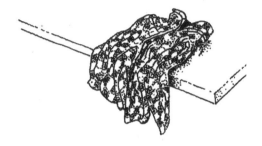

Mac waited before joining the others at the church. The signet ring Emmett left him dangled from the mirror in his truck. He took his time walking from the large new parking lot to the finished church and stopped beside the almost-completed parish center. Despite the cold, he remained there for a while.

Dark and quiet, the parish center sat in contrast to the church like an unopened gift. The walls and roof were erected, but the center wouldn't be complete until Easter. Mac tried to envision the name above the entrance: The Emmett and Abby Hodges Parish Center. The vestry had unanimously voted to name the building in their honor, and no one was more pleased about that than Mac. "There you go, you two," he said softly. "There you go."

The covered walkway connecting the parish center to the church was in place. He remembered Jake describing how it would connect the two buildings literally and figuratively. Even in the dark, Mac saw the vision.

The church looked like a house ready to host a party. The steeple was illuminated by lights Stanley and Gladys Fitzpatrick had donated. "We want the cross to be visible for all to see, even at night," Mac remembered Stanley saying proudly at one of the early design meetings. Below the steeple was the Gothic church with its cruciform shape and stained-glass windows. The granite donated by Sam and his father made the new building look as if it had been there for years. The Revere Bell was ringing, inviting the congregation to gather below. The service would be a combination of church consecration and Christmas Eve service.

A church consecration is intended to bless the building, Mac learned. It begins with the bishop and congregation standing at the church doors. The bishop knocks on the doors three times with a crozier, and the doors are then opened. The congregation enters, some of whom carry items like the Bible, altar hangings, and communion pieces that are later blessed as they are put in place. To dedicate the church during the Christmas Eve service was unusual, but the bishop knew better than to point that out.

Mac looked up at the windows and marveled at the colors and details. Standing below the nativity window, Mac could see Mary and Joseph in the stable with Jesus and the shepherds kneeling beside the manger. Angels crowned the window with wings spread wide. Those in the stable couldn't see the angels, but they were there. Mac hoped in some way his friend was looking down on them that night.

The youth waited by the fire pit, and the artists were strolling the perimeter of the church, looking at Jessica's windows before the service. Everyone else stood huddled together. It was an enormous crowd, and Mac could feel the excitement as he approached. Only one person was missing.

When he noticed Stanley standing by the new church sign, waving his arms while talking to Virginia and Sam, he went to investigate. "What's going on?" he asked.

"The sign. It's wrong," Stanley protested.

"It looks fine to me," Mac said. "Just like the old one."

"No, it is not," Stanley stated adamantly. "The quotation's wrong."

Mac looked closely. "And the word became flesh and dwelt among us," he read out loud.

"See?"

"See what? Wasn't that what was on the old sign?"

"No," Stanley said as if it were obvious. "It used to be, 'The light shines in the darkness, and the darkness has not overcome it.'" Stanley shook his head in disgust.

"Don't blame me," said Mac. "Jake was the one who insisted on being in charge of the sign."

"Where is he?" Stanley asked as he looked over Mac's shoulder. "Has anyone seen him?" No one had.

"I'm sure he's here," said Mac, "We can ask him about it after the service. I wouldn't worry about the sign. Maybe it was time for a new quotation." Mac shrugged and walked over to join the others by the steps.

"But it's wrong," Stanley called out.

Mac scanned the crowd for Jake but didn't see his familiar red-and-black-checkered jacket anywhere. It was unlike Jake to be missing, especially on a night like this. Mac asked Sara. She said she hadn't seen him all day. Virginia said she hadn't seen him since that morning, when he headed over to install the sign.

"He installed it?" Mac asked,

"Said he wanted to do it himself," Virginia replied before joining the bishop at the top of the stairs. Mac was grateful not to feel so much resentment toward the bishop. His apology at Emmett's funeral and the fact he had asked to use Emmett's walking stick as his crozier that night helped to diminish Mac's disdain. The bishop waited for the last chime from the Revere Bell to float into the air before beginning the service. The crowd hushed, and the bishop lifted Emmett's stick and knocked on the door three times.

"Let the doors be opened," Bishop Phillips cried out. Simon and another usher opened the two large Gothic doors. "Peace be to this house, and to all who enter here. In the Name of the Father, and of the Son, and of the Holy Spirit."

"Amen," said the congregation as they entered the church.

The organ began an elaborate introduction of "O Come, All Ye Faithful," and the people entered the church like children on Christmas morning. Even for those who had been a part of the construction process, it felt as if they were seeing the church for the first time. Everyone could sing the familiar hymn without the hymnals, and the joyful sound filled the space.

> O come, all ye faithful,
> joyful and triumphant,
> O come ye, O come ye to Bethlehem.
> Come and behold him,
> born the king of angels.
> O come let us adore him,
> O come let us adore him,
> O come let us adore him,
> Christ the Lord.

Jewell's banners from the mill now hung from the rafters. The church was decorated just like the old church, and the wreaths, garlands, and holly made it look and smell like Christmas. A candle sat on every windowsill. Trey and another acolyte lit each one as people took their seats. Some thought the church should have electric candles, given what had happened, but eventually, everyone agreed to use real candles. "But for God's sake," Mac said with a bellow, "let's always remember to put them out!" Jake had asked Sam's son and daughter to turn on the Christmas tree lights at the end of the hymn.

> Sing, choirs of angels,
> sing in exultation,
> sing, all ye citizens of heav'n above:
> "Glory to God,
> all glory in the highest!"

It wasn't until Mac was about to take his seat that he saw it. A red-and-black-checkered jacket was draped on the altar.

> Yea, Lord, we greet thee,
> born this happy morning,
> Jesus, to thee be all glory giv'n;
> Word of the Father,
> begotten, not created.
> O come let us adore him,
> O come let us adore him,
> O come let us adore him,
> Christ the Lord.

After the opening prayer, Virginia came forward with the Bible and placed it on the lectern. Sam and Jenny Cutler walked down the aisle next carrying a pitcher of water, which they poured into the baptismal font they had donated in honor of their children. Although they were taking things slowly, Jenny had invited Sam back into their home.

When Gladys and Jewell approached the altar with the linens, they saw Jake's jacket. Gladys looked around, unsure what to do. Mac took the jacket so they could dress the altar before Jason placed the communion set on it. The bishop came and stood behind the altar and offered a prayer of dedication. "We give you thanks, O God, for the gifts of your people, and for the work of many hands, which have beautified this place and furnished it for the celebration of your holy mysteries. Accept and bless all we have done, and grant that in these earthly things we may behold the order and beauty of things heavenly, through Jesus Christ our Lord. Amen."

The congregation sang "Angels We Have Heard on High" before different people took to the lectern, offering the traditional readings for the Christmas Eve service. The bishop read John's Prologue, as Emmett always had, and delivered one of his best sermons Mac could remember, entitled "God with Us." In it, the bishop recalled the dark days before Christ's birth when the people felt abandoned by God and longed for the promised Messiah. He spoke of the babe in the manger and how Jesus was nothing like the messiah people expected. "Those in the inn," he said, "did not see what those in the stable did." He also described the way Christ was with people during his three-year ministry. "He was with them in their boats and on the shore, in their homes and the synagogue, at candle-lit tables and rustic campfires." Mac squeezed Jake's jacket as the bishop continued. "What I love most about Jesus," the bishop said, "is that he met the people where they were and spoke a language they could understand. He taught them, and he healed them, but most of all, he helped them feel God's presence. In their darkness, he brought light; in their sorrow, he brought joy, and in their despair, he brought hope."

Mac looked over at Sam, who was sitting with his family. He saw Trey sitting in his robes behind the altar and Jewell sitting beside Gladys.

"No doubt, the disciples must have been distraught after Jesus was gone. As scripture describes it, they were gathered in a room when a mighty wind, a *ruach* as they taught us in seminary, blew through the room, and suddenly the disciples were given what we now know is the Holy Spirit. In that wind and in that fellowship, the disciples felt God's presence. It was as if he were right there beside them, still."

The bishop paused for a moment, then looked out at the congregation.

"I must tell you, that's how it feels to be gathered with you in this sacred space tonight. God is with us tonight as he has been through the turmoil of the last three years. God was with us on that Christmas morning long ago. He was with you that Christmas three years ago when flames consumed the church, with you as you sifted through ashes, asked for help, wrote checks, and designed and built this magnificent church and parish center. God is with us tonight; even if we can't see him, he's here. The Gospel of John reminds us that light has come into the world and not destroyed it, and tonight we celebrate that the Word became flesh and dwelt among us. It happened way back when, and it's happening now. Thanks be to God."

Mac remained in his seat throughout the rest of the service. Holding Jake's jacket, he watched as everyone held their candles and sang "Silent Night," then stood to sing "Joy to the World." When the service was over, Mac remained until the church was empty. "Merry Christmas," he said like a prayer to Emmett.

"And thanks, Jake," he added, "wherever you are. Thanks for everything." He stood and went to join the others outside and found Stanley and Gladys at the bottom of the steps.

"Merry Christmas, you two," he said.

"Merry Christmas, Mac," they said in unison.

After beginning down the path to his car, Mac stopped and turned around. "You know, Stanley, I'm not so sure the sign's wrong, after all. I think Jake knew exactly what the sign was supposed to say."

Study Questions

Chapter 1: Christmas Eve

1. In what ways is Emmett "a minister in search of a sermon?" Is he just looking for a Christmas sermon, or is he searching for something more?

2. St. John's has become Emmett's spiritual home. What makes it so? Why is it important to have a sacred space? What is the danger of having a sacred space?

3. *Ruach* is a fancy word for a mighty wind and was used to describe God's presence for the Hebrew people. Have you ever felt God's presence? Have you ever felt God's absence?

4. Emmett leaves his prepared sermon and goes off script. It is not what people expected to hear, or what they wanted to hear, but it made them think, as Mac points out. Have you ever gone off script? Have you ever voiced doubts about your faith? What do you suppose God makes of such doubts?

5. If you gave a Christmas sermon, what would be your message?

Chapter 2: Christmas

1. What would you do if what you cared about most was taken away? What would you do, and who would you be, if your (marriage, career, family relationships, church) burned to the ground?

2. The people of St. John's stand together watching the church burn. On Christmas morning, Emmett says maybe having each other is enough. What does he mean? Do you agree?

3. How is Emmett's sermon on Christmas morning different from the one he gives the night before?

4. Jake arrives after the service and invites anyone to "come have breakfast." Is it an invitation to the diner or something more? Has such an invitation ever been made in the gospels? (Hint: Look at John 21:1-14)

5. Emmett refers to the gathering as a eucharistic feast. What could he mean by that? What do you make of Jake offering Emmett toast after he sits down?

Chapter 3: This Is It

1. How would you feel if you were the one responsible for the church losing its insurance, particularly after a fire? How would you handle the guilt or responsibility?

2. While talking to Jake about the future, Emmett reaches out and pulls dead leaves from the plant on the kitchen table. Why is it important to pull such

leaves from a plant? How might that also be important for Emmett (and the parish)?

3. Jake's specialty is restoration. How does that differ from building from scratch? When it says in scripture, "Behold, I make all things new," is that restoration or building from scratch?

4. Can you imagine looking out (literally or metaphorically) and seeing your life's work in ruins? How would you respond?

5. In the end, Emmett decides to offer his resignation to the vestry. What led him to this decision? What do you imagine he will say in the letter to the vestry? Who would you be if you lost your job?

Chapter 4: An Undeserved Gift

1. Confession is an important part of the spiritual journey, but it's difficult. In your experience, what role has confession, or owning up to something, played?

2. Emmett feels relief after writing his letter of resignation. Why? Before entering the house, he has second thoughts. Why?

3. What do you suppose Emmett is thinking about while he waits for the vestry to respond? Why is Emmett surprised by the vestry's decision?

4. Their forgiveness is an undeserved gift. Why is this important for Emmett to experience?

5. How is experiencing forgiveness different from preaching about it? Have you ever experienced such an undeserved gift?

Chapter 5: Bringing It Home

1. Emmett is torn between the past and the future. Looking out at the ruins of the church, he has no choice but to start over. Why is this significant for him (and anyone on a spiritual journey)?

2. In what ways is the idea of home churches "risky," as Virginia put it, for St. John's?

3. What could be gained by having home churches? What could be lost?

4. Facing the financial reality is difficult, but essential, for the parish. When have you faced something hard in your spiritual journey?

5. Mac confronts Emmett and tells him he needs to go see the bishop. Emmett doesn't want to, but he knows Mac is right. Do you have anyone in your life who will (or has) told you hard truths? Is there a person or situation you fear facing?

Chapter 6: On Our Own

1. Emmett and Michael Phillips have history. What do you think is at the heart of their competitive wranglings?

2. In what ways did they come to seminary from different worlds? What were the advantages and disadvantages of each?

3. It has been said that what bothers us about someone is what bothers us about ourselves. Is that true with Emmett and Michael?

4. How does their rivalry continue in the bishop's office? Is it a divine encounter or a worldly feud? According to Mac, the bishop's refusal to help is a good thing. How so?

5. Why is Emmett's comment about being alone such an unusual thing for a minister to say?

Chapter 7: Communion

1. Emmett celebrates communion on the kitchen counter. Communion is a sacrament. What was he taught about sacraments in seminary?

2. What is it about plastic containers that troubles Emmett? What does he mean when he feels his ministry has become plastic? How has serving communion become like fast food?

3. Abby always reminded Emmett that the interruptions were his ministry. By whom is Emmett interrupted? How are they his ministry?

4. What is Marty Starnes's main concern? How is this challenging or threatening to Emmett? What objections or excuses does he offer when responding to Marty?

5. What does St. John's history of outreach say about the parish (and its rector)?

Chapter 8: New Wineskins

1. A grist mill is the last place Emmett imagines for the church. Why might it be a fitting setting for the people of St. John's?

2. What does Emmett learn about his parishioners as they come together to turn the grist mill into worship space?

3. How do the artists react to having a church in the mill? In what ways do they help the church get ready?

4. When Emmett refers to "new wineskins," is he talking about the mill or the people?

5. Prayer books and hymnals arrive from St. Barnabas Church. Why was such a gift unexpected? Why was it appropriate for a church with that name to send such encouraging gifts?

Chapter 9: A Companion

1. Jake returns and catches Emmett off guard during the worship service. Emmett asks Jake to help them. Do you think such a request is easy for Emmett?

2. What is Jake's concern about Emmett's invitation?

3. What is Jake's experience with people asking for his help? Does that experience reflect how we often approach God?

4. Jake thinks things are going well; Emmett doesn't. How can the two be right?

5. What would your life of faith look and feel like if you saw God as your companion?

Chapter 10: A Surprise Challenge

1. Emmett learns that the fire likely came from a candle left lit by Robert Prescott's son, Trey. Why is this such an uncomfortable revelation?

2. How could Emmett use that information in an unhealthy way?

3. Jake helps him see another way to handle it; some might refer to it as a "more, excellent way." How does this serve Emmett and the parish in the end?

4. Jake points out that it's only a chapter, not the story. Have you ever needed to be reminded of that in your life?

5. What reason do you think Robert has for wanting the challenge to remain anonymous?

Chapter 11: Ashes

1. According to Emmett, what is the purpose of Lent?

2. In what ways is holding the Ash Wednesday service at the old church appropriate?

3. Why does Jake have them go into the ashes instead of hiring a company to clean up the mess?

4. The people find it difficult to walk through the ashes. Does that have a greater significance than what it means literally?

5. What is behind Emmett's tirade at the end of the chapter?

Chapter 12: Debris

1. It's been said that unlearning is as important as learning, particularly when it comes to our spiritual lives. How might that be true as the people of St. John's begin envisioning the church?

2. What's more important: what the church is, or what the church does?

3. What do you think needs to be different about the church(es) you have known?

4. The dump trucks continue to haul away the debris. In fact, each time a truck drives past, it interrupts a meeting. How might that help the people remember the importance of what they are doing?

5. If you could envision a church, what would you come up with?

Chapter 13: Church

1. If you were to define the church in a sentence, what would you say?

2. Why do you think coming up with only one sentence is difficult for Emmett?

3. In what way is Emmett helped by attending the AA meeting?

4. Have you ever seen or experienced "conditional grace"? Have you ever experienced, or given, unconditional grace?

5. What do you think of Emmett's definition of the church? What implictions might it have on the work to come?

Chapter 14: Turning On the Water

1. Why is Emmett unable to see the freedom Jake saw in the bishop's letter?

2. What is holding Emmett back from being his true self?

3. What memory causes Emmett to walk down to the river? How is the memory an important glimpse of Emmett as a boy?

4. What is the significance of Emmett falling into the river? What is the significance of his father's crozier breaking in two and floating away?

5. Why does Emmett try to turn on the water?

Chapter 15: Reorientation

1. Why does Emmett change his mind about using the sanctuary for things other than worship?

2. Why is Jewell surprised to learn that it was Emmett who turned on the water?

3. Why does Jake have the people come to the church site at dawn? Is the orientation of the building the only thing this chapter is about?

4. What do you think they should do with the old church site if they reorient the church?

5. What does Marty point out to Emmett when he mistakenly thinks she's saying the guests are hungry?

Chapter 16: Railings

1. What is making Emmett restless, irritable, and discontent?

2. What is the deeper reason he is troubled?

3. What is significant about Emmett clinging to the mangled railings?

4. Why are the artists surprised Emmett wants the banners to hang in the church?

5. Why does Jake stare in disbelief at Emmett when the rector invites Sam to play the guitar in the church (and allow the AA group to meet there)?

Chapter 17: Opening the Cabin

1. Why was the cabin so important to Abby?

2. Jake asks some tough questions about faith, Mac's and Emmett's. What do their answers reveal about each of them?

3. Why does Emmett feel like the cabin's view is his church? What does Jake say about inspiration, and how does that relate to the church?

4. What was the relationship between Mac and Abby? How did he show his love and concern?

5. Jake uses the mountains as a lesson on how to proceed. How does his analogy apply to major challenges you have faced?

Chapter 18: Stars

1. Why do churches have lock-ins, or in this case, campouts?

2. Why do the youth want Emmett to attend?

3. How does Simon use building a fire to teach the kids? What do you think they learn? How can you apply the lesson to your own prayer life?

4. What do Emmett and Trey learn about each other?

5. Why are the children's memories about the church surprising to Emmett? What would Abby have been happy about at the end?

Chapter 19: A Minister

1. What is the bishop's main concern when he comes to St. John's?

2. In what ways have the days since the fire been a blessing to St. John's?

3. How does something Sam says help Emmett to begin thinking about the bishop in a new way?

4. Why does Emmett take the blame for the fire?

5. In what way does it make him a minister?

Chapter 20: Home By Another Way

1. One can look at something with scarcity or abundance. How could the people of St. John's look at their situation from both perspectives?

2. Why do you think it is important to ask Trey to acolyte at the Christmas Eve service?

3. In Emmett's sermon, he says no one can encounter Christ and not be changed. Do you agree? Do you think Emmett has firsthand experience? Has the parish changed? If so, do you think it's because they've encountered Christ?

4. Emmett says Sam's children should see him as he is, not as he was. Have you ever been guilty of only seeing someone as they were? What do you think his children feel as they listen to their father sing in church?

5. Even with $2 million dollars pledged, why does Jake think St. John's is a long way from being able to build the new church?

Chapter 21: New Thinking

1. The church needs an architect. What are the differences between their three choices? Why do they select Jake?

2. From the start, his approach is unconventional. Why does Jake begin their work in the way he does? Why does he need to challenge their way of thinking?

3. What does the clay teach them? How can you apply those lessons to your spiritual life?

4. What does drawing negative spaces teach them? How can you apply those lessons to your spiritual life?

5. What do the broken plates teach them? How can you apply those lessons to your spiritual life?

Chapter 22: Textbook

1. Do you believe buildings have a theology? If so, find one that isn't a church and see if you can discern the message it is designed to say.

2. What does the design team learn from the Roman Catholic church?

3. What is important in the Baptist church? The synagogue?

4. Walk into your place of worship (if you have one) and see if you can discern its theology.

5. What is Marty's concern at the end of the chapter? Should she be worried?

Chapter 23: Pages

1. What are the two things Jake believes hinder someone from becoming a good architect? How can these obstacles hinder other people as well?

2. How does Jake connect the parish center to the church, architecturally? Why is that important?

3. Why is reading stories from the Bible and speaking about them personally difficult for the people of St. John's? Do you share their struggle in speaking about your faith?

4. Which story selected by members of The Designers speaks to you most? If you were asked to pick a story or passage from the Bible that means a lot to you, what would it be, and why?

5. What does Trey take from their discussion and bring it into the mission of the parish center?

Chapter 24: Let the Building Help

1. What is the tension about the estimate? What is the argument for building such a church? What is the argument for using the money in other ways?

2. What does Jake mean when he says they should "let the building help"?

3. Emmett feels it is up to him to solve the financial crisis. How is the "Unveiling" a testament to the importance of working with others to solve a problem?

4. How does the parish's vision tell the biblical story?

5. How does the parish center illustrate the congregation's commitment to serve?

Chapter 25: Broken Ground

1. Although symbolic, why do you think Emmett feels it is important to have a groundbreaking ceremony?

2. Is the soil the only broken ground?

3. Why will the soil be hard to get ready for the foundation? Does that speak about more than the soil?

4. Emmett sells his beloved grandfather clock. It is a significant way to participate in giving to the new church, but does it represent more than that?

5. Emmett knows he must deliver the news about not building the parish center to Marty. What is her reaction? What does she say that is hurtful? Is she right?

STUDY QUESTIONS

Chapter 26: Death

1. In what ways is Emmett's funeral different from earlier services?

2. Sometimes, you hear familiar words as if for the first time. The opening sentences of the funeral services are known to many. In what ways do you think the congregation of St. John's hears them anew?

3. What do you think of Mac's eulogy? Should he have mentioned Emmett's achievements? What's more important about a person: what he/she does or who he/she is?

4. What's your most vivid memory of Emmett?

5. Who do you think the stranger is who arrived looking for Virginia?

Chapter 27: Resurrection

1. In what way does Emmett live on in the building of the church and parish center?

2. Long ago, Jake tells Emmett not to try to build the church on his own. In what ways is the finished church and parish center better because more people were involved?

3. What features of the building speak to you, and why?

4. What makes the Resurrection Window so special? What important message is it shining into the church?

5. Why does Jake take the people outside before heading home? How does Jake use the stained-glass windows to teach the people about the light within and how their lives should let light shine into the darkness?

Chapter 28: Life

1. It is unusual to dedicate the church during the Christmas Eve service. In what ways does it make sense for the people (besides it being the anniversary of the fire)?

2. Emmett always wanted to leave a legacy. Looking at the evening service, where is his legacy found?

3. What does the bishop say that resonates with the people of St. John?

4. What is wrong with the sign?

5. Do you think it was a mistake? Explain your thinking.

Final Thoughts: New Life

1. New life is always unexpected, both in the life given and the people to whom it is given. How is that true for the people of St. John's?

2. How is the church different from what they originally imagined?

3. How are they different from who they used to be?

Gratitude

When I heard someone say it took her 10 years to write a book, I scoffed. But then reality set it, and I found that it took me even longer! With a swollen heart, I write to thank the people who played a significant role in making this work a reality.

My editor, Richelle Thompson, and her team took my draft and made it a book. Like gifted midwives, they brought this baby into the world, and I am forever grateful. Any mistakes or imperfections are mine, not theirs.

Feel free to judge this book by its cover! Nate Rogers, who painted the cover, and Hank Bristol, who created the chapter drawings, have done all I could have hoped for in pointing the reader to the story beyond the story. I'm so thankful for the power of their work.

GRATITIDE

The seed for this book was planted during an Artist's Way discussion group many years ago. Since then, I've talked it out and shared early drafts with trusted friends. Their feedback and encouragement have done more to get this book finished than they know. I'm especially grateful to Emily Bradley, who coached me for two years and grew to love Emmett. I also promised to thank the seventh-grade Language Arts/Literature students at Westchester Country Day School (2021-2022). You taught me more about writing than I taught you.

Beyond these important souls are others who taught me what this book is really about. These include the bishops and ministers I've known, parents and siblings who believed I had something to offer this world despite my obvious limitations, and countless friends who have joined me in the sandbox of life. I am indebted to Candace Folden, my therapist, who helped me learn to see and tell my story. I also want to thank the wise and courageous souls of Alcoholics Anonymous, who gave me a vivid picture of what the church looks like.

Finally, to my children, who roll their eyes and love me anyway, and my wife, without whose patience and encouragement this would never have made it to the finish line, thank you from the depths of my tattered soul.

Chip Bristol
Greensboro, North Carolina
Advent, 2022

Made in the USA
Columbia, SC
16 December 2024

49595807R00187